Off Her Game

The Game Lords

Zoe Forward

Chapter One

"Where's the rest of it?" Tori Duarte fanned through her empty wallet. She show-and-telled its vacant pockets to the police officer across the counter.

The officer's eyes didn't deviate from his computer screen. Smells of coffee and cigarette smoke floated off him. "Musta been confiscated."

"That was mine." She needed that two hundred and ninety-eight dollars.

He shrugged. Arguing was pointless. The attitude? Nothing new. Cops profiled her based on one glance at her Cuban heritage. Besides, the cop had drawn the shortest straw in the crap-jobs lottery, condemned to hand out personal effects when people were on the way out in the witching hours.

"Take a seat. They'll call when they're ready for you." He extended a bony index finger toward two metal benches along the wall. Six taped-up crayon pictures of Christmas trees clung to the gray cinderblock wall. "Take me down" had been scribbled in pen across one. Although the graffiti came off as disrespectful, the holiday had come and gone over three months ago.

She met the gaze of the only other bench occupant. And nearly sucked in a breath. Her fellow detainee was gorgeous, with messy, short, dirty blond hair, deep blue eyes, and… *Oh my fucking arm porn.* His black T-shirt stretched tight over his biceps.

She plopped onto the unoccupied bench, landing with her back against the cold wall. Goosebumps studded her arms within seconds.

"They stole your money, too?" The guy propped his cheek on a hand, his elbow on the bench arm. Men in Tori's world of computer geeks didn't come in models like this—earring in his left ear, dark jeans, leather jacket slung across his lap, and the body of a man who didn't live on fast food or have an aversion to working out.

"Assholes," she muttered, fingering the three mini hoops along the edge of her left ear. "What'd they get you on?"

"Wrong place at the wrong time," he said. This time, beneath the cool confidence, she noticed he looked a little disheveled—uncombed and unshaven.

"That's the story of my life," she mumbled. "Wrong place. Wrong time."

A more comprehensive assessment of him and…no way. He wore a vintage *Zoneworld Warrior* shirt? Melt her heart and set flame to her panties. A fellow video gamer? Maybe he'd been caught in the same police raid as she.

You cannot be into a random guy at a police station. That's beyond desperate. He could've picked up the shirt at the thrift store.

"Gum?" He held open a Doublemint pack in offering.

"Sure, thanks." The spicy spearmint coated her parched taste buds.

Her phone dinged. She opened up the homepage to read the message from one of her eGaming team members who'd checked in to the Washington D.C. hotel where she planned to travel via train tomorrow for the competition.

Dibs on the bed by the window.

She bit back a smile as she typed. *Sure. Try not to rack up the porn bill again.*

Alex's enthusiasm over qualifying for the WorldGaming Championship this year had him packed last week and scheduled to arrive a day early. She loved him to pieces, but she and Quan never missed an opportunity to remind him what happened the last the time Alex arrived early to a competition and got bored. As the trio comprising the Dynasty team, they'd been gaming together long enough that they behaved like siblings. And, even though internationally ranked, gaming didn't pay much, so they bunked together. It wasn't anything new since they were all roommates anyway.

"You're a Trekkie?" His eyes were bright as he glanced at her home screen background image icon.

Was that a judgmental tone, or was he a fan? "Yeah. So?"

Perking up, he looked her square in the eyes. "The latest movie just popped up off preorder on my TV. The opening scene…great a second time around, but wouldn't do it justice without a kickass sound system." He left out the *which I've got,* but it hung there, implied.

She imagined him with the total gaming setup—monster high def screen, comfort seats, and a surround sound system that'd knock her socks off. Hook her up with a headset and a gamepad, and *that* was the stuff of fantasy. In reality, the guy probably had two roommates and rented a one-bedroom in Queens.

Wait a sec. The movie released in digital yesterday. He'd preordered? *Oh my God.* He *was* a sci-fi geek.

"You asking me to see your big-ass sound system?" she asked.

"Beats Tinder. One detainee to another, at least we already know about our arrest records." A smile teased the corner of his mouth. He leaned forward and said low, "Would you judge me if I admitted my nightmare is an exposed public toilet in jail?"

Giggling, she shook her head. "No. I wouldn't judge you in the slightest. I've got to pee like a racehorse, but no way was I going in the holding cell. No way. And have you seen the restrooms up the hall?"

"Me too. No way." He leaned back to rest his head against the wall.

5

"You like *Zoneworld?*" Her eyes darted down to his shirt.

"You play?" He stopped chewing his gum and gazed at her out of the corner of his eyes with a guarded expression.

She nodded.

Quickly, he asked, "Who do you play?"

"In *Zoneworld One* or *Two?*"

"*Two.*" He uncrossed his legs and faced her.

"Evelle."

He nodded and resumed chewing. "Of course. You'd choose the femme fatale."

"She gets more weapons than any other character." And, she didn't have enhanced tits or a bubble butt. In this classic role-playing game she adored the avatar for being an ordinary-looking brunette with glasses, rare attributes for a gaming character. The glasses might be a nerd stereotype, but she'd take it over a sexualized female.

"She doesn't need a single one of the weapons." His eyes flared. This was a test to see if she was only a talk-the-talk kinda girl or a serious gamer.

"That's why choosing her is a no brainer. You gotta admit the best part of the *Zoneworld* games is their storylines." She couldn't remember the last time she'd talked gaming with a guy who piqued her interest for something other than kicking his butt in front of a screen. She found herself on edge, giddy for his next question.

"Evelle is a tough play because of the level of extra work required, since she can seduce the other characters."

Whoa. Hold the boat. What, what, what? She hadn't known that. She knew a hell of a lot about the game, being ranked in the top twenty in the legit, up-and-up, non-gambling world of multi-character gaming competitions and top fifty online. Talk about shattering her love for a non-cliché female character.

Maybe he lied. Who was this guy, anyway?

He grinned wide. Dimple alert. Damn, he knew he'd surprised her. He asked, "I assume you mastered *Zoneworld Warrior One*. What level have you gotten to in *Two*?"

"Forty-one," she admitted with pride. It was as far as anyone else online had achieved.

"Nine away from the accolade. That's pretty good. Did you get stuck at the cave?"

"What's the accolade?" He'd made it all the way to the end? In the four months since the game released no one had made it that far. If he'd finished the game, it'd been offline. Unless everyone witnessed your success online, no one believed it.

He shook his head in an *I'm-not-telling* way, but no comment on if he'd mastered the game. "You've got to make it to there to find out."

"How do I get out of the cave without getting killed by a scorpion bot?"

A voice yelled, "Harrison and…" The thin cop at the exit read names off a clipboard. "Duarte."

Not now. I need this answer!

A burst of dignity backed her down from begging.

The cop held open the swinging door into the station's lobby. A floor wax machine hummed its circular wipes up the hall.

High heels that probably cost as much as had been in her wallet fast clicked against the worn linoleum in her direction. Each click ratcheted up her nerves. Did she beg for the bots answer before he disappeared or ready herself to face off with her pissed-off sister?

"Guess it's a two-for-one special tonight." Emma flicked imaginary dirt off her designer dark coat. Her sister had been the last person she'd wanted to call, but she had no other option with Quan on a train to D.C. tonight.

"What do you mean?" Tori started when her fellow

7

offender stopped next to her and shrugged into his jacket. Her flawless, had-her-shit-together sister who could maintain an impeccable facade at all times, even in the middle of night at the crappiest police station in New York City, knew this man? Emma didn't hang around gamer guys with earrings who got arrested.

Emma said, "Tori, meet my boss, Noah Harrison. Noah, this is my sister, Tori."

He was *the* Noah Harrison? The mysterious, reclusive billionaire to which her sister had risen in the ranks of his company to become his personal assistant a few months ago? The guy who co-designed *Zoneworld Warrior*?

Oh my freaking God.

She'd conversed one-on-one with one of the Game Lords? No one got that kind of quality time with one of them. At least, no one she knew. Over the past year she'd begged her sister for info on Noah since little was posted publicly about him, not that she'd found out much. Noah avoided media exposure like the plague. His business partner, Jake Allen, Game Lord number two, was the face of the company, but everyone knew Noah was the brains. Jake's line on the mystery of Noah's media reticence was that he wanted his work to speak for itself. She hadn't expected him to look like *this*.

Be cool. You will not go all fangirl crazy and creep him out.

Noah held out his hand her.

Shake it.

Crap, she'd frozen. Like a clumsy puppy she slapped her tremoring hand into his for a brief shake.

Maybe he'd autograph something. *Hello, checking out of jail.* Yeah, that'd be weird.

"*Zoneworld Warrior's* cool," she muttered. Hand to forehead slap. Dumb, dumb, dumb.

"Tori's in to video games." Emma's eyebrows shot

upward in a *what's-wrong-with-you* glare. Or maybe it was a *don't-embarrass-me* glower.

He granted Tori a small smile. Her stomach clenched. She couldn't interpret the smile. Was it a pity smile or an *oh-god-not-another-gaming-fan* smile?

He said, "Thanks, Emma, for bailing me out. Guess it wasn't too out of your way tonight."

"I hope you're not going to make this a habit." She looked between the two of them. Her scowl promised more was coming Tori's way as soon as her boss was out of earshot. "Either of you."

Outside smelled of recent rain and gasoline. The icy wind whipped through the few microns of T-shirt fabric, reminding her she'd left her favorite jacket at the Stadium tonight. No getting it back after the cops invaded. The Stadium wasn't so much a place as an event. The dark underbelly of the video gaming world commanded a lot of money, unsavory characters, and a buttload of the illegal. The competitions never happened in the same location twice. It was unlike the up-and-up, legit event she'd be attending tomorrow.

"Mr. Harrison, I phoned your driver." Emma waved at a dark sedan idling on the curb. She pasted on a professional smile. "Let's talk tomorrow."

"Nice to meet you, Tori." Noah's gaze bounced back to her. His eyes crinkled in the corners with his smile. "Good luck with the gaming."

"You too." *Please, dear God, tell me about the bots before you leave.*

Noah met Emma's gaze with raised eyebrows.

Emma pointed her finger at him. "No. Absolutely not."

"We can talk tomorrow, Emma." He gave her a pointed look before he disappeared into the back seat of his car. The driver shut the door, closing him away.

Tori fisted her hands against the desire to bang on the

window and demand an answer to get through the game level.

Have some self-respect.

As she watched his car turn left at the end of the street and out of sight she wasn't as disappointed to see him go because she didn't get the answer as because she genuinely liked Noah Harrison. And maybe there was a tad bit of hero worship thrown in.

Emma snapped, "You were gambling on those video games again, weren't you?"

"I would've won tonight." Said like a bonafide gambling addict, which she wasn't. Or, maybe she was. She'd argue until the end of the Earth she wasn't. The gambling, the underworld gaming...at first it'd been about a quick buck to pay rent. Now, she was desperate to be free of it.

Emma's lips thinned. "You always think you'll win. I'm never doing this again. I swear."

"Thanks for coming down to pick me up. Again." Her sister had threatened the same a few months ago. As polar opposites, they rarely jived on life choices. Emma was the blonde to her dark, almost black hair. Even if her sister's color wasn't natural, it fit her. Unlike her sister, Tori excelled at one thing—other than her new talent to get arrested—and that was gaming. Both playing and designing. She traveled to big gaming events, winning a pittance, but still placing with her team in the top twenty-five. Someday, she hoped to design video games fulltime and not rely on freelance coding and Twitch streaming with her teammates to pay rent, a dream that was a few months away from becoming reality.

Emma paused at the entrance to the parking deck adjacent to the police station and whirled. "Why do you do this? We can't afford a big time lawyer. I'm lucky to have found some lady at Legal Aid familiar with video gaming who worked magic to get the gambling charges dropped last time. This time sounds like they didn't have anything concrete to hold you on. You lucked out."

Tori tucked her frozen hands into her jeans pockets. "One more good win and then I'm out. I'm hoping D.C. will come through this weekend." But playing in legit competitions was a crapshoot. When the prize was good, the big names in the sport showed up. Noah Harrison's company, NJ Legacy, sponsored a twenty-thousand-dollar pot at the D.C. competition. She'd be lucky to hit the top ten and get a fourth of that. Two or three good wins, though, and her gambling debt could be paid off.

"How much do you owe?" Emma released a long sigh filled with judgment.

"Don't worry about it."

"Jesus, Tori. I'm at a police station at one a.m. bailing you out when I have to be at work at seven. Tell me how much you owe."

"You also bailed out your boss, which is…weird. How often does that happen?"

"Never. This is a first. I don't think he'd want either of us talking about it to anyone." Emma cast her a plea for silence.

"All right. I won't tell anyone I met the elusive Game Lord in jail." She bit her lip against a smile and amended in her mind that she might tell Alex and Quan, but not the whole story.

"Thanks. How much do you owe?" Emma's tone had gentled.

"Ten grand. Give or take some change." Tori toed a plastic bottle cap with her sneaker.

Emma stepped back. "Wow."

Tori shrugged.

"To whom do you owe this much?"

"Symphis." An ambitious nudge kicked the bottle cap too hard. It rolled under a car.

"There's a person who actually calls himself that?"

"He's the guy who owns gaming in New York. Not legit stuff but the underworld, monster multi-character gaming competitions." A few bad bets her pride pushed her to place and now he owned her ass until she could pay him back. Making that much money required she either gamble more in hopes of a win or play on his teams for the chickenfeed he offered as compensation for each night of gaming. If she played off her debt it'd require another sixty-three nights, which equaled to six more months of hell. Symphis's teams sucked since he assigned her hotheads peppered with low talent wannabes. If she won a big, legitimate competition with her chosen teammates then she could pay off her debt and be out. Well, that was if Symphis would let her get out. Big fat if on that. She'd heard rumors of Symphis having a cartel connection and that video gaming was their idea of next level organized crime.

"You were such a good programmer. What happened to that as a career?" Emma asked.

"I'm not an attractive hire. Not after I took time off from MIT to…you know." *Care for Dad.* "Looks bad on my resume to have a dropped out of college. Like I couldn't handle it. I could do programming or coding for a big company, but that's not for me. I design games. That's all I want to do." She cleared her throat. "A gaming company bought my game last week."

"Who?"

"Conjur Games." She'd been reluctant to discuss this with Emma, who worked for what many would argue was the most successful gaming company of the decade.

"Oh." There was judgment in her tone. Conjur was small-time with no big hits. Yet. Maybe hers would be the one. They didn't offer a signing bonus, only royalties off sales.

"It's something," Tori muttered. She also had a job interview next week to write code in a cubicle. It'd suck, but it paid money, which she needed. Her gaming team's live stream Twitch chats had starting bringing in more from ad revenue when their international ranking increased six months ago, but barely enough to pay a bill or two. The money in legal eGaming was in sponsorships. No company had the balls to sponsor a team with a girl as one of its key players, not when some of the bigger competitions still discouraged females from playing, or if they did allow them, the women played in their own brackets, gender separated from men, with little to no chance at a decent prize. Quan said they could use her uniqueness as a bargaining chip to get a sponsor, but so far it hadn't panned out.

"You know I could've helped if you wanted NJ Legacy to review your game."

"I'm not into nepotism, or whatever it's called when it's a sister doing you a favor. I'll hear more on their production plan for my game in the next few weeks." *I hope.* She had the feeling her game got shuffled to the bottom of the pile.

Emma chewed on a nail with the *I'm-formulating-a-plan* face.

Tori threw out there as distraction, "So, your boss is hot."

"Everything with estrogen agrees, although he tries to pretend they don't notice him. He doesn't really date. He works. A lot."

"Is he gay?" Valid question, but it'd shock her to be true.

Emma coughed. "Hell, no. The man's brilliant behind a computer, but awkward when it comes to women, dating...pretty much the whole social scene."

Not with me.

"What was that about before he got in the car? Him giving you that weird look." Tori wondered if he and Emma were getting it on at the office.

Emma blew out an exhale hiss of air and rolled her eyes heavenward. "I can't believe this is happening to me. Why the hell did you have to go play at that place tonight, of all nights?" She waved a hand. "I'll take care of it. You go do your competition in D.C. I'll see you there. Noah's business partner, Jake Allen, is giving a presentation on their next game release and then handing out the winner's check. It'd be amazing if your team won. The prize got boosted to one hundred fifty thousand last week when Red Bull joined as a sponsor."

Didn't know that. Every pro team in the States would be there for sure. "What are you going to 'take care of'?" Her stomach clenched. Maybe Emma would try to rig it so she won. She wanted nothing to do with cheating.

"It's nothing. Work minutia."

"Do you and Noah have a thing? I mean, he's certainly lickworthy." Oh, this was bad. Of all people to be jealous over, her sister wasn't someone she could compete against and win in the dating ring.

"Eww. No. He's my boss. Sure, he's pleasant on the eyes and works hard to stay in shape, but he's not my type." Emma's forehead crinkled. "Lickworthy?"

"Those arms. That earring." Tori fanned her face. "You've got to have noticed."

"No. You can forget about it. He doesn't do dating."

"He seemed interested in me," Tori challenged.

Emma shook her head and covered her face for a moment. "Tori, once again, you were in the very wrong place at the very wrong time."

Chapter Two

"How far is she into the game? Beyond level twenty yet?"
Noah asked while he paced behind the bank of monitors and
computers in the cramped hotel security room.

Sam, Noah's head of IT security for his company, NJ
Legacy, looked up from his laptop where he'd been monitoring
Tori Duarte's progress in the competition. More like fan stalking
her. Sam had gushed for almost five minutes about her being one
of the infamous Dynasty who'd been placing in the bigger
eGaming competitions over the past year. Turned out she was
one of the most talented players to hit gaming in years.

Sam scrubbed a hand over his recent buzz cut and ran a
finger over his three eyebrow bars. "She's genius. I'd never
thought of some of her moves. Hell, I've got an e-boner over this
girl's badassery. The guys on her team are also pretty good, but
not like her. I mean… Holy hell, did you see what she just did to
that cyber-hawk? She's less than two hours in and already this
far into the game. No wonder she made it to the final round."

"He didn't ask about her skill. We need to know what
level she's on." Tom, leader of the FBI task force assigned to the
underground video gaming investigation, click-clicked his
ballpoint pen. He yanked off his fleece vest and tossed it over the
back of a chair. Tom had a cool, organized tenacity Noah
imagined made him excel at the job. However, the pen clicking
might drive Noah over the edge.

Noah didn't want to screw up her chances of winning.
But, ironically, his assistant's sister might be the key to
unlocking a year of investigations into the deaths associated with

illegal gaming and gambling in New York and shut it down. Tori's assistance hinged on her not winning today.

"Level twenty-one." Sam's frustrated glare met Noah's gaze.

"It's time. Get out there and distract her. Make her screw up," Tom said. *Click click. Click click.*

Jake, his co-CEO, strolled in. His dress slacks and button-down shirt were wrinkled, highly atypical for Jake, who always had a change of clothes handy. His dark hair, however, maintained its perfect styling. He must've come direct from the airport.

Jake plunked a white paper bag by Noah. Maybe not so straight from the airport.

"You stopped for doughnuts without me?" The booze-flavored doughnuts from the Mom and Pop place they found on 8th Street were his favorite in the country.

"Saved a bourbon butterscotch for you." He rolled his eyes heavenward with an ecstatic smile.

Noah reached in to the bag to grab around one of the sticky concoctions.

Tom snapped, "There's no time for food."

"There's always time for *these* doughnuts." Jake gave Noah an encouraging smile.

"I didn't think your plane got in until the afternoon, Jake." Noah's stomach clenched at the thought of what he had to do. He grabbed a napkin, wiped off his hand, and rolled the top of the bag down. His mind rumbled along in slow motion bouncing between *I don't want to do this to her* and *this has to happen.* Tori was perfect for the FBI's infiltration plan. If only he wasn't also considered ideal—because he'd met her and he was single—then he could waltz his ass far away from this impending debacle.

"Thought it best if I was here for the kick-start to this plan." He squeezed Noah's shoulder as he walked past to lean in

and stare at the monitor with Tori's image. "Catch me up."
Tom click-clicked the pen twice. "Noah needs to get out
there and distract her. Right now. He's getting cold feet."
"I never said that. Don't put words in my mouth." Noah
leaned closer to the monitor directed on her. A sexy dragon
tattoo on her inner wrist flashed as she pulled her long dark hair
out of its ponytail and up into a messy bun in the break between
levels. How many other tattoos did she have? "She looks pretty
focused. I'm not sure I can make her mess her up."

Him involved in this plan guaranteed it would get messed
up. He regularly misread people and said the wrong thing.
Awkward moments didn't just sneak up on him. They clobbered
him over the head, especially with women. Talking to women
was like conversing with a beautiful but terrifying alien species.
When confronted with an attractive woman he'd break out in a
cold sweat and invariably say wrong thing.

The worst was when he misinterpreted a first kiss
moment. Like the time he leaned in for a kiss at the exact
moment she turned to open her car door. He got a mouthful of
hair. Shocked, she'd whirled. Her head slammed into his nose.
The catastrofuck ended with one of his hands stemming the
hemorrhage from his nose and the other gripping hers in a lame
handshake. Of course, he never called her again. That kind of
humiliation was why he hadn't been on a date in months. No,
years.

When he'd discovered online gaming, eGames, after a
life-altering humiliation as a freshman in high school, for the
first time in his life he wasn't awkward. In those early days of
eSports, gamers played for fun. None devoted their every waking
hour to gaming, formed pro teams, or calculated how to rake in
bucketloads of money from sponsorships like they did these
days. As an avatar he could do anything he dreamed. People
didn't recognize him as the overweight kid who starred in a viral
video.

That night in the jail with Tori, though, everything had gone different. He hadn't freaked out about talking to her. He'd even come off marginally cool. Something about her being as screwed by the system as he put them on equal footing.

"We need a reason for you to meet her. To draw her away from the competition floor and get her on board with our plan. Come on. We went over this a zillion times." Tom threw up his hands and paced away from the screens. "I'm not feeling your commitment here."

"You got this, man." Jake stress smiled. Not comforting. "We need you. The future of the gaming world needs you."

No pressure there. "I don't like this. I'm not a player. Video games I can do. Women, though? I'm sure as shit not good with dating or women. Me showing up out there won't be enough to distract her. I can't talk to her. I mean, what the hell am I supposed to say? You should do this, Jake. You're better with this kind of stuff." Noah watched Tori's facial expressions as she battled imaginary creatures on screen. God, she was pretty. Not drop-dead beautiful. Thank God for that. Beautiful women with perfect hair, unblemished skin, and honed seduction techniques ramped up his unease. And turned him into a babbling idiot.

"This is about stopping this crime organization before it spreads across the world, killing more than just your brother. Don't you want to bring your brother's murderers to justice?" Tom asked from the back of the room. "I need someone who can get inside the operation without suspicion. That someone is her."

Tom pushed off the wall and paced. "When you came to us seven months ago after Kaleb died you were the one worried about a future where the best computer programmers and designers are tricked into working for criminals. They'll be sucked into an underground world where they'll be forced to hack and program to survive. This is about preventing that reality. They're already luring in retired pro gamers, disgruntled coaches, and those who almost made it."

His neck tingled. He glanced around to find his assistant glowering at him.

Emma crossed her arms. Her gaze bounced between all of them. "I don't like any of this. At all. I wish she hadn't been there, that you hadn't met her, Noah. She's a person. This competition is real to her. This is how she makes money to live." She pointed at the monitor. "That's my sister we're talking about manipulating. You're putting her life on the line."

"I get that." Noah swallowed his compulsive need to apologize. Angry Emma scared him a bit. She could go from cold to hot in milliseconds. Emma could bulldoze a polar bear and have it begging her for forgiveness. It's why he'd come to rely on her and respect the hell out of her. But Emma had been riding his ass since yesterday morning to find someone else for this. Gently, he said, "She's in deep shit. The way she's going could end like Kaleb."

Emma breathed out a protracted sigh. "Fine. All you have to do is get her attention. She'll mess up. You're you, which in her world means you and Jake are the Game Lords. You're gods. She also thinks you're hot, Noah. Be ready for her to be bitchy, though. This is important to her. She's a horrible loser."

She thinks I'm hot?

Jake said, "No offense, man, you're the smartest guy I know, but you'll never be a player. According to Emma, Tori wants out of the illegal gaming as much as we need in. This is going to be a win-win. Remember that. All this is for show because we know the guys of the illegal world have spies everywhere. They're always watching."

"We need answers," Tom said.

"Only if she agrees. We're not forcing her into anything," Noah confirmed, casting a glare at Tom.

"Sure." Tom clicked his pen once more. The FBI agent would do almost anything to break this case and find the kingpin who controlled the Stadium. Coercing Tori to help ranked high on Tom's list of must-dos. He wanted his own spy.

Noah gritted his molars and met Jake's gaze.

Jake shrugged apology for the direction everything had taken as Noah brushed past him out of the door. Yesterday, Jake wrangled a promise from him to never again try to do things on his own. No more illegal eGaming events, even if him going had given them their first break—a contact on the inside.

As the security room door clicked shut behind Noah the willowy brunette he recognized as the hotel's events coordinator stalked his way up the hall. What was her name? He sucked at names. He couldn't return to the security room or duck into a nearby room. No escape.

The closer she got, the brighter her smile, and the tenser his muscles became.

"Noah. Is there *anything* I can get for you? *Do* for you?" She'd stopped so close her perfume clogged his nose. Her tongue darted out to moisten her sculpted bright pink lower lip.

Was she hitting on him? Maybe she was just being nice. Fuck if he could tell. His tongue felt swollen. Sweat broke out on his back. The expected reply didn't come. Finally, he blurted, "You're great."

And he walked off.

You're great? What the hell? He'd meant to say she was doing a great job. He should turn around and fix his misstatement. Nope. He'd blunder himself into a bigger mess.

His racing heart slowed as he strolled onto the dark competition floor. He missed the adrenaline rush of competing and the anonymity of playing an avatar. Of course, he couldn't compete today, not on the game he co-designed with Jake. He hadn't sat in a competition chair since they started their company six years ago.

The hotel ballroom, low lit to facilitate optimum screen exposure, was a cacophony of groans and cheers from headphone-wearing finalists and excited murmurs from the audience who watched the competition on a jumbo screen. Truly humbling that he and Jake had programed a game that captured the imagination and enthusiasm of so many. It'd hit the world two years ago and taken off like wildfire. The game offered an ever-changing world with a few static fixtures on each level and the ability for the player to do some building of structures, weapons, and stationary items. Players couldn't get enough of it.

She's had to work for everything she's got. The testosterone crap she's up against when gaming has made her cynical and hard. Emma's words ran through his mind.

He'd recognized a kindred ambitious spirit in Tori when they met. He respected hard work. Her edges made sense once he'd discovered her to be one of the two top-ranking female players worldwide. In the jail he'd liked it when she'd looked at him with honest lust, when she didn't know who he was. She wasn't another girl looking for five minutes in the spotlight or a gamer looking to score so she could brag she'd fucked one of the Game Lords. Tori was none of that.

He tried to swallow his emotions but remained so conflicted he wasn't sure how to get through what needed to be done.

This sucked.

Remember the plan. Distance yourself from all of this...her. Do it for Kaleb and the future of gaming.

Awareness slammed into him when he saw her sitting cross-legged in concentration, wearing headphones that were way to too large for her. How could he have forgotten how petite she was? In black tactical BDU–style pants with a loose graphic tee, her determination and stubbornness intrigued him. That and all the soft curves. Damn, he'd really liked her when they met in jail. Something about the jail after an hour of interrogation about why he'd been at the illegal gaming event made him vulnerable to all the feelings he usually kept sealed in an airtight container.

He could've told the police he was working with the FBI on the case and saved himself the stress, but he'd wanted to avoid the embarrassment of Tom or one of his FBI peons bailing him out. He hadn't wanted Tom publicly scolding him for going to the event without approval. In retrospect it seemed stupid, but he had a life-long aversion to public humiliation.

Seeing Tori again tonight, he wanted a conversation with her instead of twisting her arm. Maybe they should trust she'd do the right thing.

What he wanted wasn't an option. Too many things were already in play. Too many other people outvoted him.

He didn't need feelings to get in the way of the plan. This would be a business arrangement.

He stepped up behind her screen and stared at her. Distracting her was a violation of gamer code. *Don't want to do this.*

Look up.

Moments later, her incredible eyes lifted from the screen to him and widened.

Even in the low light he picked up the light blush that stole across her cheeks and pert little nose. Blood thrummed through him to have her full attention. *Say something.* His mouth wouldn't work. He raised his hand and silently mouthed, "Hi."

She stared at him for several more glazed seconds. Then her gaze bounced back to the screen. "Shit."

After a series of animated moves over several minutes and many curses later she threw off her headphones. "Dammit, you made me mess up. You know better than to interfere with a player. I lost on level twenty-three. *Twenty-three.* That's humiliating. How could you?"

He flinched. "I'm just here." *What in the name of God did that mean?* He couldn't think of anything else to say, being the focus of her glare.

"I had this." He could've sworn he heard her mutter, "I

needed this." She cradled her face in her hand. She mouthed a silent apology to the guy next to her, a teammate. As per the rules, this was sudden death. If a player's character died, no second chances. The person was to leave the floor.

Noah followed her at a distance. As she stepped away from the banks of gaming stations a guy with a backward ball cap over shaggy dark hair, ill-fitting board shorts and a dark tank top leered at her chest. "Tori got her ass kicked, did she? Maybe she's ready for this." The guy rolled his junk suggestively at her.

Noah's hands fisted.

Tori stepped into the bully's space. "You didn't just adjust *that* in front of me like I'd want to jump on for a ride, did you, *Martin Rodriguez?*"

"It's War Dawhg." His leer fell. He tugged at his sagging shorts.

Tori said low. "Do that shit to me again and I'll break what you're so proud of and kick your balls into your abdomen until you squeal like a fifth grader for the rest of your life."

Snickers surrounded them.

"Oh yeah. She wants me," Martin sneered to his friends.

She took another step toward him.

Martin backed up with his hands raised.

She poked him in the chest. "You're a decent gamer, Martin. I respected you online when you were with the MPG team, but out here, come on. Girls don't go for this sort of crap." She leaned in close to say low, "No one wants to see your grundies. Small hint: buy boxers."

Fuck me. I think I'm in love.

Noah approached her at the back of the room where she hovered over the remnants of the breakfast table laid out long ago. She gazed at the stale bagels, doughnuts of undesirable flavors, and broken pastries.

"I'm sorry. Didn't think I'd distract you." So lame. He'd be surprised if she didn't kick him in the balls.

"Are you sorry? Really? That seemed intentional." Her eyes narrowed. Smart girl.

"Should I cover myself before you kick my balls into my abdomen?" He bit back a laugh.

She moistened her generous lips. Her eyes slow scanned down to his crotch before returning to his eyes. The tiny little nose stud on her left nostril glinted in the low light. "Bet you've got more to offer than Martin in that department."

Said dick went on full alert. This woman was hands down a full-blooded goddess. *Remember the script.* "Let me get you some coffee. They've got a room for us where the coffee is fresh. I swear it's ten times better than the crap out here."

Not quite on script, but okay.

She glanced at the coffee carafes, which probably hadn't been replenished in hours. Her arms crossed, causing the oversized dark shirt to fall off one shoulder, revealing a black bra strap. Maybe her panties matched, too.

Was she a thong kind of girl?

Was that the tail of another dragon tattoo under her bra strap?

Head out of the gutter. This is about saving lives.

She said, "Sure. Whatever. This stuff smells disgusting. You still owe me an answer on the bots question."

He suspected she wouldn't let that go. He wouldn't have forgotten had he been in her shoes. Four doors down from the main ballroom he punched in a security code to a locked ballroom, not the security room, but the designated meeting space for the next step in the plan.

Inside, all the tables were stacked except one, where Tom, Jake, and Emma sat. Only a few of the lights had been lit, giving it a closed-down quality. Light from the huge glass windows at the far end added an eerie glow to the space.

"What's this? An ambush?" Tori blanched. She glanced at the door they'd just entered as if preparing to bolt.

24

Emma skirted around a table to her and gave her a hug. "I'm sorry. So sorry he made you lose. I hoped you'd win this weekend, but they concocted a plan to get you out of the illegal stuff."

"Losing *was* intentional." She glared the promise of payback Noah's way.

"Sorry," Noah said.

"Why're you apologizing?" Jake whispered to him.

Can't help it.

"They want to talk about the illegal gaming and gambling," Emma said. Noah noticed Emma's hair had frizz and her earrings didn't match her outfit. His assistant never appeared imperfect.

"Emma, a moment." Tori grabbed her sister's arm and dragged her to the far end of the ballroom away from them.

They argued in hushed voices until Emma took Tori's arm and tugged her back toward them. She waved at the men. "You need help to get out. This is help."

"My plan was to earn the money free and clear at this competition, then pay off my debt. Then I'd be out." She stepped away from Emma and crossed her arms.

"You probably wouldn't be free," Noah said softly. Paying off whomever the guy was that ran the illegal competitions wasn't a guaranteed end. It hadn't been for his brother.

She rounded on him. "You sneak in to one event uninvited and think you know all about it?"

"It happened to my brother. Kaleb made some bets, got into debt. He agreed to work it off, but he was a horrid player. Instead, he programmed for the guy. He told me they modify *Zoneworld* to make it impossible to win. The changes are subtle enough those who know the game well won't notice."

Tori's eyelids drifted closed. "The bastards. I knew it didn't play like it should. That's how they keep us in debt and control the bets." She frowned. "I thought it impossible to break in to any game from your company. No one can figure out the key to bypass the security code, which is amazingly well written. I've heard praise from hackers who've tried. Any attempt to bypass the security code shuts down not only the game, but also their computer."

"It is impossible unless someone steals it. Kaleb gave them the code to the first game. We've been fighting pirating ever since."

"Nightmare," Jake muttered.

"Kaleb used to be on the team that programs security aspects of our games. Getting the code was easy for him. He paid off what he owed to get out and gave them the code but still couldn't shake free. First came cyber threats. Then they tore his life, his credit, everything apart. He got paranoid about everything. One day he disappeared. His body surfaced a month later in Ithaca shot full of heroin like he'd OD'd. My brother wasn't a drug addict."

"I'm sorry about your brother. Maybe you didn't know everything about his situation, though. The Stadium can be stressful. Many turn to drugs—uppers and downers. The shit is all over the place there." She wrung her hands and stared wide-eyed at her sister.

Noah hadn't known drugs floated around the competition space. Made sense.

"We've got to get you out." Emma's eyebrows drew together. "Give them a chance to tell you their plan. You can say no. But, please, listen. I'm worried you'll end up like Noah's brother."

"I'm screwed. I might end up in a casket no matter what I do. Stay in and be a slave, and eventually turn to drugs as a way out. Get out and be terminated. It's a no-win situation." Tori massaged her temples. "What kind of whacked plan did you come up with?"

"I'm Tom Smith. Special Agent, FBI task force." Tom stepped forward and held o ut his hand to Tori. "We need your help to pin a series of murders on Symphis. All killed were gamers who'd gotten sucked in to playing at the Stadium."

She glared at the offered hand, but didn't shake. "FBI, huh? You don't give two craps about me. You're after Symphis."

Tom dropped his hand back to his side. "Won't lie. I want him."

Tori chuckled. "You're going to cuff Symphis, huh? How long have you been chasing him?"

Tom shuffled his feet. "A while."

"You know his real name?" she asked.

"Do you?" A hungry glimmer lit Tom's face.

Tori cocked her head and crossed her arms. "No. No one does. He doesn't make appearances at the Stadium. He's got heavies to do everything for him. Manages the whole thing remotely."

"That's what we thought."

"You've assumed Symphis knows you're after him, haven't you? He's likely manipulated every bit of info you have on him. That means he might know you've targeted me. So, all of you doing this might've expedited his interest in getting rid of me. Thanks." She glanced at each of them. "If I end up dead tomorrow, it's on you guys."

"Sure, we've assumed that." Tom's obvious lie stank. "We've been careful."

"You've got no idea who you're dealing with. Rumor is Symphis can own you—anyone—in about thirty seconds. That he's a certified Mensa genius."

"We know he's smart." Tom crossed his arms.

School his ass, Noah thought, suppressing the laugh itching to break free.

"If he's got you checkmated, you're done," Tori said. "Okay, that's the rumor. That's what floats around the Stadium.

In fact, the rumors go further. Most say you won't know you're toast until he pushes enter on his laptop. No need for weapons. He can do anything digitally. Any. Single. Thing. He'll make all your money disappear. Tank your credit. Make you a wanted felon. Hack your car, your computer, or your iPhone. Make your plane crash. Put a hit on you. If he doesn't have the know-how, he's got someone who owes him that does."

"If that's rumor, then what do you think is real?" Tom asked.

Tori gazed at him in silence before answering. "I think he's probably a good gamer. Maybe even an entry-level hacker. The fact he has to leverage people with gambling debts and then use them to do his dirty work tells me he's not brilliant. This might've made him rich, but I doubt he could hack the Pentagon or drain a bank account himself. He might have someone he can apply pressure to who could do that for him, though. If he were such a great hacker, why would he stick to gaming, gambling, and drugs? That lacks imagination. Seems so small time. This doesn't mean he's not dangerous."

"You're going to help us," Tom ordered.

"I don't think so."

Can't lose her. Noah didn't know if that came from concern over the FBI investigation or personal drive not to let this goddess walk out of his life. "Can I talk to you in private, Tori? Without all them?"

"You going to spin bullshit about rainbows and happy endings? Or are you going to talk straight to me?"

Damn, he liked this girl. "Straight talk. Detainee to detainee."

A smiled teased her lips.

"Outside?" He pointed toward the glass doors at the far end of the ballroom.

She preceded him onto the concrete veranda. The moment the door closed behind them a chilly blast of wind pushed at them. "I have a proposal for you."

"I'm listening." She wrapped her arms around her and shivered.

"I should've known it'd be freezing out here. Sorry. I don't have a jacket to give you. Here, you stand in front of me. I'll block the wind as best I can." He adjusted his position to make himself a barrier. Windy gusts blistered his back, not that he cared.

"Thanks." Her eyes softened for the first time.

He stared at his hands. *Talk to her. Say something.* He cleared his throat. "You're the first person to offer us a glimpse of the inside. You're already in. A lot of people—programmers, coders, and hackers—have died over the past year. Most by what seems like drug OD, but some in accidents that don't make sense. The FBI's in it because it qualifies as serial killing."

"You're in it for your brother?"

"That, and what this means for the future of gaming. If they target all the most talented programmers and hackers to suck them into their world of debt, that's a more powerful army than any on earth. Okay, that sounds melodramatic, but this is about way more than us or my brother. Maybe it's just about a future where gaming is illegal and goes underground, which I don't want. We're cooperating with some of the other gaming companies to help with the investigation."

"I knew that bit about caring about my life was bullshit."

"I care. I can't speak for Tom. He's a hard-ass. We'll guarantee your safety." Noah didn't know if they could get her out and keep her safe, but he wanted to protect her. "We'll get you free of the illegal gaming."

"Why me? Can't the FBI infiltrate an agent like they do in the movies?"

"They've tried. Twice. Both ended up dead."

"That stinks. Wonder who they were. Most of us know each other in this circle, even if we're not all BFFs." Her face scrunched up. "Assuming that it was possible to get free by catching Symphis, is there anything else I have to do other than provide information?"

He cringed. "We have to give you a connection between us other than your sister to get that information from you and to you. I can't hire you to work for NJ Legacy because we don't usually hire gamers. Emma said you're single. I'm single. So, we need to date."

"What?" She threw back her head to glare up at him. At least she wasn't laughing. "You want us to *pretend* to date? You and me? The two unlikeliest people to end up across a table from each other?"

"That's the plan they came up with. I don't think we're all that unlikely."

"Seriously? I'm an unemployed gamer with illegal gambling debts and way more arrests than you can imagine. You're a CEO, which means although rich, you're likely stressed, stretched thin, and don't have time or interest in dating someone like me."

"Not all of that's true. I'm totally into badasses, and you're about the most badass woman I've ever met." Damn, that came off as cool. Something about her didn't make him stumble all over himself like he did around most women.

Her cheeks turned an appealing shade of pink. "This better not be because I look like the Giselle avatar in *Zoneworld One*."

She did have long dark hair and a petite curvaceous hourglass figure. Based on her mean face she was super sensitive about being attractive.

He rushed to say, "No. I mean *no way*. No, I don't mean you're ugly. You're pretty, don't get me wrong, but it's not like I associated you with some gaming character and wanted to use this as a weird angle to get you into bed. No." He shook his head.

"Just checking." She hadn't relaxed and continued to

scowl at him.

He massaged his forehead. "I'm not asking you to like me. We don't need to actually be in to each other. This is just a show. A few dates. A week or two, perhaps. I'll pay."

"You're not expecting full benefits of dating, are you?" She moistened her lips as she let her eyes drop down his body.

Full benefits? He wished it could go that way. Oh, hell, did he want that. *No, she just established this couldn't be about that.* "Show only. We might have to kiss or act like we're in to each other once or twice in public. Might have to sleep together, depending on how long we have to continue the charade." His face went hot. "Shit. Sorry. Meant you might need to stay over. In the guestroom."

"You're not some Joe Schmo I can take to a seedy Chinese restaurant on a date. You're the Game Lord. You're a god in this circle, and if word gets out about you and me—and it will—I'll be scrutinized closer by Symphis." Before he could reply, she held up her hand. "I don't want to be followed around by FBI agents or wired while we're on our dates. That's got to be you and me doing whatever we'd be doing on a date. If you have info to pass to me, then you tell me. Nothing via email or text or phone message. Nothing written. I can slip you a flash drive or something, but I don't want to look over and see two steroid junkies in beige suits watching me."

"No agents."

They both stumbled when another gust of icy wind hit. Her hand landed on his chest, inciting a tangle of sensation. His startled gaze dropped to her gaping shirt. The swells of her breasts and...another tattoo?

One of her eyebrows quirked.

He jumped away. "Inside...go in. I mean it's hot. No, cold."

Now both of her eyebrows shot upward.

"I swear I didn't mean to look and see the tattoo," he said.

31

"But you did look. Is this kind of looking going to be a problem?" She took a step away from him. Did she want him to look or not? He couldn't tell.

He shook his head. "I'll only look at what you want me to look at." Damn, that sounded idiotic. This was turning into a clusterfuck. *Escape.* He pulled open the door and glanced to the opposite end of the room where Jake and Tom had remained at the table. "They'll want to know if you're you in or out."

She closed her eyes and sighed as if kissing her plans for the future goodbye. "So, how're we supposed to have met? In jail?"

"No. No one can know I was there."

"Records of detainees are public."

"The FBI is going to adjust the records, if they haven't already. I made you mess up today and asked you out as an I'm-sorry." He shrugged. "Not too far from the truth."

With a resigned tone she asked, "When's our first date?"

"Day after tomorrow. I'm taking you to a French place. Emma will get you the details."

"Dressing nice, then," she muttered. "My price for this first date is you getting me through level forty-one.

***

Tori slammed the door of the hotel room she shared with her teammates. *Let them not be here.*

"Why haven't you been answering your phone?" Alex called out from the bedroom of the two-room suite.

Her eyelids drifted closed before she braved the bedroom. *You can handle this.* "Why aren't you on the floor?"

"I messed up on thirty-one after you blew up. The maze always gets me when you're not there to throw cover fire for me, but you? Twenty-three? What the hell? You had a fifteen-plus storm shield and built yourself cover. How?" Alex perched on the windowsill. He pushed his glasses up his nose and rolled the Tootsie Pop in his mouth to the other side. His lucky vintage

Punisher T-shirt had a half-inch hole on his left side where white skin showed through, but no one could convince him to wear anything else during a final competition round. She bet he hadn't washed it in a long time out of fear it'd disintegrate.

"I know. I suck. Sorry." She swiped aside a few of Alex's discarded clothes and the swag he'd picked up to make a spot on one of the twin beds.

"You're usually one of the last players standing. I haven't seen you do this since the time Chris What's-his-name distracted you at the Daytona playoffs." He pulled out the lollipop and stared at her over the top of his glasses. "Who got your panties in a wad this time?"

Was she really that predictable? "Noah Harrison messed me up. Didn't you see him at my station?"

Alex's eye went so wide behind the glasses they looked as if they'd pop out of his head. In a hushed tone, he asked, "A Game Lord spoke to you? You're messing with me. *The* Noah Harrison? The guy who hates social events is actually here?"

She nodded. "He's pretty hot in reality. I got a date out of it."

He touched both sides of his head and pulled them away in a mind-blown mime. "You have a date. An actual go to a restaurant and have sex afterward date with *him*?"

"You don't think I'm hot enough for him?" She waved at herself.

"You know I think you're hot. Is this you finally saying yes to me?"

"Not willing to ruin the good thing we've got going. Besides, your idea of a great date is frozen pizza and cheap beer while playing *Visionquest Warrior Twelve*. I've got standards." She bit back a laugh when he gave her a *yeah-so-what* shrug.

"He's taking me to a restaurant in the city day after tomorrow as his way of apologizing. He was sweet about it after I bitched him out."

"The Game Lord distracting you is a decent excuse for messing up, but you better get something outta this. Like inside info on *Zoneworld Two.*"

Great minds do think alike.

"You think he'd autograph something for me?" Alex asked. "I'd die to have him sign my *Zoneworld One* original soundtrack CD case."

"Why in the world did you want the game soundtrack on CD and not digital?"

"It was a two-part box set. I like to workout to it. It's got a good beat." He examined the lollipop as if it'd become fascinating.

"You haven't stepped foot in a gym since high school. Admit you wanted the commemorative poster that came with it." She laughed and threw a pillow at him.

"Oomph," he groaned when it hit his stomach. "Maybe. Hey, you hear from Conjur on their plan for your game?"

"Nothing."

The door opened and closed. Quan dumped his backpack and put his hands on his hips. "Got anything you want to tell us, Tori?"

"About?" She waited. With Quan, he might be upset about her play failure downstairs, or Mr. Obsessive Compulsive might be having another meltdown about the refrigerator rules since she stuck leftover pizza in the mini-fridge. Tall and lean in slate-gray jeans and a gray-marled T-shirt he radiated the epitome of cool. Quan was an avid runner. He ran almost ten miles several times a week and entered races a few times a year.

"I ran into Alonzo, the dipshit, downstairs coming off the floor." Quan's eyebrows rose. He pushed his good-luck sunglasses higher into his spiky pomaded hair.

Oh no.

"He told me you played on *his* team night before last, *Selene.*" Color spread across Quan's cheekbones.

Her Stadium nickname. Super oh crap. Tori chewed on the inside of her cheek. What more could she say?

"What were you thinking? You played in the Stadium? It's a con. They send out a scout who dangles the carrot of making a little easy cash for a night of eGaming. All it takes is once and then the Game Master owns you. I warned you never to do it." Quan fisted his hands and then relaxed them. His voice softened. "How far in are you?"

Tori fiddled with a few pens on the bed next to her. "It's bad. I shouldn't have gone, but two months ago Jar invited me. You remember him? He's the guy who won second down in Florida last fall. I didn't think it was what you were talking about, but I was wrong. I'm working a new angle to get out of it."

Quan sat next to her, put his arm around her, and pulled her into his side. "You should've told us. I don't know what we can do, but we'll figure it out. We'll get you free of it. Alonzo said you went to jail the other night when they raided the Stadium. That true?"

She nodded. "Emma bailed me out. I'm sorry I didn't say anything. Hate that I didn't have the cash for rent last month."

"We covered you. Alex is raking it in off his new app, the one you helped him write. I'm doing okay." Quan squeezed her shoulder. "We can always go to Plan B. Move to Sierra Leone, make apps, and disappear."

"There's always Plan B." Sounding better to her by the minute.

Alex said, "She got distracted by Noah Harrison today. The Game Lord, himself. He asked her out on an I'm-sorry date."

Quan whistled and pulled away from her. "What would he think about you getting arrested for playing his game on an illegal circuit?"

Not what you'd think.

35

"It'll probably be a one-time thing, anyway. I'm good at scaring off guys."

Chapter Three

"You're kidding, right?" Tori stared disbelief at Noah.
"About what?"

"A motorcycle? I'm wearing a dress." *This is one of two that I own.* "When Emma said you wanted to pick me up, to drive us yourself, *this* isn't what I expected."

"The dress is nice. Really nice." His gaze slid to the low dip above her breasts. As a man, his DNA was programmed to look. And maybe she'd chosen this dress to make sure looking happened.

"You could ride sidesaddle? Come on, sometimes you gotta live a little." He held out a helmet.

"You want me to mess up my hair, too? I don't put product in my hair for anyone, but because in the normal world I'd probably be super into this date, I did." She touched the long, dark tresses, which with product waved like she had a perm.

"Your hair should shake out without a problem."

Said like a man who didn't have long hair or work for the past two hours to make sure the curls happened.

"It's a gorgeous night. Seventy-five degrees in March is almost unheard of. I wanted to get her out of the garage, but I didn't think... Are you scared?" His brows drew together.

Was he calling *her* chicken? Oh no no no. "A few tattoos and piercings and you assume I'm a bike girl?"

"Nothing like that." He ducked his head. "All right, maybe it was like that."

"I've been on a few bikes. Sidesaddle is for movies and dipshits. It's not the bike that's the problem."

He rubbed a hand down his face. "I'm sorry. Totally didn't think you might not be into it. If you want to change clothes, I can wait, but I like the dress. This was a stupid idea." He fiddled with the helmet he'd offered her. His fluster was kind of cute.

She nibbled on her lower lip. Might as well just throw it out there. "I have this thing about the helmets. They're tight."

"Tight? They're for safety. They have to be tight."

"I know. They kind of freak me out. I have a claustrophobia thing."

"Forget it. I'll park it here and call my driver to pick us up." He pulled out his cell phone. "Damn it. I should've texted you before, but it was a spur of the moment decision."

She touched his arm to stop him from sending the text. "It's a nice night."

On a deep inhale, she pulled the helmet over her head. *One, two, three...* She continued counting until she reached fifteen, then opened her eyes. Her heart jackhammered against her ribs while she struggled not to feel like a cat crammed into a hamster tube.

"You okay?" His voice echoed inside the helmet. "I'm serious. We don't have to."

"I'm good." Way too much stress packed itself into the words.

He mounted the bike and held out his hand to help her on behind him.

There wasn't a way to climb on the bike with grace. Being a shorty sucked. She tucked her purse under an arm, hiked a leg, exposing all the way up her thigh to straddle the Ducati. About half of the dragon tattoo that trekked up her inner leg showed before she tucked her dress tight.

"That was a dragon." He said it in a way she couldn't tell

if it was a question or comment.

"I've got a few of them." *Got yourself a good look, did you?* No giggling. A firm lip compression kept any noise from escaping. She could've flashed less skin, but she'd wanted him to look. Call it payback for making her put on this helmet.

"How many do you have?" His stupefied fascination was so adorable that a small giggle noise escaped her. She cleared her throat to hide it.

"I'm not sure I know you well enough yet to have a tattoo discussion, Noah."

"Right. Shit, this date is a train wreck, isn't it?"

A laugh burst free. "Then thank God it's not real. For future reference, ink discussions involve showing. Mine are in spots that require lack of clothes. Show-and-tell costs some talented tongue action first."

"Oh, fuck me," he said hoarsely. His imagination was probably doing backflips.

She laughed harder. "Stop it. You're making me cry and I can't wipe my eyes with the helmet on."

The bike lurched off the curb. She wrapped her arms around him, putting her chest tight to his back. "Was that on purpose to get me to hold on to you?"

"It's what you get for giving me visions of dragon ink and you naked. The offer remains open that I'll park the bike and call my driver."

"I'm not getting off at this point until we're there."

Something about Noah's comment about living a little seeped in. She might not make it through the whole Symphis–eGaming business. Why not throw caution to the wind and experience something new, something crazy out of the norm? Why the hell not experience rather than worry for a few hours?

Noah parked between two cars in front of a chichi restaurant she'd heard about but was far out of her budget. Her meals usually consisted of prepackaged ramen and applesauce.

A mix of modern and Old West décor greeted them on the inside, which was weird for a French restaurant. Of course, weird was the new chic.

She dragged her gaze off Noah's wide shoulders as he checked in. He hadn't let go of her hand since he opened the door for her, which was awkward and simultaneously sweet.

This is bad. She liked him, maybe even *like* liked him a little bit.

Focus on freedom. And the deal. This is for show and not real.

A hostess with an elegant bun and low-cut black dress tossed Noah a flirty smile. The girl thrust forward her ample cleavage, which pulled the v-neckline of her top even lower. "Mr. Harrison. Your table's not quite ready."

When Noah didn't glance at her chest right away the girl flipped her hair.

Noah's eyes dropped to her cleavage. As if suddenly realizing the girl was hitting on him and that he was staring at her boobs, he jerked his free hand, accidentally knocking the toothpick dispenser off the counter. With a curse, he dropped to a knee to pick them up.

Tori leaned over to help, but he came up at the same time, slamming into her chin.

"Oh, shit. Sorry. You okay?" Horror crested on his face.

"I'm fine." She compressed her lips against a smile as she helped him pick up the rest of the toothpicks. Once done, she suggested, "How about we wait at the bar? A drink sounds good."

"Text me when the table's ready," he threw over his shoulder without glancing at the hostess again.

He gripped her hand tight as they waded into the clamor of Saturday night sexed-up twenty-somethings packed around the bar. He paused, staring at the bar. His eyes wandered around as if scanning for something.

"You okay?" She had to lean in close to ask him.

"I'm good." It came out tight. His eyes met hers. "Thought we should get a drink. I was looking to see if there's a line, but I can't figure out what's going on at the bar." Anxiety fled his gaze to make way for dread. "Someone I know is headed this way. Damn it. Everything's about to get more complicated. This might go south." He muttered, "He's going to tell Mom."

The object of Noah's glower strolled up with an easygoing smile and smooth confidence. The man flashed a straight line of white—but not too white—teeth and ran a hand through his graying dark hair. He held hands with a tall blonde in a silky dress. The blonde did her best to avoid eye contact, which initially seemed snobbish but the stressed fear in her gaze when it skittered into Tori's suggested otherwise. The blonde's skin was so pale Tori could see the blue veins running beneath, yet it didn't detract from her elegant beauty.

"Noah, you're out? Is this a date or a friend thing? I didn't even know you had female friends." The man's tone suggested these two knew each other with a familiarity closer than work colleagues. Yet, whatever rested between them bittered their relationship.

"Michael, you and Darcy having a date night?" Noah granted the blonde woman a fleeting glance before meeting Tori's gaze. His stress level was so high over this encounter he'd forgotten introductions. Emotion flashed for a moment in Noah's eyes before his face glazed over into stoicism. He'd seemed pained or sad or something else. She didn't know him well enough to read him. Fake date or not, she'd take his side on whatever happened.

Darcy stiffened and looked away. Bad personal history between Darcy and Noah, perhaps. Based on the gigantic diamond on her left hand she must now be engaged to Michael. Awkward.

"We didn't expect to run into you here." Said like if

they'd known he'd be here they'd never have chosen this restaurant. Michael's gaze slid to Tori.

"This is Tori," Noah introduced. "Tori, this is my brother, Michael."

Michael nodded her way. He continued to stare at Tori as if there was something wrong. Maybe her hair was messed up from the ride. A brief look in the mirror behind the bar showed it to be flatter than it started tonight but not a disaster.

Tori said, "Why don't I grab those drinks we talked about, Noah. I'll be right back."

"Sounds good." Noah's icy gaze remained focused on Michael.

She pushed between bar couples engaged in the pre-hookup game to order some beers. She hoped he liked beer. While waiting she messaged Emma: *What's up with Noah's brother Michael and his fiancée?*

She tapped her foot. *Come on, Emma. Check your phone.* She watched Noah stiffly talk with Michael. Darcy didn't engage in the conversation at all. The woman barely glanced at the guys.

Finally, her cell vibrated with Emma's response: *Michael is engaged to the woman Noah dated a time or two and then he found her naked with Michael. Happened three years ago. She used to be NJ Legacy's CFO.*

Her heart ached for Noah. She texted Emma, *Thanks.*

She sent Noah a text.

With a beer in each hand she marched back to Noah. The cool glower Noah centered on Michael bothered her.

"Here." In a show of juggling the two sweaty beer glasses she slid in next to him and handed him his beer. After he took his with a muttered thanks she wrapped her free hand around his waist and scooted in close. His startled gaze met hers, but on the up side he no longer had the icy look.

Noah's phone dinged.

She butted into their conversation, "Your phone dinged,

didn't it?"

He whipped out his phone with his free hand. His eyes widened as he processed the message from her: *Hey, wanna ditch them? Just offering an excuse for you to tell them you have something you have to go take care of.* :)

Michael leaned in to try to read, but Noah darkened the screen.

"We've got to get going, Michael. I heard the call for us." Noah shoved his phone back into his pants pocket. He met Michael's gaze. For a few silent moments something passed between them. Then he nodded a silent goodbye, put his hand around her back, and directed her back toward the entrance.

Once they were out of earshot she said, "Hope you were okay with that."

"I could handle…" He halted halfway back to the hostess podium, his gaze fixed on the people waiting for tables. "Oh, shit."

"What's wrong?"

He grabbed her hand and pulled her down the dark, quiet hallway behind the bar. Restroom alley. A server closed a closet door and walked off. He tugged her into the small closet and flipped on the light.

"Why're we in here?" She glanced around at the rolls of toilet paper, mop, and various cleaning aids. She set her untouched beer on a nearby shelf.

He glanced at his watch. "Let's just stay in here for a few minutes."

"Seriously, this is weird. What's going on?"

He covered his face. "There must be a fuck-Noah convention going on tonight."

"Noah, you're freaking me out."

"Of all nights, of course John fucking Willard would choose this restaurant. He works on Wall Street so I usually avoid clubs and restaurants on this side of town. God, the last time I bumped into him…" He ran a hand through his hair.

"I've never met John fucking Willard. Need a bit more info to understand why we're in here." She gave him a pointed glare.

"In high school, there was a thing that happened to me. He caught it on video."

"High school? Everyone did embarrassing stuff in high school. Can't be that bad."

He grunted.

She glanced around. "Since I'm in a janitor's closet on my fake date, I think I deserve the whole story."

He gazed at her in silence. She was a staredown contest champion. *Bring it on, Noah.*

Finally, he blinked. "This doesn't leave this room."

"Promise. This stays in the janitorial closet." She traced an X over her chest.

"Homecoming football game. Freshman year. I agreed to fill in for the mascot when he got sick at the last minute, whose absence in retrospect I'm pretty sure was on purpose. God, I was a gullible dipshit." He shook his head and blew out an agitated sigh. "Of course, I jumped at the chance to be found cool by seniors when the football team captain asked me to help out. The fake fur mascot suit was so tight and hot that I had to take off almost all my clothes to fit into it. Back then I wasn't…" He glanced down at himself. "In shape."

"None of us rocked high school." She wanted to give him a hug, but held back.

"I ran through the paper banner to open the game and…*surprise*. They hit me with a fire hose water spray. No one knew there was a pressure problem with the hydrant they used. It blew the mascot suit off me. And my underwear. Ended up swimming naked in mud."

"Oh my God. You can't be…"

"The video John, the fucker, took of it went viral."

She clapped a hand over her mouth to suppress her laughter. "No. Can't be. You're Naked Chicken Boy?"

His eyelids drifted closed as he put his hands over his face. "For the record, it was a hawk outfit. Not a chicken."

"Sure looked like a chicken." A bit of laughter escaped. "God, I'm sorry. That video was epic. That was you?"

"I hoped John would move away from the city." He rolled his eyes heavenward. "I go out there right now and he'll show the video to his new New York friends. Then someone will snap a photo of me. It'll end up online as a *look-at him-now* thing. It'll get shared with all nine hundred in my graduating class. The old video will have an upsurge in interest. Then I'll be reliving the nightmare of being Naked Chicken Boy for another few years."

"Is this why you don't like the media?"

"Yeah."

She leaned in and kissed him. Brief. Not at all satisfying, but an invitation. She pulled back to let him make the next move while a hint of *shouldn't-have-done-that* swamped her in uncertainty.

His chest rose and fell for endless seconds as he stared at her mouth. He was going to kiss her back.

Her breath hitched as he leaned in. The fabric across his chest tightened.

Her body tingled as she waited for the press of his lips against hers, but just when she thought he was going to close in on the final few inches, he cleared his throat and slowly pulled away.

"That was a pity kiss, wasn't it?" His eyes narrowed.

Yeah, it had been. She put a hand on either side of his face. "There's something about you, Noah. It makes me a little crazy."

"Then, what was it? Felt a lot like pity."

"You're overthinking it. Let that ridiculous video get you something positive for a change." She threaded her fingers through the soft strands of his hair. "Kiss me. You want to."

"This is a line we shouldn't cross. I won't deny I want to." He slid his hands up her arms. Cupping her neck, one hand gently twisting in her hair, he pulled her head back an inch. On an audible gasp, her eyes widened in surprise at the dominant move before he brought his mouth a whisper from hers.

He paused.

Oh, for God's sake, do it!

Eyes locked, she anchored her hands in place on his upper arms. Holding her breath, her skin prickled with awareness, with the knowledge he might think himself right out of doing this. Maybe they needed one of them to be cautious because leaping-before-thinking didn't always turn out well for her.

He said, "We shouldn't."

"Probably not."

He cut the distance between them, his lips touched hers. On a sigh, she melted into him, relieved.

Tentative at first, they explored, their lips light and not quite fusing.

She moved her hands to the back of his neck as if to keep him from pulling away.

Mouths opened. Grips tightened. The lightest touch of tongues.

He pressed her against the door and delved deeper while his thumb caressed the pulse point on her neck. His mouth left hers to kiss behind her ear. "How many tattoos do you have?"

Hoarsely she asked, "Does it matter?"

"The one on your thigh makes me want to tear off your thong and press my tongue against the dragon's flame. Then I can show you what real fire feels like."

Holy badboy in disguise! The heavy pants of her breaths echoed in her ears. Her attention was riveted on the heat of his lower body, now pressed tight to her. "How do you know I'm wearing a thong?"

"I might've gotten an eyeful when you got on the bike. I'm not apologizing." The exhales of his chuckle tickled her skin as he kissed down her neck.

"Not asking for an apology. I might've intended for you to look." She smiled.

"Jesus, you're sexy." He nibbled and kissed down to her collarbone, fingering the strap of her dress. "Another tattoo? How many do you have?"

"I'll tell you about my ink if you tell me about yours."

With a groan, his mouth crashed onto her lips. His tongue tangled with hers in a way meant to dominate. Her leg wrapped around the back of his, linking them together.

Each tangle and taste... She was falling fast with the kiss so deep, so intense with each thrust of their tongues.

Tentatively, her hands explored the divots of his broad chest. But she was fearful of the unknown, of what this was. Yet the craving for him was so freaking electrifying that everything else slipped away.

Until he stopped.

"We shouldn't have done that."

His rejection hurt. But he was right. That should *not* have happened. She scooted out and away from him, grabbing her discarded beer for a fortifying gulp.

He added, "I don't regret kissing the hottest gamer chick on the circuit."

She froze, the beer half way to her mouth for a second swallow. Did the kiss only happen because she was one of the few girls who competed? Was he a pig like too many of the other guys on the eGaming circuit?

Calm down. You started the kissing out of pity. She set down her beer. "You don't kiss like a fellow game designer."

Aw crap. Hadn't meant to let that slip out. Anger always unlocked the filter between her brain and mouth.

Noah's eyebrows almost reached his hairline. "You design

games?"

Now he'd judged her to be another programmer angling for him to see her work. She was *not* a desperate designer, not anymore. "Yes, but I make ends meet by freelance coding and ads on our Twitch streams. I might've gone to MIT, but after a two-year break for personal reasons everyone assumes your skills suck."

Stop blathering.

***

This woman kept shocking the hell out of him. The fear of motorcycle helmets. Kissing him. And now she designed games, with MIT as her alma mater, too? Hard to believe this was Emma's sister. Where his assistant was polished, Tori had hot as hell rough edges.

And that kiss… It'd rocked his goddamn world.

He wanted to know more about her. He didn't want a fake dating scenario. This want wasn't just about jumping into a physical relationship, although the wish to do so dominated everything south of his navel at the moment.

He asked, "You went to MIT?"

She nodded. "Didn't graduate, though."

His gaze drifted to the plunging neckline of the black dress. To peel off the silky creation and see the concealed ink tempted him. *Fake date, remember? It'd been a pity kiss for Naked Chicken Boy.* Not a real kiss. He needed to tell himself that about a hundred more times.

Felt pretty fucking real.

"Let's go out there and get our table. He's probably gone," she said. "I know that look." Her gaze darted to the door. She lowered her voice. "You and I can't be taking this to *that* level. It's not a part of the deal, remember? I don't regret the kiss, but I shouldn't have. It was impulsive and I'm sorry. Our date is for show. Me in the guest bedroom when necessary. Everything about this freaks me out. You're trying to help me to help yourself to help the FBI, which is totally screwed up." She reached out for his arm. "We should call this all off. The whole thing is ridiculous."

"No. This is important to try to get you free. It's bigger than that. This is for the future of eGaming." His gaze locked on her delicate hand where it touched him. His whole body exploded at the one small touch. The tattoo on her wrist caught his eye.

She released him as if she'd been stung and glanced around. "What the hell are we doing? Us pretending to date is a real dumbass idea."

"Pretend. This is pretend." *Keep saying it.* Not that it sunk in. He took two steps away from her. His heart pounded against his sternum. His dick pressed against his zipper so hard it'd probably have metal tracks permanently imprinted onto it.

She stared at his mouth. Was he supposed to go in for another kiss? If he did, and she hadn't intended it to go down that path, then he'd be an asshole. After years of misreading social cues he'd conditioned himself to wait, to evaluate, and to remain inactive until someone else indicated the right way to behave. He held his breath, more than hoping she wanted to kiss again. He waited for her to say something, anything. To move. To breathe. To give him some sort of signal.

Any signal.

"We have a table waiting on us," she prompted.

Each of his breaths echoed loudly between his ears. Was she saying she wanted to exit or stay in here? She didn't seem to be moving to leave.

Just as he swayed toward her his phone dinged with an incoming message. What usually came across as a soft tone sounded like an alarm in the small room. They both jumped.

He viewed the notification their table was ready on his cell phone. "Table's ready. Second message."

"Let's get out of here. I don't know what you think might be going to happen, but..." She shook her head. "I'm sorry. Let's forget about all this." She smoothed her dress.

You started it. "How many tattoos do you have?"

"Five. All dragons." She blinked up at him, wide-eyed and vulnerable. "How about you?"

"Back. Bit on my arms." He fingered a roll of toilet paper. "Why dragons? I mean, a gamer girl should have sexy tattoos, but dragons?"

Her eyes narrowed. "A gamer *girl* is expected to have tattoos? Why? Because it helps me seem tougher? Edgier? Maybe more butch and therefore not a threat to your idea of femininity?"

"That's not what I said." Damn it, he'd stuck his foot in his mouth, as usual.

"Sure as hell sounded like it. I like ink. It hasn't got anything to do with gaming." She waved her hand. "Forget it. This whole night is a study in insanity."

He reached for the doorknob. "Thank God this isn't for real. I suck as a date. I can't figure out what's going on and I always say some something asinine like the tattoo thing. Let's go get our table and get this over with." He yanked open the door and held it for her.

"Look, I'm sorry." She paused outside the door to glance up at him. "I'm used to a lot of shit coming my way from gamers. Makes me assume the worst."

"I'm sorry."

"You're apologizing for all the other gamers who toss shit at me or are you apologizing for yourself?" A small smile tugged her lips upward.

"Just take it as an overall for everything. Are you okay? Like really okay? I mean, are they threatening you or anything? Have they hurt you?"

She poked him in the chest. "Don't do that."

"What?"

"That whole nice-guy thing. Going from bad boy to possible asshole to nice guy... You're officially driving me nuts."

"In a good way?" *You did not just say that.* "Sorry. Didn't mean to take it there."

"It's..." She stepped back, putting a few feet between them. "You're complicated. I'll handle my end of this arrangement. You handle yours."

"You'll let me know if you get threatened or in trouble, right? More trouble than you're already in?"

"What'll you do? Charge in with the FBI or the police? Sweep me away in your limo to your penthouse?"

"I don't know. I haven't formulated a plan yet, but I'm working on it. I don't like the thought of someone hurting you."

A genuine smile lit up her face. "You're the real deal, aren't you?"

"What do you mean?"

"A genuine nice guy."

He put a hand over his heart. "The kiss of death. I've earned the *nice guy* label before we even finish our first date. There's no hope for me now."

She put a hand on his arm and laughed a glorious freeing sound that made him smile.

"Come on, Mr. Nice Guy, let's do this."

Chapter Four

Why couldn't this be a real date?

Because Noah Harrison would never go out with someone like me.

Noah hot, bothered, and naughty one moment, to stumbling all over his words, to saying the wrong thing, to caring and sweet the next rattled Tori.

The man could kiss. Fake date or not, the spark she'd felt in the police station wasn't a fluke.

Oh boy. She was in trouble.

Half a glass of wine and a string of meaningless chitchat later, she reminded herself to slow down on the alcohol. *You're on the road to getting wasted.* Didn't sound bad, though. Then maybe she'd forget this whole night. The smooth white wine Noah chose floated down her throat without the normal aftertaste she associated with wine. The bottle cost more than she made in a week. Of course, given her current negative income situation anything on the menu cost more than her weekly income.

She nodded in the direction of the storage closet. "I don't know what happened in there. I'm sorry. It's been well over a year since my boyfriend decided monogamy wasn't his thing..." She clapped her hand over her mouth. Damn alcohol. She had no tolerance.

"You've kept that fire pent up for a year?" His eyes sparkled.

Her cheeks burned. "You're really good at this pretending to be into each other thing."

His eyebrows rose.

Was he pretending? Oh God. Maybe he wasn't? The desire etched into his face did crazy things to her insides. Her eyes locked on to his, unable to break free from his mesmerizing intensity. "We need a topic change because this is messing with my head. We've got to stay on game here. Pretend, remember? Tell me something about yourself."

He swirled his wine and stared at the rivulets of liquid as they slid down the inside of the glass. "I'm blind without glasses or contacts. My glasses in grade school used to be a half-inch thick. How about you?"

"Twenty-twenty." She laughed when he fake glowered. "Oh, you wanted to hear something real. All right. I'm addicted to eighties horror movies. No one can beat *Jason* or *The Crypt Keeper*."

"They are pretty cheesy. I'm partial to early Stephen King films."

She got a sixth sense of someone staring at her. Behind Noah, a group of men leaned in around a phone, casting furtive glances Noah's way. Laughter broke out.

She stiffened. Had to be the John guy Noah worried about running into.

"Did you hear me?" Noah asked.

"What? Sorry." She double blinked at him.

"He's behind me, isn't he? John Wilton."

"I haven't met him so couldn't be sure, but I think the guys at that table know you from somewhere."

Noah cranked around. "Shit. It's him."

***

Tori's forehead furrowed. "You okay?"

No. This was high school all over again. Feeling humiliated to the point he wished the floor would swallow him whole. He hated it.

Years of therapy meant he should be over this. All those awful sessions hadn't done one iota of good, not when faced with the person who'd exploded his life by shooting a video of a prank gone wrong.

She fiddled with the hoops on her ear, something he noticed she did when agitated. "Why don't you go over there and tell them all to go to hell? You're a god in the gaming world. You're a self-made millionaire, maybe billionaire, wildly successful, and hot as hell. Why should a video of something that wasn't your fault continue to bother you?"

"Naked Chicken Boy had six million hits within six months." When it popped up in his Twitter feed a few months ago he'd spilled coffee all over his keyboard.

"So you were an internet sensation years ago." She chewed on her lower lip.

"You think I'm hot?"

Her cheeks flushed. "You know you're hot. You're also pretty good at kissing, which must come from years of practice because women probably throw themselves at you all the time. Hell, I was one of those women, wasn't I?"

No witty comeback popped into his mind. Making out on a fake first date in the janitorial closet of a restaurant? T-otal turn-on, but a first for him to be tempted by a woman to move so fast. Something about Tori challenged him. Everything with women in the past, although enjoyable, had been premeditated, almost to a predictable tee. Definite yawn-fest in comparison to what hijacked him minutes ago with her. He also didn't geek out and go all clumsy with her.

But he didn't want to admit that. For a brief moment he reveled in being wanted.

He wanted to know more about Tori. To see if they clicked as he suspected they would on more levels than just physical. Beneath her beautiful exterior, which it seemed she rarely let shine, she was a techie nerd. A programmer. He could talk things with her he'd never been able to with the other women he'd dated. His conscience crashed in. This was about Kaleb and freeing Tori from the dangerous eGaming underworld. Not actually dating.

Tori's glanced beyond him and stiffened.

"This isn't working," he finally said.

"What, us dating? We already knew it'd be a shit show."

"No, us trying to have a conversation with John over there. Let's get out of here."

Chapter Five

"I'm sorry about the viral video thing ruining everything tonight," Noah said as they approached the motorcycle.

"Not your fault that guy's an asshole." Tori stared at the helmets attached to the motorcycle in dread. "You can drop me at home." *Or we say goodbye here and I'll hop on the subway.* "When do we get to have this much fun again?"

"I owe you dessert and a hint on forty-one. There's this Italian place near the Flatiron with the best tiramisu."

"You can't be serious. This date was about the two of us being seen together, right? Mission accomplished."

"Please, Tori. Let's have coffee. Let me make this evening better." He picked up her hand. Heat focused on the point of contact. For a single moment she longed for another kiss. Maybe more.

She removed her hand from his. "Why? What's the point? No need to keep pretending."

"Even though this is what it is, I want to make sure you have a nice time. We didn't even get to eat. We can't end a first date like this."

She traced a crack in the sidewalk with the toe of her shoe. "Let's reality check this, okay? This isn't a real first date. A real date between us never would've happened. Guys like you don't date girls like me. You might want to fuck a girl like me as a curiosity, but not date. This is why *this*"—she waved her handed in an inclusive back-and-forth between them—"makes no sense. It doesn't even make sense for us to do a date number two." She stared at passing cars, unable to meet his gaze. "We can talk about level forty-one next time since we're required to have a second time."

"True, I've never dated anyone like you. Come have dessert with me. I haven't spent time with a woman who's a Trekkie since high school. Well, other than my mom, and there're a few ladies at work, not that I'd be taking them out anywhere. Come talk to me about the new movie, not the one that just came out on video but the one scheduled to release next year. We can even talk about the bots, if you like."

Trekkie talk did tempt her. She had a few hours to kill until she found out if she had to be at the Stadium tonight. "Not too long, though. There's a meet tonight. I'm probably going to get called in, which I know you want."

He released a breath as if he'd been anxious about her reply. He nodded to an idling car across the street. "We're driving this time. I texted my driver. He brought a friend to ride my bike home."

"Oh, thank Jesus," she muttered. *Oops.* Her cheeks blazed. He chuckled.

"I meant, how very thoughtful of you." She followed him to the waiting car.

As he slid into the car next to her he made a call, "This is Noah Harrison. I've got two for dessert. Do you have a table? I'd prefer the one in the private room where we won't be bothered." There was a pause. "Excellent."

Outside an unfamiliar Italian restaurant minutes away from the restaurant they just left, he took her hand and led her to the front of the throng waiting to be seated. She liked how big and strong his hand was around hers.

The hostess smiled broadly. "Mr. Harrison, your table is ready."

The hostess led them to a table in an isolated private room at the far back of the restaurant. Soft guitar music played in the background while the smell of garlic swirled around them.

Tori examined the dessert menu. "How'd you manage to get a table? This private one in particular? They're super busy."

"The owner's son works for me." He fiddled with his silverware and wouldn't meet her gaze.

A short, round Italian in white chef attire scurried to their table. He grabbed Noah's hand and pumped. In a thick accent, he said, "Signore Harrison. Such an honor. So pleased you have come tonight. So pleased."

Noah's eyes softened when he spoke to the chef. "Antonio, let me introduce Tori."

Antonio clasped her hand between both of his large hands. "La signorina, it is an honor to meet one so beautiful. Signore Harrison hasn't brought a lady with him in a long time." Antonio said low, conspiratorially, but not low enough that Noah couldn't hear, "We'd do anything for *him*. Anything. He took in my son when life beat him to the gutter. He give him job and saved his life." He released her hand to dab at the moisture gathering in his eyes. "We owe him everything. My boy was headed nowhere good, probably to die in gang fight, but now he's a success and about to give me a grandchild." He turned to Noah. "What may I make for you tonight? On the house. Anything."

A blush suffused Noah's cheeks. "I enjoy everything you make. Are you hungry for dinner, Tori, or just dessert?"

The sweets addict in her screamed for a fix. "Dessert works."

"Tiramisu, double portion. Two forks," Noah requested.

"And a coffee." She had a long night ahead.

"Decaf for me." Noah smiled at the chef.

"Of course. But you never pay." With a hand flourish, Antonio bustled away as fast as his large frame could weave between tables.

She bit her lip against laughing at Noah's unease after the chef's gushing. "What's the story? You gave the chef's son a job?"

"Antonio's son had a rough time before he came to me. Barely squeaked out of high school. Multiple expulsions for skipping school and there was an incident of spray painting public property. Rejected at all colleges. It took me about five minutes to figure out his kid's a genius when you put him behind a computer screen. You know some of us computer folks excel at little else."

"I get that. He applied for a job with you guys? He got your attention with no resume?"

Noah shook his head. "I was having dinner here and while chatting with Antonio I found out his son's story. I offered he send his son down to the office for a day. I thought it'd be a big brother situation, but I swear his kid is brilliant. He's become one of my top creative designers. A lot of the newer ideas on the second *Zoneworld Warrior* came from him."

Her heart squeezed. "That's amazing you gave him a chance. I'm sure half the gamers in the world are jealous."

"Are you?"

She shrugged, grabbed her water for a swallow and stared at the doorway through which Antonio disappeared.

"So you design video games?" he asked in a leading tone.

"I didn't mean for us to talk about it." She shifted and re-crossed her legs.

"What kind do you like to write?" He nudged his fork away from his plate and slid it back.

"Fantasy."

"Did you finish one?"

"I did, but let's discuss something else." She met his gaze for an instant.

Noah leaned forward, his eyes sparkling. "Tell me about it."

"You don't have to fake interest so we can have small talk."

"Gamers make the best designers. They know what

59

irritates the hell out of people and what draws them in. You had decent training if you went to MIT. I went there, so I'd know. Tell me what you came up with."

She chewed on her lip. She'd already sold her game. She didn't need Noah's opinion or interest, but she liked talking about it. "In undergrad I had this idea for a game and recruited a friend to help me fill in the gaps. I'm good at content like characters and visuals and ideas for the building aspects. I can code with the best of them, but my friend did artificial intelligence. He moved on from it when it was in its neophyte stage. My game is in a different category from what you created."

"In what way?" He maintained eye contact without a hint of ennui.

"It's fantasy. A royal assassination sparks a war between the dragon-keepers, elves, humans, and elementals. Players can choose which avatar they want to play. They can be whatever they want, be it mage, elf, drunk, whomever. They work to figure out who's evil, who did the assassination, and save the world. There's traditional slash-and-hack fighting, guerilla warfare, and advanced building capability."

"Is it single pathway or multiple?"

"There're hundreds of hours of quests, caves, dungeons, forts. It's a classic RPG where you can create your own experience within the storyline. You could tip cows for an hour if that's your thing."

"Sounds interesting. I'd like to see it."

"Really?"

Oh, crap. I giggled.

That kind of airheaded noise couldn't have come from her mouth. Her stomach did belly flops while *he wants to see it* played over and over in her brain.

"Yes. I want to review it. I'm looking for something new." He dug his cell phone out of his pants pocket to read the screen.

"I'm sorry. I despise texting in restaurants, especially when with company, but I've got to reply to this."

She waited until he was done. "Business? Or a girlfriend who's pissed you're not already home?"

"I said I was single before we started this. Are you jealous?" He seemed genuinely confused. Her typical date would've jumped all over her with joking snark about jealousy.

"Maybe."

"Serious? This is you jealous?" He flashed his dimples as his lips split into a killer grin. He put his phone back into his jacket. "I had a call scheduled at eleven tonight, but I arranged to move it to tomorrow morning."

Did he assume they'd end up at his place? In his bed? Uh-oh. She was thinking like this was a real date. "You didn't need to reschedule. Not for me."

"It's done." He rested his chin on his hands and studied her until she had to fight fidgeting.

"What?" she finally asked. "Do I have food on my face or drool on my chin?"

He laughed. "Drool on your chin?"

"You know what I mean. You're staring. It's not polite."

He laughed deep and low in a quiet way that caused her stomach to clench. "I find you different."

Different? She jerked her hand so abruptly she knocked her fork into the plate with an ear-splitting clatter. What the hell did that mean?

He compressed his lips as if holding back a laugh. His eyes crinkled at the corners.

She pushed the fork far away from the plate to avoid a repeat incident. "I'm not sure what you mean by *different.*"

"I meant you're unusual. Kind of bizarre…but exciting. No, that doesn't sound right." He cleared his throat. "I'm sorry your last boyfriend cheated on you. That turns one off of the whole relationship thing."

"The asshole stole my work, made a fortune off it, and cheated on me. Talking about exes isn't good first date material. They don't make good second date chitchat, either. Let's not go there, especially after you called me weird."

Noah looked like he was standing in front of an oncoming semi-truck, but was so wide-eyed frozen he couldn't move. "I... Uh..."

She waved a dismissive hand. "Lucky for us this isn't a real date. If it was I'd say it crashed and burned. Under normal circumstances I'd leave after being called weird."

Dessert arrived.

"I didn't call you weird. I'm sorry. I meant to say I think you're an interesting person." He gazed at the dessert and lifted a fork as if waiting for her to take the first bite.

"Sorry I overreacted, then." She took a generous bite. "This is good."

Many silent minutes later they stared at the decimated remains of the tiramisu.

"So... I guess I still owe you a hint on forty-one," he said.

She couldn't tell if this was a peace offering or something else. Still, she'd more than earned her reward. "You do."

He gazed at her intently for a few seconds. "Let's go."

"What? You're not going to tell me right now?"

"Not yet." He smiled elusively and left a generous cash tip.

Outside, the chill of the March night had descended over the city. The honk of cars echoed in the streets during the rush of late Saturday night. Heavy bass music lingered in the air from several doors down.

Her cell phone vibrated inside her clutch. Symphis texted. *Tonight. Midnight. Don't be late.*

Symphis docked her fifty bucks for being five minutes late last time.

She shivered as she shoved the phone back into the mini-purse. The cold wasn't only from a blast of cool wind, but also at the thought of the Stadium. "I'm on for tonight. Midnight."

They stared at each other in silent understanding of this as the start of *game on.*

He slipped his coat around her shoulders. "You look cold."

His warm hand slid around hers and he led to the waiting car. After he scooted in next to her in the back seat he finally said, "Come play the level with me and I'll show you its secret."

A laugh broke free. "As far as come-up-to-my-place lines, that was probably the most original I've ever heard."

"I didn't mean…" He seemed legitimately perturbed like every time tonight she'd pointed out a dating faux pas. Perhaps his ingenuousness was legit.

Hadn't Emma said something about him avoiding the social scene? Now she felt like crap for being tough on him. Her go-to behavior with the opposite sex, born from years in the eGaming world where sexism ran rampant, made her quick on the offensive.

"Maybe we should talk about the game level another time," she suggested. "In the fake dating world it'd be moving a bit fast, don't you think? In the non-fake world me going to your place feels like a step beyond our agreement. I'm not angling for anything serious to come out of us fake dating."

"Your call. I'd like to spend more time with you for real, not for this farce. But I didn't mean to imply… I'm not looking for anything serious, either."

"Nothing serious then. Just fun? Okay, clarification. Fun as in playing the game. That's it."

"Yes." He looked relieved, but also jazzed.

"You better play your best, and realize I'm going to win. We're not starting from level one, though. Not enough time."

She bit back a smile at his suppressed enthusiasm. A fellow gamer geek hid inside the body of this socially maladroit Adonis.

She related, not the body part, but the chance to play and have some genuine competition. That she totally got.

"If we play, *you* better bring your A-game. You have no idea what you're in for."

His tone suggested he wasn't referring to playing the game. She narrowed her eyes.

"Just the game." His shirt pulled tight across the strong muscles of his chest as he shifted in his seat. She'd liked being pressed against those contours. And that kiss... This was bad. Temptation and resistance—two words that never worked for her.

She said hoarsely, "Okay. One game. We'll start on forty to get warmed up to forty-one. Being the game's designer I assume you have the ability to skip to a higher level from the start. You can't play Rys."

His eyes flared wide. "How would you know he's my choice?"

"I've played this game since its release against gamers that can make even the most experienced player beg for mercy. I can read personality character choices. I see people as their character choices sometimes, especially when it comes to this particular game."

"Why can't I be Rys? That's not fair. I know you want to be Evelle."

"Rys has those *Emei* daggers from hell. Whoever plays that character is always ramming one in Evelle's leg on level twenty-one. You know, the one with—"

"The swinging bridge and the helicopter air attack. I hadn't thought of that. Perfect ambush for Evelle. But we're not playing level twenty-one."

She crossed her arms again. "No Rys. His knives irk the hell out of me."

The car stopped. She glanced outside to his apartment building in uptown Manhattan.

He hopped out of the car and held his hand out for her, "One game, two levels. I owe you at least this."

She took his hand. Her heart raced while her brain spun with a case of second-guessing.

Chapter Six

Noah swiped sweat from his forehead. Finally, level forty-one. He'd witnessed Tori's skills at his game, but he'd almost gotten his character killed twice already. He glanced at her sitting beside him on the floor in front of the flat panel screen compressing her lips in concentration. Besides being out of practice, he didn't like playing any character other than Rys.

Bullshit. She's better. He should've pushed a littler harder to play Rys but feared if he had she would've left. So he chose a less familiar character with a sword.

Their characters faced off as a team against hostiles at the top of the waterfall. She focused her avatar on fighting while he moved his to the access point where they could go over the edge.

She drawled, "So, Evelle can seduce? How does that work?"

"As if I'm telling you how after you almost beat my high score on the last level."

Tori's character killed off the last hostile. She squinted in concentration and pushed her character into a hip swagger. Noah's avatar dropped his jaw. He yanked at his controller, demanding his character move without effect.

"Whoa." She scowled. "Did you program her?"

"Yeah. Cool, huh?"

"No, this isn't cool. This is disgusting. Evelle was the first non-sensationalized female avatar who could be awesome because she was a regular person. Now she's got this, which makes her like every other cliché female in games." She shook her head.

"It's a powerful tool."

Tori didn't look impressed.

Their characters jumped over the falls onto the rock shelf several feet below. Their characters now stood at the spot no player internationally had moved beyond.

"Now what?" She glanced away from the screen for the first time. "This is where I die every time. I've been through every cavern. I've pushed every rock, played in the water, and jumped off the falls. Everything's booby-trapped. Ugh, here come those freaking robotic scorpions."

Noah smiled. "It's not about the caverns or the bots."

"They're distraction. I've tried going other ways or finding a secret button."

"Ignore the doors. Use the rope," he instructed.

"What rope?" she asked dully.

"The one we picked up on level twelve."

"Oh, yeah. I remember a rope. And then what?"

Noah's character killed off the three scorpions.

She grunted. "You made that look too easy."

"It was easy." His character looped the rope over a rock and then propelled downward in the middle of the waterfall's cascading water."

She made her character follow. They swung onto a rock shelf. "I didn't know we could go down farther. Cool." The screen flashed *Level Forty-Two*. "Hot damn."

Noah's character moved in next to hers as the level opened. He swung a lethal pivot and decapitated Evelle. Her screen flashed *Game Over*.

"How dare you?" She threw her controller at him.

He dodged and grabbed her when she dove for him. She managed to get a solid punch into his stomach before he alligator rolled her beneath him. She bucked up against him and cursed, then her body relaxed. He pushed upward away from her.

"You're a piss poor loser," he grumbled.

"You're a sexist double-crosser."

"I didn't promise anything about playing forty-two." He couldn't figure out if she was pissed or into him. As always, he waited. *Give me a sign.*

Her eyes dilated and dropped to his lips while her fingers traced up and down his spine. "A hot sexist, though."

He fit two fingers under her chin and tipped her head up. "We can keep playing if you want."

"Forget the game. I'll figure out forty-two on my own." Desire darkened her eyes. Her pulse ticked rapidly in her throat. The same floral combination that had teased him in the car saturated his nose.

Before he could slam on the brakes he leaned in. He caught himself mere millimeters from her parted lips. Her breath hitched.

Eyes closed, he drew in ragged breaths, trying to remember why they'd gone on this date tonight and the barriers between them. Why he shouldn't do this. His lips on hers crossed the line. Sure, it wouldn't be the first time tonight and it'd been so goddamned good the last time, but this felt different.

Her hand moved to his neck, pulling to encourage him to close the distance.

He ducked away from her lips to kiss the side of her neck with his hand resting on her stomach. Her body arched up into his hand, silently asking him for more.

He was going to lose his mind trying to avoid her lips. But he complied with her demand for more. Inch by slow inch he guided his hand to just below her breasts. When he halted a displeased groan escaped her.

"Noah, please."

He squeezed his eyes shut, trying to find willpower. Her fingernails dug into his scalp, guiding him to her lips.

Her lips glided across his, her tongue diving into his mouth. Someone was moaning. He wasn't sure which one of them made the noise, but it was vocal and sexy. Moving his hand higher, his fingertips grazed the bottom of her breast. So soft. Round. He caressed below her nipple, never touching, just teasing.

"God, Noah..." Her body rocked against his, bringing on a fresh wave of longing.

This is getting out of hand. He pulled away, gasping for air. Distance. They needed distance even if doing so was going to hurt.

"We could up the ante. I'll give you a level hint for every tattoo you show me." The words hurt him to say. She'd think him a total dick, but if the offended gamer girl reared its head, she'd back off at a hundred miles an hour. He forced a smile.

She froze. Her forehead creased and face fell flat with disappointment. "We're not doing this."

***

"What's wrong?" he asked.

How could he not get it? Tori glared. "Level hints?"

"I meant it as a good thing. Tongue action...tattoos...right?"

She wasn't going to whore herself for level hints. She had *not* fallen that low. No way she'd become the gamer slut every guy assumed of her before they pushed some of their bullshit prejudice on her and got their nuts crushed.

One glance toward Noah and her stomach plummeted at his devastated look. Had she misinterpreted again? Maybe he really didn't understand how demeaning the suggestion had been. He also didn't seem to understand how him programming Evelle with a secret seduction power was a crushing disappointment.

She stood, righting her dress and pulling back on her shoes. "I'm not going to mess around just to get level hints. I'm smart enough to figure it out on my own."

"I didn't mean to imply you weren't."

She massaged her forehead. "I think you really don't get how deprecating it is to assume I'd do that for game hints." She held up a hand. "This is my fault. I gave you the wrong impression from the get-go, wanting a game hint in exchange for a date, even if it was a fake date. Then I kissed you. I should've known it'd go this way. Let's forget it. You and me...none of this is real."

"I didn't even think of it that way. I'm a dipshit, I guess. Whatever's going on between us feels pretty real, but it's best we not be involved. You're right. It'd be too complicated. But you felt whatever this is, didn't you?"

He was cute in his socially inept way. Yeah, she felt it.

"Look, right now has to be for show only. There's too much at stake for us to throw the mind fuck of sex into the mix. I can't lose focus. You shouldn't, either. Let's not go in this direction. Let's work to figure out how to take Symphis down."

"You're right. Sorry." His hair stuck up at odd angles. Her doing.

She compressed her lips together as she admired the long lines of his shoulders and his strong arms. "Pretty sure I'm 51 percent responsible for what happened. Apology unnecessary."

"I've got something for you." He pushed up to a stand and went over to his hall table. He held out a small, round item. "Tom said to take this. It's a listening device and tracker. Take it with you to the Stadium from now on."

"Looks like a button." She scrutinized the tiny piece.

"Stick it in your pocket or something. Keep it with you all the time. If they frisk you they shouldn't care about it. It won't get picked up on a metal detector."

She shoved it in her pocket and trekked to the front door. Once there, she glanced up. Mistake. The desire to dishevel him further and feel his lips on hers once more burned her from the inside out. She bit her lip against a litany of excuses and justifications to convince herself, more than him, that she had to go. *You said your piece. Stick to it.*

"My driver is downstairs waiting at the front for you. Seems like as a date I should go with you to take you home, but you're right, we need to back away from what happened here."

Having a driver take her home sounded luxurious and way, way, way out of her comfort zone. "I can get home on my own. This is the safest part of the city."

"If you're not taking my car, then I'm going with you to make sure you make it home safe." His face got tough.

"Fine. I'll take the car." She hugged her arms around her body.

He opened a closet and handed her a fleece jacket. "Take it. I don't know if it's getting cold outside or whatever. You can give it to me next time." Before she stepped out the door he said, "I'm sorry the date sucked. Be careful tonight."

She turned and glanced up. Oh dear. The concern in his gaze tempted her to lean into him and accept the comfort he offered.

He put his hand on her shoulder and lightly squeezed. "You'll be okay, right? You can do this?"

"Oh my God. Stop it."

He pulled his hand away. "What?"

"Being so freaking nice. It's killing me. I can't handle it." *No one's ever this kind to me.*

"Just promise me you'll be okay." He gripped his hands together.

"I can't make that promise. There aren't any guarantees with this." She gazed at the elevator, reluctant to leave. "I gotta go. I'll see you later." Because this was a pseudo-date she threw over her shoulder, "Text me or something."

In the elevator, her phone dinged with a message from Anonymous. Aside the surprise she got good reception in an elevator, the text contained an image of her in an elevator. No, couldn't be *this* elevator. She enlarged the picture and recognized the gold rings on the carpet. Goosebumps raised on her arms.

The elevator lurched. The lights flickered off and then back on.

Coincidence. Right?

Could she reach the panel in the ceiling to get out, if needed? No. Too high.

With a finger extended to press the red emergency button a new text came in from Anonymous: *I see you.*

She glanced around. Then up at the camera.

Anonymous: *Fun date? Sure hate for something to happen to you 'cause you can't keep secrets.*

Had to be Symphis or one of his lackeys.

The elevator continued its downward journey. Heart hammering the inside of her ribs, Tori jabbed the button for the next floor and kept jabbing until the elevator doors opened. She jumped out, threw a hand against the wall, and slumped to her knees. Oh, crap, she was in a lot of trouble.

* * *

Noah stared at the closed elevator doors for several long moments, barely breathing and not moving. He worried about her safety at this time of the night and where she was going. He considered chasing after her, but the two of them alone in the back of a car would end in him kissing her. Again.

Letting her leave had to happen. He hadn't wanted it. He'd wanted her to stay, not for sex, although their combustible chemistry would've made it inevitable had she remained, but to be safe from everything about the Stadium. If anything happened to her, he'd be devastated.

Tori...hell. Everything about her was new. Although the

small taste he'd gotten with her might've shattered all expectations, it was a dead-end street.

He hadn't gotten her up here with any sort of long-term hopes. He might've had a few plans for right now…a lot of right now. And, maybe a few plans for a bit more.

He wished things were different. That he could have real time with her, not fake dates. Time to explore her curves and tattoos. Time to see the game she'd programmed and play the rest of *Zoneworld Warrior* against her. He wanted to see her expression when she reached the accolade. That was far more plans than he should've made for someone he wasn't actually dating. Someone he was using.

Damn it. She was a means to an end.

He released a frustrated snort. He both liked and hated the complication of actually liking Tori.

Chapter Seven

Tori's eyes adjusted to the dim light of the Stadium, tonight located in a modified basement in an old office building near Columbia's campus. Rows of tables and already-claimed computer terminals sat in the center of the room. The only allowed light came from the blue glow of the computer screens. Players already hooked in grunted, groaned, yahooed, and cursed.

She zipped her fleece-lined hoodie to ward off the super-chilled air. Frequent air exchange helped control the smell of sweaty men and fast food, although its real purpose was to keep them awake. Her usual sense of homecoming when at a gaming event evaded her. Tonight, she wished to be back with Noah, playing for fun and not competitively. She longed to be in charge of her fate, not owned by an arrogant, power-tripping narcissist and by Noah's FBI agent.

She fingered the button inside her hoodie pocket. If something happened here or on the commute, someone would hear. That didn't mean whoever listened at the other end could send help in time. Still alone in this endeavor.

"Selene." Rand, Symphis's first lieutenant, gave her a lewd chest scan like she was a character in a game he wished he could redesign to have bigger boobs and a smaller waist. He took a sip from his Monster. As one of only two women who competed in the Stadium she experienced constant sexual objectification. This middle-aged creep could jerk off to fantasies all he wanted. It wouldn't get him anywhere. Her typical disgust didn't roll off her like it did in the past.

Did he know about Symphis's elevator threat? Her heart thrashed inside her chest.

Her stomach churned. *No puking. Relax. Be yourself.*

Rand adjusted his calf-length, split-leg leather coat. The new piece was probably custom made as some sort of cosplay costume. The way he flapped the edges together hinted he longed for her to comment. When she said nothing and remained unimpressed he said, "You're on the Red Team tonight. At least you made it on time, unlike last time."

"What're we playing?" Good, that came out bitchy.

Rand snorted and rolled his eerie pale eyes. "Symphis texted you the schedule weeks ago. It's *Unholy Wars.*"

"Great." She fake smiled. *Unholy Wars* was her least favorite play, even if she was one of the top fifty scorers in the world. When it first released two years ago she'd obsessed about it, memorized maps, remembered enemy patterns, and bombed every square inch of the three cities in the game. As time passed and she mastered all the levels, it bored her.

"You on your game tonight, Selene?"

"Yep." She liked that he didn't call her by her real name. She wasn't under any delusion Symphis didn't know or couldn't find out her real identity. Selene, in this world, kept her more detached, even if it didn't keep her out of jail.

"If you're betting, Xion's handling it tonight." He nodded toward the back. He pulled his long, thin, white-blond hair out of its ponytail and redid it. The style accentuated the disappearing widow's peak of his receding hairline.

"Got no money to bet." She gazed at the oversized screen at the far end of the room that showed the other cities with teams who'd be logging in to play tonight. Like a horse race, the odds for each team flashed beside their name. Bets could be called in, placed online, or in person. The Stadium had grown to involve ten cities in the past three months, which was terrifying. The FBI and Noah were right to be worried. Illegal eGaming was so much bigger than New York, not to mention those who disagreed with Symphis ended up dead.

"Oh, Selene, I heard you had an interesting date tonight," Rand called out.

"Did I?"

"Noah Harrison. We weren't aware you two knew each other. Your sister works for him, but we didn't think you…"

Her heartbeat thudded between her ears. "I met him at the game in D.C. He made me mess up and lose early. The date tonight was my consolation prize." She didn't like the thoughtful look on Rand's face.

He pushed his ear where a communicator plug rested. "Symphis thinks maybe you dating him could be beneficial for all of us. He offers to clear your debt if you get the key code to unlock *Zoneworld Warrior Two*."

"Oh, sure. That's dinner date small talk."

"You might have to do more than talk to get it." His eyebrows rose as his gaze dropped down her body.

"You want me to blow him and in the middle of it go 'Hey, can I have the key to unlock the copyrighted code to *Zoneworld Warrior Two* so this guy I know can hack it or sell it or do something that's definitely not legal?'" Her eyebrows smashed together into a cynical *are you shitting me* look.

"I think with your mouth on his dick he'd probably give you anything you wanted." He stared at her mouth. "I might."

Eww. "I'd need a second date, which isn't certain yet." This was a test to feel out her usefulness to them.

Rand cocked his head and ogled at her chest again. "You went up to his place tonight…"

"I'll get back to you if we're going out again. Symphis will clear my debt for it. Really?"

"We heard the FBI approached you in D.C."

No use denying it if they knew the FBI talked to her, but how did they know? They probably had a mole either with the FBI or NJ Legacy. Her head throbbed. *Must calm down.*

"They cornered me at the competition in D.C. I told them to fuck off. I've landed in jail enough not to trust those conniving shitheads."

"What'd they want?" Asked in a tone that was a little too curious.

"They wanted to know about this and to get my cooperation to recruit Noah to help them since they somehow know you have us play *Zoneworlds*. They found out about our impending date."

"Why would they want Noah Harrison's help?"

"Don't know, but, like me, he was ambushed in D.C. by them. He seemed pissed. They tried to twist my arm into cooperating, but they didn't have anything on me to do the twisting."

He smiled a sinister show of braces-laden teeth. "So long as you're telling the truth."

"I'm here. I owe Symphis. I know the stakes." She put her hands on her hips. "I've been to jail three times over the Stadium. Have I blabbed once? No. So, back the hell off."

"Don't forget what's at stake."

"I won't." As she sauntered away she saw Rand push his ear and heard something about Jersey. Was Symphis in Jersey? Might be another Stadium event location, though.

She nodded at the familiar faces she passed. None smiled at her. One guy shot her the finger, perhaps because she'd nixed his character last week on level ten. Symphis demanded "cooperative team spirit" within each assigned squad, but nixing the guy's avatar last week improved the crappy squad's performance.

Nearby, Jar, her recruiter, accepted something from a known drug dealer. He popped whatever pills he'd acquired into his mouth. Clothes hung off his used-to-be-XXL frame. Stress and drugs made for an unbeatable weight loss program.

"How're you doing?" she asked him.

Jar vacant stared at her as if accessing memory proved difficult. "Tori, right?"

"Yeah, it's Tori. You okay?" They'd competed against each other for years with a friendly smack-talk rapport.

Deep bags drooped beneath his eyes. As she brushed past him when he didn't answer he grabbed her wrist in a brutal grip and leaned in to whisper, "If they offer you drugs, don't do it. Get out now. Just get out."

With a yank she freed her wrist. "Uh, okay."

She wove through table clusters to find the Red Table.

"Aw shit. Tell me, we didn't get the *girl* on our team," a barely fifteen-year-old groaned.

Ugh. The fifteen-year-old was a notorious hothead who didn't comprehend the concept of teamwork. Her other three squad mates were mid-twenties greenhorns on their first or second night of play, identified by the nametags they were forced to wear. This group guaranteed a shitshow performance.

She tested the suppleness of the only open chair. It wobbled. Pet peeve number one when gaming was chair issues. She dragged the chair away from the table and exchanged it for one from a nearby cluster. The new one's wheel squeaked, but it didn't wobble.

The gigantic countdown timer on the wall signaled three minutes until the competition started. She glanced around, expecting someone to offer to be team leader. Fine, she'd be the one to ask. "Did we already discuss strategy?"

"Fuck you," the fifteen-year-old muttered.

Tori scowled. "That's a piss-poor strategy if we're doing this as a team."

None of the others met her gaze. Typical. They judged her to be the unskilled token female player. "If you can't play this game, then tell me now. Assuming you can, I need to know your strengths so we can decide who does what."

Nothing. One of the guys had the audacity to leer at her chest.

"If we win or place in the top ten, then we'll get a minimum thousand credits." It'd get her one step closer to free of debt.

The fifteen-year-old snorted. "We're not gonna win. Not with this group of shitheads. So, who cares? We get out there. We shoot and stay alive. Move to the next level. End of strategy."

"Have you ever played this game? It's not about shooting hostiles. It's about—"

A horn sounded. Thirty second warning.

She pulled on her headphones. Too tight. She fiddled with them but in the dark she couldn't see the mechanism to loosen them.

Double horn blare. Her screen lit up automatically. The game's intro launched.

Ninety minutes later, twenty-six levels in, the greenhorns already out, she made a mistake by moving through the indiscriminate fire line of her teammate. The cocky fifte-year-old whose finger never let up on his fire button accidentally shot her. Maybe it wasn't an accident. He'd positioned himself in a way that made it almost impossible for her not to cross through his active fire line.

She tried to compensate for the error, but as expected, her character died within a minute. This game was sudden death. One life. No extra life credits. She ripped off her headset with a curse. No matter whether this was real or show, she despised losing.

"What the hell?" Rand slammed his hand down on the table beside her.

She jumped. "My teammate shot me. Blame him."

79

"You never mess up this early. Did you screw up on purpose?"

"I don't mess up on purpose. It hurts my reputation to lose. You want me to do better? Then assign me people who actually want to work together. But that's not the point of this circus, is it? As long as we keep screwing each other rather than working together we remain in debt. Right?"

Rand's face mottled red. "Get out of here. Get some practice in for next time. Go blow Harrison and get us what we want. If he won't give it to you, steal it. Don't disappoint us."

Chapter Eight

Tori batted at her alarm without cracking her eyelids, but the electronic ringing didn't stop. She rolled over and glared at her bedside table. The noise culprit wasn't the alarm. Who called at 6:05 a.m. on a Saturday? Her cell phone's insistent beeps stopped. With a relieved groan, she relaxed into her pillow. Seconds later, the noise resumed.

She grabbed the phone, recognized the number and grumbled into it, "What?"

"Tori. It's me," said Emma.

"It's six something. This better be an emergency?" The blue light of dawn filtered through the apartment window. She needed five more hours of uninterrupted sleep.

"How'd the date go last night?" asked Emma.

"You're calling for a play-by-play at six freaking a.m.? I got through it." Kissing Noah dominated her mind. "I'm hanging up now."

"No, wait. He wants to go to breakfast with you."

"Then why isn't he on the other end and not you?" *Not interested in waking up yet.* "I got in bed three hours ago. Need sleep."

"Mr. Harrison had a Skype meeting this morning and it's running late. He sent me out to contact you. They just bought a small gaming company. The sale came up really fast." Emma took a breath. "Oh dear. It's Conjur. I didn't even think of you and your game…"

"What?" Tori sat upright so fast her brain swirled with dizziness. That game was her foot in the door of a new life. "Are they keeping all of Conjur's acquisitions?"

"They'll sort through Conjur's backlist, but there's so much it'll take a while. They'll only keep a handful. The rest they'll let go. I'm sorry."

Would they choose her game? With her dating the CEO, even if it was a fake relationship, keeping it might be perceived as she screwed her way into it. They had to pass on her work.

Just like that her future financial security turbojetted out the window. Man, her life sucked. Tori fell back onto her bed. "Don't tell them."

"Might be good if they knew. They might like it."

"No. Promise you won't tell them. With me and Noah dating…it'd look bad."

"Fine. They'll eventually figure it out, but maybe it'll be when everything is over. Mr. Harrison says you two having breakfast is *important.*"

Her gaze caught on the tracker button on her bedside table. Her sister sucked at subterfuge. "I'm going back to sleep now."

Emma rushed to say, "If you can't make breakfast then he has a brunch event this morning he'd like to take you to. It's business and socialization. Company brunch."

"No way." Her have to deal with both Noah and a company event on too little sleep? Uh, no.

"He texted me to say last night was good."

"What does that mean?" Her heart pounded. "Did he go into details? The date was a bomb of epic proportions. He called me weird. I called him a sexist." *Did good refer to the date or the kiss or her in the Stadium?*

"Guess it didn't go as bad as you thought."

She settled under her comforter and dozed off.

"Tori?" Then silence. Then Emma yelled, "Are you listening to me?"

"Sorry. Phased out. Really tired. I'm not going out today.

Tell him it's a no."

"On the one hand, you don't say *no* to Mr. Harrison. On the other, this is a great opportunity for you to meet some people in the company and might be important for your game's future."

She released a sarcastic snort. "This doesn't have jack to do with my game."

"I can help get it out of the slush pile. Noah actually asked me about it."

"He did? Scratch that. No. Promise you won't do anything to draw attention to it. Noah's kidding about interest in my game. He's trying to make you feel good about us dating before our next date." She rolled over and snuggled deeper under the covers. "I wanna sleep. Please."

"This will only take a few hours of your time. It's a brunch thing. You spend an hour or two with him and then you can go back to sleep." Emma added softly, "I love you, Tori. Please, this is important."

Damn it.

Do not cave.

She pounded her fist into the bed. Her plan for a lazy morning vanished. "It didn't go well yesterday."

"I think Noah really likes you."

Did she mean that for real or did she say it in case anyone was screening her calls?

"You should wear a pink suit today," Emma suggested.

"Pink? Who in the world do you think you're talking to? Since when have I ever done pink or a suit? I took your advice last night. Wearing a dress backfired. Did he tell you he brought his motorcycle?" She stumbled into the bathroom and leaned close to the mirror.

Oh my. Stubble burn trekked across her chin. Maybe that's what Rand had been leering at last night.

"Tell me he didn't show up on that bike," Emma said.

Tori snickered. Noah was about to get his ass ridden all

over by her sister. "Yep. Imagine me straddling that thing in a dress and heels. This time I'm wearing whatever I want."

"You can go to my apartment and pick something out of my closet. Please choose something that isn't black. This isn't a dressy event, but you're going to be with the boss. Black is for evening dates. Don't wear those clunkers you love. Noah wanted to pick you up but I said you'd meet him at his building at ten this morning."

"You already knew I'd agree."

"You like him. Lickable, remember? So..." She hit three octaves on the word. "You went to his place last night?" Emma asking a leading question meant Emma didn't know exactly what happened last night.

"We played a video game."

"Of course, you did. What else would two gaming junkies do on a date?" Disgust lingered in her tone. "Remember—this, you participating, is important. Really *important*."

Code for: expect the FBI.

A single message dinged its arrival on her phone from the Anonymous she'd relabeled as Symphis.

Get the code

.

***

Tori chewed her lip on the elevator ride up to Noah's penthouse. As the numbers increased her dread of another message from Symphis grew. She glared into the camera in the corner.

Outside the elevator she exhaled long and hard. False bravado aside, she'd been scared shitless the elevator would fritz again.

Her phone dinged.

Symphis: *You enjoy the smooth ride up?*

Her heart pounded so hard inside her chest that she felt

84

dizzy.

Symphis: *Go get what I want.*

Her lungs locked. After a few wheezes she coughed. She stared at the ceiling in search of cameras. Had to be one there. How else would he know?

Symphis: *Tell Tom I know he wants to recruit you. I own you.*

She slapped her palm against the wall for support but instantly hated she'd shown the jerk how upset he made her.

He knew about Tom? Yet he thought her dating Noah was real?

With a glare at the closest ceiling camera, she made a show of turning off her phone and jamming it into her jacket pocket.

Noah's door loomed ahead. She needed to see him. He'd help her feel safe, even though there wasn't anything he could do to save her.

She knocked. No answer.

Hand raised to knock again, the door flew open.

"You're late. Thought you might've bailed." Noah gave her a once over. Maybe she'd underdressed in jeans and T-shirt, but the jacket upgraded the outfit. And she hadn't worn her "clunkers," having traded them for heeled boots.

She wanted to dive at him for a hug, but her gaze darted to the ceiling camera. No way she'd show that level of weakness after a few subtle threats.

She dwelled on what Symphis wanted her to do with Noah. Her interest in the actual doing had nothing to do with the code. She wanted to see this man lose his mind because of her. Heat crept into her face. He looked so hot. Dark jeans encased his muscular legs. The blue button-down shirt drew focus to his eyes.

"So, it was *good* yesterday?"

He folded his arms across his chest. She wanted to rip the

buttons on his shirt open and kiss his chest, maybe find his ink. His eyes dilated as if he picked up on the fantasy swirling in her head.

"I did say that." His eyes narrowed as his hand dropped off his chest. "You think your mouth could be persuasive enough to get *anything* you want?"

That meant he'd already been briefed about what happened last night. And knew what Rand expected her to do to get the code. Hopefully the hallway cameras didn't pick up sound. It took colossal effort not to glance at the cameras.

With a slow smile she said, "I've got skills."

Color suffused his cheeks.

Her gaze trekked south. She stepped into him, pressing tight to his erection. "You'd like to sample my skills, wouldn't you?"

"Fuuuckk," he whooshed out.

She pushed him into his apartment and slammed the door behind her. She whispered, "Symphis is watching me on the hall cameras."

"That wasn't for real?"

A laugh broke free. "I'm not sure you can handle me, if this was for real."

He snagged an arm around her waist, leaned in. "I want to yank off those ridiculously tight jeans, rip off your underwear, and have you against the wall. For real. Right now. It'd be deep and hard until you scream and we both say to hell with this brunch and everything else. It'd be *me* that makes you lose your mind. You'd give *me* anything I wanted."

She might.

Oh, hell, for the dirty-talking bad-boy side of this man she would. Anything.

Breathe, she ordered herself when her lungs closed up.

He stepped away from her. "What do you mean he's watching?"

She excavated her cell phone, pulled up the texts, and rotated her phone for him to read.

Noah frowned. "How long has this asshole been doing this to you?"

She shrugged.

"Jesus, Tori. I'm sorry. This guy's seriously messed up." He handed back her phone.

"He's controlling his asset. I think he believes you and I are real."

He snort laughed. "After that little show he thinks you're getting down to business."

She rolled her eyes heavenward. "I hate this. Hate being played like a gaming character. Hate all the pretend. Hate that some faceless person controls me."

He released her. "All of this sucks."

"How long do you think is reasonable for us to be in here before we can go and him believe I gave you a blowjob?"

"The real question in that is how good are you?"

She forced a scowl, although a laugh itched to break free. He laughed.

Her smile over the absurdity of everything couldn't be suppressed. She laughed so hard she swiped away tears. Then she dramatically rolled her wrist to look at her watch. "Yep, I'd say four minutes is plenty of time for you to come apart in my mouth. But we have to make you look a little less together after that." She leaned in and tugged his shirt out of his pants. No missing his erection.

He sucked in air when her hand swiped close to touching.

She couldn't resist leaning her body into his to be sure to press her pelvis tight to his arousal. Hoarsely, she whispered, "You'd totally give me the code, but I'd enjoy every freaking moment of making you lose your mind."

"Are you fucking with me right now?" His entire body remained stiff with his hands at his sides.

"No." She fisted a wad of the cloth of his shirt over his pecs in each hand. "I don't know what it is about you, but I feel whatever this is between us. Believe me, I'm tempted. And, Noah?"

"Yeah," he said on a ragged exhale.

"I'm not good at saying *no* when I'm tempted." She leaned in and put her nose against the exposed skin of his upper chest and inhaled. She rolled her head away to rest her ear against his chest, hearing the thump-thump of his heart. He smelled amazing. "Not good at all."

"Tori, take two steps away or I will have you against the wall. I'm not a saint."

She forced her hands to release his shirt. Before she stepped away she whispered, "This doesn't mean the wall scenario doesn't tempt me. But I won't be manipulated into it by a gaming asshole."

He gripped the back of her head and leaned in. Kiss coming. She put her fingers over his lips. "Stop. I want it, too. Don't get me wrong. But now isn't right."

After he sucked in a breath he straightened and backed away from her. "Let me grab my wallet and we'll head out."

"Why exactly am I here this morning?" She wished for more sleep, but she liked seeing him. And making him come unglued.

"FBI meeting during the brunch." He disappeared into the kitchen and reappeared a moment later. "Let's go."

"No. I shouldn't go anywhere near the FBI, not after Symphis's text."

"How much do you want that code?"

She wasn't sure, but if there was a chance they might give it to her, then so be it. "Just remember he's watching us the moment we step outside your place," she said.

As they rode the elevator down she prayed for the numbers to move faster. God probably didn't listen to her anymore, but it didn't stop her hoping this once he might. She'd been a solid Catholic kid growing up, although she hadn't attended a service since her father died several years ago. Maybe she should go this week. She needed any and all positive juju possible.

Her stomach growled.

He gazed at her grumbling stomach. "Skipped breakfast?"

"Late night." She smiled wryly. "I was kind of in a hurry to get going after I got the call this morning. No time for food."

They rode in silence for a few moments, each gazing at the other.

Hoarsely, he said, "You've got to stop staring at me as if you'd be happier if I ripped off your clothes." He cleared his throat. "I had a good time last night…just now, didn't you?"

"I did." She glanced toward the cameras in the corner and then met his gaze. His deep blue eyes drifted off her lips and up to her eyes leaving no question he'd been dwelling on things to do with her lips.

The elevator floor numbers seemed to be decreasing at an epically slow pace. Sweat gathered between her breasts. "We've got to get out of this elevator."

He leaned in close to her ear. "Why? Worried you can't keep your hands off me?"

More concerned Symphis will do something again. "I'm worried about you doing whatever comes with *that* look and my lips in a public place."

He chuckled low and suggestive.

She scooted to the far side of the elevator. "There're cameras in here."

"You're the one thinking about doing *that*."

"That's it." She pressed the button for the next floor. The elevator stopped. "I'm taking the stairs."

With one foot out the door he pulled her back inside and pushed the button to close the elevator doors. "Don't be ridiculous. I'll behave to the lower floor. Do you think you can?"

She crossed her arms and backed against the opposite side of the elevator.

A deep belly laugh rolled out of him. "This should be an interesting morning."

Chapter Nine

"Why's the car stopping? This isn't your workplace." The car sat double-parked in front of a small bustling bakery.

The driver hopped out and opened her door.

"Breakfast. No one does bagels like this place." Noah reached for his door handle.

"I thought you were in a hurry to get to your work event. Isn't it a brunch, which means there'll be food?"

"We're going to have breakfast first at a place that doesn't have cameras." He flashed her an encouraging smile before he slid out.

She scooted out next to him. A quick phone check reassured no new texts. She shoved it into her pocket.

His hand closed around hers, large and reassuring. He led into the crowded bakery. The smells of cinnamon and freshly baked bread pushed her complaining stomach into gurgly begging. Minutes later, they sat at a window table so small she had to smash herself next to him to avoid touching the lady beside her.

She could feel the press of the solid muscles of his arms. Incredible arms with a smattering of freckled tanned skin peeking beyond the point he'd rolled up his sleeves. Every inch where they pressed together sizzled. This was hell. Temptation hell. Her gaze snapped up to his.

He whispered on a rough rasp, "I'd probably give you anything you asked for if you..."

She nodded, unable to speak.

His eyelids drifted closed as he bit into his cream cheesed bagel. "The bagels here are the best. I think they put drugs in their cream cheese or something. I wish I could get down here more often."

She sipped her chai and nibbled at a bagel.

"I like your hair down," he said.

"Oh? Thanks. You said that yesterday." She smoothed a hand over her hair. Her stomach somersaulted. If he continued to do things like feed her and give her compliments she might just fall for him.

His wide smile coaxed her to smile back.

He gave her a long look full of intensity. "Is Tori your real name or is it short for something else?"

"Really?" A laugh erupted. She'd expected him to delve into deeper waters.

He bit into his bagel and shot her a questioning gaze.

"Victoria," she admitted.

"Emma and Victoria. Very…"

"Jane Austin-esque. My mom loved that time period."

"I was going to say classic. Emma said she grew up in Virginia. Are your parents still living there?"

"Dad died recently. Lung cancer. He wasn't even a smoker. My parents divorced when I was fourteen. Mom moved away. I haven't seen her in a while, but we're in touch."

"I'm sorry about your dad. I can't imagine losing my dad, but it's coming. He's got early onset Alzheimer's." His eyes saddened.

"Your dad is lucky you can be there for him." She squeezed his forearm, meant as a comfort but it reminded her of her desire to see all of his arms out of the shirt. "My father had his ups and downs. He had a mean streak."

Noah's gaze turned dark. "Did he hurt you?"

"Not physically. I wanted to move with Mom when she went west, but we were in high school. With my brother in his senior year they decided we should stay with my father until we graduated. We were pretty good at knowing how to handle Dad when he had one of his moods." She leaned back from the table and stretched her shoulders. "Enough of that super light topic. Do you have any siblings other than Michael and Kaleb?"

"A younger sister. She left to attend Berkeley a few years ago. She was in town last weekend, but I didn't get to see her for more than a quick lunch. Work's been busy recently."

"How do you have time for anything other than running the company?" she asked.

"I don't, even with two of us splitting the duties."

"Is that by choice or because you're truly busy?"

He sipped his coffee. "It is what it is."

She propped her chin on her hands. "That's not an answer. Do you make yourself busy to avoid things like dating?"

"You're an armchair psychologist, too?" His look became inscrutable.

"Sorry. I get nervous and start overanalyzing everyone else's issues."

"You went to MIT. Why aren't you out there designing what you want for a video company?"

She cringed. "I didn't graduate."

"Neither did Jake and I. Who cares. An MIT–trained programmer doing websites and freelance coding doesn't make sense."

"Maybe I sucked at it." She fiddled with the edges of her paper napkin.

"Do you?"

She shrugged. "I took a few years off between dropping out and looking for a job."

"You weren't sure this was the right field for you?"

She picked at the lid on her cup. "This is what I want to do. My dad needed someone to help him navigate treatments once he'd been diagnosed with cancer. It was a tough ride to the end." She met his gaze out of fear she'd see the too familiar sympathy.

"That was brave to put your career on pause for someone who wasn't always nice to you."

Damn, this man was too much.

"I built a web design business during that time. It was pocket change, but it helped pay the bills. I also started gaming and earned a reputation."

"Did you study under Professor Wingate at MIT?" He touched the top of her hand, drawing small, mesmerizing circles with his finger on her skin.

"The Dew Man. Of course." She smiled as she remembered the professor who constantly misplaced his glasses and roamed his lab mumbling about it incoherently until he found them again.

"Did he guzzle Mountain Dew when you were there?"

The circling of his finger on the top of her hand shifted direction. Tingles skirted up her arm. "Since he became diabetic he'd switched to sugar free. He complained about it nonstop."

He lifted her hand and laced his fingers with hers. "Why didn't you self-publish your game?"

She teased a napkin around the table, but didn't remove her hand from his. "I guess my dreams are bigger than what can be done going it alone."

"Frank ego. I like it. Why is someone so talented still single?" His tone was light and playful.

"How do you know I'm talented?"

"You studied with the Dew Man. He's selective. You're single because..." His eyebrows shot upward, prompting an answer.

"Ex talk again?"

"Yep."

"I choose the wrong guys. After the last jerk I decided to avoid the dating scene for a while."

"This is the guy who cheated on you?"

"It didn't end well." She pretended absorbing interest in the napkin. A side-glance found the quiet couple seated next to them focusing on their e-readers, but she bet they were eavesdropping.

"What does that mean? Bad breakup?"

Her eyelids drifted closed on a long sigh. She removed her hand from his to cover her face. "I warned you ex talk would be bad, but okay, here goes. We'd worked together to design a pretty cool program that would allow easy integration of medical records between a few of the common medical data programs without requiring manual reentry of data. A true game changer. Any hospital changing to a new system would want it. Okay, I pretty much did all the work while he provided moral support. He stole it, sold it, and sued me when I claimed designership. I didn't have any money to hire a lawyer and fight it. He dropped the case when I threatened to take him to court for assault."

"He assaulted you?" Noah tensed.

"He didn't take well to the idea of breaking up and losing his programming hookup. He slapped me when I confronted him about cheating. I kind of kicked the crap out of him." She glanced up, wondering if this would freak him out. "Who knew a black belt in karate would come in handy."

"A secret ninja. I'm glad you kicked his ass." He grinned.

She smiled back, but soon lost it. She leaned in to whisper to avoid eavesdroppers. "This whole thing is only going to get worse. Much worse. I'm not scared for myself, but for you and Emma and my roommates, and anyone who can be targeted. If anything happens to them or you it'll be my fault. You should get out of this. Walk away."

"No." He wrapped an arm around her and whispered back, "None of this is your fault. We both got into this knowing it came with risk."

Chapter Ten

"Have you ever visited NJ Legacy?" Noah asked as they crossed the threshold into the skyscraper where his business occupied the upper five floors. He waved at the two security guards at the check-in kiosk. Good guys. He usually talked baseball for a few minutes every Sunday with them. One of them triggered the gate to the elevators.

"I put in an application last year." She surprised him by rocking onto tiptoes to smooth his hair. The wind must've done some rearranging. "Better."

"Thanks." He scrutinized his reflection in the elevator's mirrored doors and finger combed. "You applied to work here? I don't remember that."

"There wasn't anything available. You guys have low employee turnover."

"We always have room for talent." He punched the button for the top floor.

"Guess my resume got hung up in HR or something. It's not like you see every application. You also don't know if I'm talented. I might be a talentless amateur."

"Somehow, I highly doubt it."

Her eyes darted around as a flush stole across her cheeks. The woman didn't like compliments. She leaned close to whisper, "You think he can watch us in this building? How careful should we be?"

"I put my security guy on it yesterday. He said he has every feed in the building protected."

"How good is he?"

"I hired him away from the NSA. We have a much better compensation package it turns out."

"I'll bet. Emma mentioned this was a brunch. I kind of phased out on the details beyond that." With each higher floor number her shoulders notched themselves higher. She chewed on the inside of her cheek. "I think this is a bad idea. Not so much the brunch, although that'll be awkward since I'm Emma's sister, but because I shouldn't meet with...you know, them. I should go." She scrutinized the ceiling, perhaps searching for the camera.

"Let's see if they have a solution for everything. But first, this is a social event. I have to mix a bit. It might be weird since I've never brought a date. There might be more than a few who're interested in you."

"How, uh, into each other do we need to be? We talking a kiss before I walk away to get coffee, holding hands the whole time, or some social distance?" She met his gaze, wide-eyed like a bird in a cat's mouth. "I don't know if I can pull this off, especially with Emma there."

"Where's the girl who almost castrated a guy in D.C. for taunting her after losing?"

"I'm not pissed off right now. That brings out a different side of me." A small smile touched her lips.

He mentally fist-pumped as if he'd won a competition. "You're a badass, Tori. These are your people. They're gaming geeks who, like me, will find everything about you from the nose stud to your tattoos sexy as hell."

"You think I'm sexy?"

Noah cast a look heavenward. "Hasn't it been obvious since the moment you argued with the police officer over the money they lost?"

"They didn't lose it. They stole it." Her eyelids drifted to half-mast as she glided close to him. *Danger alert.*

"Elevators are an issue for us. Want me to hit the

emergency stop button?" Her finger reached out toward the red button.

He stopped her hand. "I still wouldn't give you the code."

"Uh-huh." She wiggled her hand free of his grasp to trace a path from his chest down to his waistband. She moistened her lips with a flick of her small pink tongue.

"Christ," he muttered as his imagined those lips around him.

She leaned in to press herself against him. "Do you like it soft and shallow or hard and deep?"

Yeah, he'd totally give her the code, his passwords, and any account numbers she wanted. He'd never been the recipient of attention from anyone like Tori.

The elevator dinged its arrival. She stepped away as the doors opened onto the glassed-in top floor. Fifty to sixty people already hovered around the food stations.

He adjusted himself like a damned teenager.

"Got a little situation you'd like to bargain for me to take care of before we step out of the elevator? Perhaps, in your office?" A deep, almost hoarse laugh erupted from her when he glared at her.

"How about if I grab us some coffee and we meet in the center?" she offered. "What's your preference?"

His eyebrows shot up as his gaze drifted to her lips.

"Coffee. We're talking coffee, remember? How do you take yours?" She compressed her lips against a laugh.

"Black." His strangled voice entertained her.

"Back in a few." She pivoted and left.

Something about that man made her lose her freaking mind. The choked noise he made when she teased him had been priceless.

She managed to weave through the crowd and avoid all conversations in a beeline for the coffee station.

On her way back to Noah, she spied her brother, who worked in the marketing department. Yes, small world but Emma had encouraged him to apply when he'd lost his job at the sports clothing company. Their eyes met. He headed her way.

Not good. He wouldn't know about her "arrangement" with Noah.

"Hi, Tori." Jason smiled. "What're you doing here? You come with Emma?"

"Uh, not exactly. Where's your wife?" Maybe distracting Jason with his wife would make him give up the questions. She scanned around for Noah, spotting him close to the exit. She'd give him his coffee and then take a bathroom break, one that might just last the rest of the brunch. Good plan.

"Jillian is at home. She's got a cold she's been fighting all week." His gaze darted to Noah who met their gazes with a smile and a wave. "Why is Noah Harrison waving at you? How in the world do you know him?"

A svelte blond guy moved in close and gave her a speculative scan. "Hey, Jason. Who's this?"

"This is my sister, Tori."

"Good to meet you. I'm Chris from marketing. I work with Jason." The blond leaned in to Jason to ask low, "Have you heard about Noah?"

Jason shook his head. His worried gaze met hers.

"You know I'm tennis partners with his brother. The three of us have known each other since preschool. Michael mentioned this morning that Noah was dating again. Is that true?"

Jason sprayed out his mouthful of orange juice on a cough. He wiped at the orange droplets on the guy's shirt with his paltry drink napkin. "I'm so sorry."

Tori compressed her lips to hold back her laughter, but a few chuckles broke free.

The blond hit Jason on the back. "Yeah, that was my reaction, too. He hasn't jumped back into the dating game since… Well, you know since the whole Darcy fiasco however many years ago that was. I mean, good for him. The man needed to get laid."

Jason subjected her to a double eyebrow *what-the-hell* that had her shifting on her feet. Little got past her brother. Her at his work brunch was weird enough. Noah waving at her? Yeah, he'd figured it out.

Chris continued, "Michael ran into Noah last night while he was on his date."

"Last night?" Jason's gaze snapped to her. His eyebrows couldn't go any higher.

Tori shrugged in response to Jason. She wished she could prevent the heat in her face. "Great to meet you, Chris. I've got to get going." She shot Jason an apologetic smile. "Call me later."

She moved quickly to Noah, finding him with a young mother and her son. The boy couldn't be much beyond kindergarten or first grade. With a smile Tori handed Noah the coffee.

The lady asked her son, "Can you thank Uncle Noah for coming by your class last week, Max?" She glanced up at Noah, "They were so happy to meet you."

Noah smiled. "It fit in the schedule and it was fun. What'd you think, Max?"

Max beamed up at him. "It was awesome. And when you let us do the vextual realty it was great."

"Virtual reality," his mom gently corrected.

Max gazed solemnly at Tori. "He's not my real uncle. He's my fill-in uncle while Dad's in Afghan-stand. He's been gone a long time."

Tori struggled not the laugh at Max's earnestness. "You're very lucky to have such a great fill-in."

"I am," Max said, dead serious. "There's no one else like Uncle Noah."

"We're so proud of what your dad is doing over there," Noah said. "I heard he's coming home next month." The soft smile he gave Max did crazy things to her chest.

Excitement blazed on Max's face. "That's what Dad told us last weekend when we Skyped. We're going to do my birthday again since he missed it." He gazed sadly at his mom.

"It's good to see you," Noah said to the lady. He squeezed her arm before leaving. He said to Tori, "I've got make a call to Tokyo, if you'd like to come with me for a few minutes." His smile made her stomach flip-flop.

Did he really have a call or was this him giving in to temptation?

Please, let it be the latter

.

***

He had to get her out of this crowd. If he didn't, someone would notice he couldn't stop staring at her ass. God only knows what she'd been talking about with Chris. Bringing her here was about outing their relationship. Tom thought it'd be easier to perpetuate the farce if him dating became water cooler gossip.

Just as he had his finger reaching out to push the elevator button someone shouted, "Hold up, Noah."

Damn. He dropped his hand. With a slow turn he faced his childhood friend, now company marketing manager, Chris. He plastered on an impassive look.

Chris eyed him. He swiped a hand over his blond crew cut. "We think it'd have a huge impact if you joined Jake at the GameCon next weekend in Colorado to talk about the new tech we're launching."

"No. I can't…" He might as well wear the Chicken Boy suit if he attended. He cleared his throat. "I don't do media stuff. Our agreement is I stay out of it. That's not about to change now."

"Think about it. Please. You're reputation as the genius behind the scenes means your opinion means a lot more than Jake and his marketing spiel. Jake is good, but the press is desperate to know you." Chris didn't move even though he seemed done.

"Anything else?" Noah asked.

"Uh, you got anything you need to tell me about your life? Anything *new*?" His gaze darted to Tori, filled with curiosity, but then dismissed her as a possible candidate for *the girl* Noah now dated.

"No." Noah folded his arms over his chest.

"We been buds a long time, man. Michael mentioned this morning that you might be getting in the game again."

"Even if I was, it's none of your business." Chris might've known him since he was barely out of diapers, but he didn't need to know everything.

"Oh, come on, Noah. This dry spell of yours has been…" He sucked air through his teeth. "Well, I'll be happy to see you less stressed."

"You think sex will fix my stress?"

"It might help." Chris shrugged her way apologetically.

Tori's lips twitched upward. A snort laugh broke from her. With an abrupt turn she faced the wall. Her shoulders shook with silent laughter.

"See. Even Jason's sister thinks you're, uh…grumpy." Chris patted her back.

"I never said that." She wiped tears from her eyes as she turned back to face them.

"Do I seem like I'm in a better mood today?" Noah asked Chris.

"As a matter of fact…" Chris grinned. "You're back in the game. This is great. Congrats, man. When can I meet her?"

"Chris, I'd like you to meet Tori. My date."

"But you're Jason's sister." Chris's face flushed scarlet.

"I'm sorry about... Oh, hell."

"No worries." She lowered her voice to whisper to him, "Can't keep my hands off him. I mean, he's sex on a stick. I could lick him all day. Believe me, I'm working on making him far less stressed."

Chris's face flushed even deeper red.

She grabbed Noah's hand, stepped into the elevator, and pushed a random floor to make them start going down.

"You can shut your mouth now," she said as the car started moving.

He snapped his jaw closed and put a hand over his face. "You're trouble."

"Do you really have to call Tokyo?" She picked at a hangnail.

"I have to deal with some leftover details from this morning. I didn't think you wanted to be up there alone." Now all he could think about was her licking him.

"Thanks." It came out tight.

As she turned to stare at the doors he examined her profile and the sleek line of her jaw. The memory of her lips against his...nope, those images went right back into an off-limits box in his mind. But, Jesus, she was beautiful.

"Stop it," she whispered.

"What?"

"That hot and heavy you got coming from over there. We've got to figure out how to deal with small spaces. You start something right now and I'm going to lose control. We'll get caught naked."

Chapter Eleven

The elevator opened. She audibly released her breath.

"Wrong floor," he muttered, pushing another button. The elevator resumed its downward trek. Air got tight in her lungs again. She glanced his way and didn't even realize she'd turned to face him or that she'd moved toward him. Or that she was laser focused on his lips until the doors slid open.

His gaze remained fixed on hers. He didn't move to exit. The smoldering heat in the depths of his eyes activated crazy fantasies of pushing him against the wall and kissing him deep and hard.

"Door," she muttered, waving half-heartedly at the opening.

The doors slid to close. Noah's hand shot out to trigger them to open again. "You're right. Elevators are a big problem. Come on."

She jumped away from him and waved for him to lead the way.

Once inside his office he said, "There're drinks in the fridge. Grab something if you'd like. Give me a few minutes to make a call." He waved at the bar area and sat behind his desk, scrolled his cell, and then dialed on the landline.

Tori roamed the office, eavesdropping on Noah's phone conversation, but lost interest when it seemed to be about some future meeting. Movement from beyond his door caught her attention. Jason waved wildly.

She fast walked into the hallway. "How'd you know I was

up here?"

"Chis the motor-mouth couldn't stop talking about Noah taking his date, my *sister,* to his office." Jason pulled closed the glass door of Noah's office behind her. Noah might not be able to hear them, but he could see them.

"What are you doing on a date with my boss? Did you actually sleep with him?" Jason's face mottled several shades of red.

"First date was yesterday. I've got some scruples. Not many, I'll grant you, but some. So, no, I didn't sleep with him."*I would've, but it's not like that. Once more time in an elevator, though, and I might.*

"How in the world did you end up on a date with Mr. Harrison?" Jason squinted at her in silence.

She folded her arms. "I don't need a big brother butting into my life. What's wrong with me dating him? Don't think I'm not good enough for him?"

"He's a CEO and you're…you."

She smacked him in the arm.

"Oww." Jason massaged his arm. "He doesn't date. That's his M.O. Why in the world would he randomly decide to start dating and go out with you?"

"Why not?" She narrowed her eyes.

"Tori—"

"You two doing okay out here?" Noah interrupted.

Jason and she whirled to face Noah, both silent.

She stared at Noah wide-eyed, unsure how Jason would play this. Her big brother could go protective in a heartbeat. Aside from a hot temper, the other thing the Duarte kids got from their Cuban father was a clear family-first mantra.

Noah said, "Bet this was a surprise. Tori and I met in D.C. the other day. I fucked her up." His face flushed. "I mean I made her mess up when she might've won. Didn't mean to. Took her out last night to apologize, but we turned out to hit it off."

Please let Jason buy this had been a pity date. Kind of bruised her ego, though.

Jason's eyebrows rose as he met her gaze. Her brother clearly thought she'd slept with Noah last night. Perhaps, she'd taken the farce too far.

"Call me when you get home, Tori. Let's chat." Jason pointed at her in a clear "behave yourself" before he strode back to the elevator.

"Sorry about Jason." She shrugged.

Noah held open his office door for her to reenter. A glance out the windows showed the city moving far below. "God love my big brother, but he can be a pain in the ass. He's going to dwell on the fact me and you together makes no sense. Hope he doesn't blow things."

"He's the least of our worries…" His voice trailed off. "Would you like a coffee or soda? Maybe a water?"

"Water is fine."

He grabbed a water whose designer bottle looked more expensive than the twelve pack of el cheapos in her fridge.

"I have something I want to show you." He waved her to follow him.

Her mind immediately flashed naked fantasy images. *He didn't say naked.* His tone didn't sound remotely suggestive. This guy was trouble with a capital A for addictive.

She followed him into a back hallway past a restroom and then down several doors into what looked like a studio with a huge TV screen. To a non-gamer the room looked like someone picked up a bunch of exotic chairs and chucked them haphazardly into a room. To her it offered every available style of gaming chair—beanbag, gaming rockers, memory foam, leather office chair or a classic sofa.

He threw her a controller and waved for her to pick her chair of choice.

She put the water on the floor by her feet and settled onto

the sofa.

"Put this on." He handed her a pair of lightweight wrap-around sunglasses and a controller. "Think of this as your living room."

He pushed a few buttons and the surround sound blasted the intro music to *Zoneworld Warrior One*. The lights dimmed into darkness. "Put them on. Helps get the best visual."

She slipped the glasses on, expecting some sort of image color enhancer. *Holy crap.* It was as if she was in the game. Virtual reality.

"Wow. This is incredible." She removed the goggles to examine them in the dim light. So small and comfortable.

"Let's play the first level," he suggested.

A half hour and five levels later she ripped off the glasses. "I love these. Please tell me I can get my own soon." As she squinted into the room lit by the jumbo screen her eyes adjusted to the light. Her breath hitched when she made out Noah in the gaming chair nearby. He'd rolled up his sleeves and leaned forward as if the position got him closer to the screen while he continued to play, even though he too wore a pair of glasses. His strong forearms mesmerized her. So masculine. Appealing and incredibly sexy.

"You're quitting?" He straightened but continued to maneuver with the controller.

She rubbed the back of her neck as she watched his hands on the controller. Her body hummed, her need for him becoming all-consuming.

He took off his glasses and faced her. "The limitation to virtual reality has been quality and comfort. The other companies market those bulky goggles. Those who've tried to make them smaller lost quality. With this, we have it."

Was it her imagination or did his gaze just wander to her breasts while spouting that PR mumbo jumbo? She wanted to believe he too felt a little bit out of control by whatever it was pinging between them. "Why're you showing me these? Aren't you worried I'll talk to someone?"

"It's not like anyone else could design what took us years in development."

"Someone could reverse engineer them."

"Not before we launch them. We're looking for the right new game to release at the same time, something we'll tweak to impress in virtual reality." He set down his controller and glasses and moved to sit beside her. He took her hand and smoothed his thumb in circles along the skin of her palm.

His touch was so gentle. It made her feel cherished—such a foreign feeling.

Fiddling with the glasses in the hand he wasn't holding, feeling a bit off-kilter, the only words that came out were, "All right."

"I want to see your game, Tori. I'm serious. We're looking for something new. Something different."

Tori dragged in a ragged breath, drawing the clean scent of him into her lungs. He was talking about her game, the one he already owned but didn't realize he owned. *Focus.* He wasn't trying to make this physical, although the hand-holding and thumb swirls sent mixed messages. *He's* keeping it professional-ish.

He wanted to see her game. *Oh. My. God.* The possibilities of her game with this system were endless. "I'm not sure it's what you're looking for."

"Let me be the judge."

Everyone will think I slept my way into getting you to like it. "I'll think about it. Thanks for the sneak peek. If the glasses are affordable, then it's going to revolutionize the gaming world. I'll be first in line to buy it and upgrade every one of my games to be compatible. Everyone I know will want them." That came off good, relatively platonic. Right?

"I thought you'd appreciate it." His lips shifted upward

into a smile as he released her hand to take the glasses from her, but he didn't move to stand.

There was nothing platonic about the way he gazed at her mouth. He had to feel the crazy pull between them. She wasn't a fate and destiny kind of girl, but meeting him in jail and now being here with Noah made her wonder.

She wanted his lips on hers just to experience the earth-jarring connection once more. Deep in her gut the draw to him terrified the bejesus out of her. It was a game changer and she wasn't sure she was ready for it. She feared what it might mean...where it could go, if anywhere.

One more taste was the path to a steady spiral downward into losing any ability to stay away from him.

Yet, not diving into him now was hard.

Closing her eyes, she took a deep breath.

He touched the side of her face, sliding hair away from her eyes. Goosebumps erupted down her arms. Cupping her neck, his opposite hand twisting gently into her hair, he pulled her head back and leaned in, pressing his lips to hers.

Scooting closer, she wrapped her arms around him, her fingers digging into his back as he deepened the kiss. So intense with each thrust of his tongue, each mingling of their lips. Every intake of a desperate breath had her falling into the abyss of the unknown.

She pulled away. "Slow down. That's what we need. I mean, the kisses are..." She blinked up into his confused and disappointed face. "Wow. But..."

He whispered, "I want to make love to you more than I want to breathe right now."

She shivered as the answering *me too* fought to be vocalized. "This has to be the product of us forced together. Let's remember why we're here. Your brother's death. The future of gaming. Me getting out of the Stadium and not dying. Stopping Symphis." When he didn't seem convinced she added,

"We're not even really dating."

"This whatever it is has nothing to do with all that. It didn't in the jail. This is something else going on here. Something real."

A noise came from outside the room. Both of them froze. She whispered, "Who's out there?"

"Maybe Tom. Meeting, remember?" He straightened his clothes, swiped a hand across his lips to remove all lipstick remnants, and combed his fingers through his hair. He still looked like he'd been doing far more than playing video games.

"Do I look acceptable?" She wiped a finger over her lips. His look wasn't reassuring.

"For God's sake, it was just a kiss. We can't have done that much damage. Maybe I could slip out a back door. I should skip this thing with the FBI. Can't you give me the summary tomorrow or whenever we go on a date again?"

As they rounded back into Noah's office a surprised male said, "Oh my God. Tell me you two weren't…"

Chapter Twelve

"We've been in the conference room for over an hour. Waiting. I think you two are taking this fake dating too far." Tom scrunched up his face and clicked his ballpoint pen.

Noah snatched the pen out of his hand. "We're on our way to the meeting now."

"Give me back my pen, please." Tom held out his hand and wiggled his fingers.

Noah longed to crush the plastic into bits. Instead, he threw the pen on his desk and selected a non-click pen from his top drawer to hand back.

"This isn't my pen." Tom held the new pen between two fingers as if it were a shoe smeared with dog shit.

"It is now." Noah cast Tori a stern look when she giggled.

"Come." Tom marched out ahead of them.

In the conference room sat Emma, the two other members of Tom's team, his IT expert, Sam, and his co-CEO, Jake. All of them were three deep in Styrofoam coffee cups. Projected on the whiteboard were images of the building where the Stadium had been last night.

One of the FBI agents locked the room after they entered.

"Thought you were going out of town again. You have that thing in Florida, right?" Noah asked Jake.

"Don't need to be there until tomorrow afternoon." Jake's gaze bounced between Noah and Tori. He cast Noah a smile that was all about knowing he'd been up to something that wasn't pretend dating.

"Let's get to work." Tom clapped his hands.

"Symphis knows about you trying to recruit me and Noah," Tori said before Tom could start whatever spiel he'd prepared.

"What?" Tom froze in the act of changing the picture on the big screen.

"He sent me a text about it, specifically mentioning you."

"I saw the texts," Noah said. "He knows you've tried to enlist her help. Not clear he knows your effort worked."

"That's bad." Tom sat down. "Real bad. Did he hurt you or do anything physical?"

She shook her head. "Just threats. I think he still believes Noah and I are a legit item, which is useful to him."

"I want her out now." Noah sat next to Jake. "You can relocate her, can't you? Do a witness protection or something like that?"

Tom said, "We can only relocate a witness crucial to a case, not someone who's simply in danger. She hasn't actually seen Symphis. All she can testify about are the people at the Stadium. We already know all those guys." He met Tori's gaze. "I'm sorry, but you're stuck in this unless you think you could walk away and be safe."

Tori sat next to Emma. "We started this. Let's end it. But this has to be the last meeting like this I attend."

"Can we buy you out of debt?" Jake asked.

"We could try," Tori said slowly. "I don't think they'll let me leave that easily, but I could try. Emma already said she'd let me borrow it."

"Yesterday, while listening to you at the Stadium we realized they compete against groups in other cities," Tom said. "We knew there were other operations but didn't know the networks communicated. These are the other spots we have intel that a Stadium exists." He waved at a map on the screen.

"I know." Tori folded her arms on the table and stared at the red dots across the country projected on the big screen. "You missed San Francisco and Tampa. Everyone bets against each other—outsiders, players, administrators, and support crew. Can you hack Rand's cell phone to know who he spoke with last night?" She didn't express any sort of emotion, but Noah realized the less she showed externally, the more freaked out she actually was. He wanted her out of all of this and far away before it moved beyond threats to action.

"We already looked into who Rand spoke with last night." Tom typed on his computer for a bit. "All caller IDs unlisted. But we do have location of the people he spoke with. Three calls to Atlanta, one incoming call from Orlando, an outgoing locally, and two calls to Jersey City. You think he spoke to Symphis?" He glanced up as if listing off cities should make her know instantly more about Symphis.

"Not helpful," she muttered.

"When do you think you'll be asked back to the Stadium?" Tom asked.

"They play once on the weekend, usually Saturdays, and then on Wednesdays." She swirled a coffee cup that sat in front of Emma and raised her eyebrows. Emma nodded. Tori sipped and grimaced, but took another swallow.

"Three days." Tom said.

"Are we going to talk about it?" Tori asked.

"About what?" Tom shrugged.

"They want the full code to *Zoneworld* with the key to unlock its security. They want it at any cost." Color bloomed on her cheeks.

"We heard." Tom looked toward Sam.

"Hey. I'm Sam. I run IT security at NJ Legacy. I thought what you did at the competition in D.C. was brilliant. I was sorry we had to mess you up. Maybe someday…" His gaze snagged on Tom, which stopped him. He slid a flash drive toward her. "It's got code for the first three levels of *Zoneworld Two* free of the security lock."

Tori stared at the drive but didn't take it.

Sam continued, "I built a back door into it. The second it's opened I'll know. It's like a virus that'll allow me to do anything to whatever computer it's used on. Once I'm into the system, it's mine."

Tori fingered the flash drive. "Is the back door detectable? The guys who Symphis will have hacking the game will be good. They're going to scan."

"Probably not as good as me." Sam met her gaze, challenging.

Tori asked, "You guarantee they won't pick it up. That it won't cause a single blip of malfunction?"

Sam nodded.

"Three levels will let the kid taste the milkshake, but not have it. He's not going to like this." After a deep inhale she took the flash drive. She rose. "If this is the whole point to my being at this brunch thing then I'm done, right?"

No one voiced a denial. *Come on. Someone keep her here.*

"We can't have another meeting. This is the last one. We've got to assume he knows you're here in NJ Legacy's building today. And I'm here. I'm going to have to convince them you didn't recruit me..." Her gaze darted to Noah and filled with concern. "Or Noah. You guys are making this more difficult." She headed to the door, but paused by Noah before she left. She held up the zip drive and whispered to him, "I'll tell them this cost way more than a blowjob."

Chapter Thirteen

Tori's phone rang. Unknown number. Maybe Tom decided to breach cell phone silence protocol since she left twenty minutes ago. "Hello?"

"Tori, Tori, Tori," said a computer modified male voice followed by disparaging clicking. "You force me to teach you a lesson."

"Who is this?" Sweat broke out over her body. She glanced around the subway. The other ten or so people in the car avoided eye contact.

"Keep looking. You won't find me, but I can see you. An FBI meeting again? I thought we understood each other. You're going to make me need to hurt you or Emma. I thought you understood the FBI isn't interested in helping you. Not like I am."

"Is this Symphis?" Tori kept looking around. She glared at the area where the cameras might be in the subway car.

"You're my girl, Tori. Mine. Not Noah's. Not Tom's. I want to reward you, but I'm afraid you forced me to do this."

"Leave Emma alone. What do you want from me?"

The call ended.

She dialed Emma. No answer.

She got off way before her stop. As she jogged to her sister's apartment through rain that couldn't decide if it wanted to drizzle or pour she tried calling Emma two more times. The second time she left a voicemail, "Call me."

Once up to her sister's place and inside, she paced. Still no call. She tried twice more. No answer. She phoned direct to NJ

Legacy. No answer at her desk. No main receptionist working on a Sunday.

***

"What are you doing here?" Emma asked as she entered her kitchen, putting down her shoulder briefcase. "It's four o'clock in the afternoon."

Tori bolted upright. She hadn't meant to conk out with her head on Emma's kitchen table. "I tried calling you at least ten times. Why didn't you answer?"

"I did call you back a half hour ago. You didn't answer."

She turned over her phone and saw she had a voicemail. Crap, she'd turned off the ringer when she was on her "date" with Noah this morning and forgot to turn it back on. "You're okay? Nothing weird happened?"

"Well, I stopped by the ATM on my way home and my card didn't work. My phone app says I have no accounts. I called the bank's help line and they said I don't have any accounts with them. So, no, I'm not really okay."

"Shit." She covered her face with her hands. "I'm sorry."

"Did you hack the bank and erase my accounts?"

"What? No. I think—"

Emma jumped forward and put a hand over her mouth. She held up a finger to her lips and pulled Tori into her small bathroom. She flicked on the fan, whose racket made Tori wonder if it might shake itself off the ceiling.

Emma said, "Tom warned me I've been bugged."

Tori's eyes drifted closed for a moment. "I can't believe my fuckups got you into this. That we're forced to have a serious conversation in your deodorized, froufrou bathroom. I'm sorry. I got a call on my way home. On the subway. I think it was him. Symphis."

"A call? Has he ever personally called you before?"

116

Tori shook her head. "Could've been one of his peons, but it sounded personal. He said he had to punish me for meeting with Tom today. He was going to do something to you."

"You think he wiped my accounts as a weird way to punish you?"

Tori nodded.

"It's a pain in the ass, but not the end of the world. I've got credit cards. I've got back up of all the account information. Tom told us to back everything up before we started in case of this. So, I'll be at the bank when they open tomorrow. We'll get it figured out."

"It's only a first step. You get that, don't you? I don't want you hurt because of this. Can you take a vacation, leave the country or something?"

"As if someone who can mess online can't get me in another country?" Emma's gaze bounced around the room. "They can't control this. Tom thinks he can, but this gaming network is elusive, well funded, and it sounds like they eliminate anyone who threatens them. Tom didn't tell any of us that he had another guy infiltrated before they recruited you."

"Who? I thought all his previous spies were dead." Tori wondered if it was a gamer or one of the extraneous extras needed to haul equipment or a programmer. Wait a second, she said *had.*

"I heard him say Ravi or Tavi. Something like that," Emma said.

"Indian kid. About twenty. Sweet guy, terrible at the early levels of *Zoneworld* but pretty good beyond level five. He was always drinking neon-colored sodas. What about him?"

"Someone dumped his body in the Bronx early this morning. Official cause of death is heroin OD." Emma nibbled one of her manicured nails.

"Oh God." That could've been her. Later this week when she disappointed Symphis it might be her. Or it might be her sister or one of her roommates or Noah. No, it wouldn't be Noah so long as she had the connection with him, which made him useful. But once she wasn't useful anymore, once she couldn't produce what Symphis needed or wanted, he'd eliminate her and maybe take out Noah as a way to wrap up a loose end. However, even if she gave him what he wanted, then she might not be valuable any more. The gears in her brain churned, searching for a solution, be it quasi-legal, illegal, or fear-based. "I warned them. These guys don't care about laws or rules. Or human life."

"They weren't listening. Tom thinks he *knows* this guy because he took a few computer classes in college. And he took down a fantasy football league with heavy gambling that had turned dangerous in Boston last year."

"I want to disappear to Europe or some Caribbean country for a few years. I'd even consider Siberia, but I won't go to Asia or Africa. The snakes, you know." She shivered. "You guys can take down Symphis and then let me know it's safe to come back."

"There're snakes in the Caribbean, too, you know. Symphis will find you the second you logged in online. There's no way you could spend two years off the grid. You're safer here with us. With people in the government knowing what's going on." Emma didn't look convinced.

"Like Ravi was safe? Bet they can't pin anything on anyone, can they? Looks like another garden variety OD." Tori wedged the heel of her hand to each side of her temple. Her butt slid down the wall to sit on the bathmat.

Emma knelt in front of her. "Your contact is Noah. You need to take your phone to him so he can get it to Tom or tell Noah in person so they can try to trace who phoned you."

"I'm sure it was blocked or a burner phone."

"You have to try. He phoned you. Based on what the FBI said that's not his M.O. Wonder why he's making this more personal." Emma chewed on a nail. "Dammit, now I ruined a nail."

"He better not have phoned me because I'm a girl."

"Whatever the reason, you need to go talk to Noah tonight."

"Okay. Is his place bugged, too?" She didn't know what'd happen if she and Noah were alone again.

Emma shook her head. "Sam's crew sweeps his place twice a week to be sure."

"All right. I'll go talk to him. Please, be careful." She pulled herself to a stand.

"What took you and Noah so long to get to the meeting this morning?" Emma asked.

Her gaze popped up. She didn't need to answer that. This was classic Emma distraction and redirection. She and everyone in that room knew they'd been doing something, probably suspected a blowjob.

"Look, we might've kissed. Made out for a bit, but we were gaming for a while, too." Tori chewed her lower lip.

Emma's lower jaw dropped. "You and my boss made out? What's wrong with him? It's like he got hit over the head by a dose of crazy since he met you in jail. Last week this man couldn't talk to a woman. If he did, he'd fall apart with nervousness and eventually give up before he even drummed up the courage to ask her out, if he could figure out how. Now he's making out in his office and going on dates. His drive for dates isn't because he has to. He's into it. Like really freaking into it...and you."

Yeah, she liked him, too. Going to his place, phone excuse or not, might end in a lot more than kissing.

"Do you like Noah, or is this fangirl worship?" Emma asked.

"I didn't make out with him because he's a Game Lord. I only played the game with him because of it. It would've stayed a friends-only thing but he allowed me to play on his new virtual reality system today, which by the way is incredible and is going to make so much money for NJ Legacy. It was an amazing experience. Then we kissed and it almost spiraled, but he remembered the meeting." *That sounded totally implausible.* "There's some sort of super-warp chemistry between us."

Emma held up her hand. "Hold up a second. Let's rewind to where Noah showed *you* his virtual reality glasses."

"They're cool."

"That project has been kept hush-hush. I haven't even been invited to see the prototype. I think there's maybe five people in the whole company who've been allowed to try it out. He must really like you to have let you into his top-secret domain." Emma whistled.

"The system they developed is amazing." Tori got back to her feet. She splashed water on her face and wiped it off, pausing to stare at herself in the mirror. Not her best look right now with frizzy, dark hair in a messy braid.

Emma sighed long and loud. "Out of all this crap comes something unexpected and maybe good. You really like him, don't you?"

"It's a dead-end that can't start right now. We like each other, but I can't handle the mind calisthenics necessary for a relationship on top of the Symphis thing." She fingered the doorknob. "I'll go to Noah's and tell him about the call so he can pass along the info. I won't make out with him again. I promise."

"Is that you trying to convince yourself, because I'm not buying it."

"I've got to go home tonight. Got to figure out how to pay next month's rent."

"How much do you need?" Emma asked.

"I didn't mean that you needed to give me anything. Don't worry about it."

"Tori, I'm worried. I'm not picking you up at the jail again. I'm going to wire you a few thousand as soon as my accounts are back in order. Once this is over you should—"

"I'll get a real job like an adult. I promise." She yanked open the bathroom door.

"As if I believe you'll do that." Emma examined her cell phone.

"I have a job interview at six on Tuesday. For a real job that involves coding in a cubicle. It's an entry level position at CyberBee. I know they do mostly kids games, but still it's gaming. It's a foot in the door. It's experience. And I need real money. See? I'm working to become an adult." She picked at the edges of the pink fleece pullover she'd borrowed from her sister's closet to get out of her wet shirt. Not her color, but she'd been cold.

"You have a job interview on Tuesday night? Why not during the day?"

"Truth is the six o'clock thing's a date. I had to agree to go out with a friend of a friend as a favor for him pushing my resume to the front of the line since he works as an assistant in CyberBee's HR department. I don't want to do this date, but I made a promise. What's a drink and a meal? I've done a lot of first dates."

"Some guy is so desperate he's leveraging a friend to blackmail you into a date in exchange for a job interview when it's not even a guaranteed job?" The *are you shitting me* gaze Emma cast her made Tori squirm.

"Sounds pretty stupid when you put it that way. I think it's more a friend setting up a friend. Whatever. The industry is cutthroat these days."

"I can't believe you have a legit job interview and a date in the middle of dating Noah. Please let me tell them about your game."

"No. I'll do this my way. I don't want to be seen as sleeping into getting my game published. Is he at his place?"

Emma chuckled and typed on her phone. "I guarantee

he'll be there in twenty minutes."

Chapter Fourteen

The doorman scrutinized Tori in the pink fleece, drenched from the torrential downpour. The hair plastered to her head probably didn't help convince this guy she was the type of woman a penthouse tenant would want to see. This wasn't the same doorman she'd met before.

"Just call him. I've been up to his place before." She added for good measure, "Please."

Her phone dinged.

Symphis text: *Good girl. Go get my code.*

A small tremor shook her hand as she shoved it into the fleece's pocket.

"Miss? Miss!"

Tori jumped. Her attention snapped to the doorman. Crap, she'd zoned out.

"You're good. Go on up," he said, hand shooing her toward the elevator.

"Sorry," she muttered before shuffling toward the mirrored doors of the elevator in a daze. Her gaze remained fixed on the camera in the corner, determined to stare down the asshole watching her.

Noah's door opened within moments of stepping out of the elevator. He glanced at the hall camera before ushering her inside. "What happened?"

"Are you sure, I mean absolutely 100 percent sure you're not bugged or wired in here?"

"I did a sweep when I got home with the machine Sam's

team gave me last month. Didn't find anything."

He wore the same clothes as before, which were so sexy they almost made her forget why she was here. Almost. But reality crashed in.

"You want me to hug you or something?" he asked. It wasn't said like he felt obligated to do it, but was reluctant. He sounded baffled over the right thing to do.

She flung her arms around him.

He held her. "What happened?"

"He called me. Symphis...on my cell phone."

"He's trying to get into your head."

"He's in there, messing me up. Scaring me. I hate this." She clung tighter.

He held her in silence for a few minutes. When he pulled away his blue shirt was now wet. "You're freezing and soaked. Get out of those clothes."

She laughed. "You say the most romantic things to get me undressed."

"You're shivering. Let me grab you something you can change into. Then you'll tell me the whole story." He disappeared down the hallway.

She hadn't even noticed the cold or wet until he pointed it out.

Before, she hadn't taken time to appreciate his place, which occupied the entire upper floor. He hadn't offered a tour last night. A glance at the high ceilings, which, in addition to the large windows with natural light, made it feel palatial, made her think she needed the grand tour. The hardwoods weren't the scraped-up, decades-old crap like hers, but a textured pattern that screamed *no cost spared*. She wandered through the TV room where they'd played the game last night and into the kitchen.

Oh my.

Outside the kitchen through a pretty glass door he had a lap pool in his freaking apartment. Along the far deck was a bevy of exercise equipment.

"Here." Noah held out a T-shirt and a sweatshirt. "I don't have any pants that'll fit you. You can go in there." He pointed to a bathroom she hadn't noticed.

The marble bathroom's accouterments could not have been chosen by Noah. No man thought about embroidered hand towels or throw pillows for the bench. Who had a half bath big enough for a bench in the city?

When she emerged he took her clothes. "I'll throw them in the dryer."

Once her clothes were happily spinning in warmth he faced her and waited.

"He called me while I was on the subway home." She scrolled through her phone to bring up the "unknown" incoming call as proof.

"What'd he want?"

"He used something to modify his voice, made it robotic sounding. He was mad the FBI was at NJ Legacy this morning. Said I forced him to teach me a lesson. He wiped all of Emma's accounts." If she was a crying sort of girl, she'd have moist eyes, but she wasn't.

"None of this is your fault, Tori. You have to remember that." He pulled her into him again for a hug. "Tell me you understand that. He's a psychopath who's using you. He's manipulating you."

She nodded. Understanding didn't change the fact Noah near her put him at risk.

He held her against his chest. "We gave you the code free of security for the first few levels. That's something."

"It's not enough." She rocked her head back and forth. "Nothing will ever be enough. I can't do this, Noah. I can't."

"You're not alone. I'm with you in this. I take responsibility for myself, for putting my life in danger."

She liked the idea of the security he offered, even though

it wasn't something he could guarantee. "Emma said I should give you my phone. That's why I'm here. Tom can do whatever he can to trace the call, but I'm not sure there's much that can be done."

"I don't know that they need your phone for that."

***

He'd hold her all night to confirm she was fine if she'd allow him, but that stepped over the line, didn't it? If only he could take away her fear, even though she realized safety was an illusion with this predator.

"You could stay for a while, if you want. Maybe you can show me the game you designed."

Him seeing her game kept this in safe waters, somewhat professional. That was bullshit. Him reviewing her game was about as personal as it got. Like looking into a programmer's soul.

She stepped out of his embrace and chewed her lower lip. "I don't have it with me, but…"

He'd been made aware they'd acquired her game this afternoon when the team leader reviewing Conjur's backlist saw her name and recognized it. Nothing like a dedicated team who worked even on weekends.

"You found it in Conjur's inventory, didn't you?" she asked. "They purchased it ten days ago and hadn't even discussed with me their plans for it."

"I found out today. You could've told me."

"Emma wanted to tell you, but I told her not to. To the world, we're dating. It'd look like I slept my way into you being interested in it. That's not me. Did you already see it?"

He shook his head.

"You can access it from here?" She glanced at his TV.

He nodded.

She rolled her eyes with a sigh. "Fine. Let me show it to you, but let me explain it a bit before we turn it on. I designed a RPG game with characters *female* gamers might like to see in a game. That being said, it's not some sort of feminist propaganda. I just wanted to take the misogyny out of the avatars, plot, and goals."

"Not all gamers or game programmers are sexist pigs." He hooked a laptop into his gaming system.

"I know, but sometimes during programming the sexual stereotypes are assumed. Unfortunately, the sexist gamers can be pretty loud. I've been called a bitch whore and much worse more times in chatrooms and on different social medial platforms than I care to remember. I probably should've chosen a more gender neutral gaming name than Selene, but, damn it, I don't want to pretend I'm not female like other gamers do. Game developers, being that they're usually men, habitually make the female characters have big boobs and little waists or walk with swaggers or have their midriff exposed. In the non-gamer real world it's the quiet women in glasses who're the most dangerous. So, why not make those avatars the most deadly?"

"Interesting." They needed more women on the development team. They'd discussed this a few weeks ago because they were sensitive to the issue of gender bias as an industry norm. They didn't want to promote it anymore, but, as she said, sometimes the programming happened unintentionally. Intuition urged him to remain neutral while she talked. He booted up the game and grabbed each of them a controller.

"The problem isn't just with the games. The industry is dominated by men, especially the ones who control gaming media. They bias what gets attention. There's a problem with the culture. It's this pervasive idea that white, straight men are the primary audience. No offense."

He shrugged, but deep down he did take offense to it. He tried to not be like that. Apparently, they weren't doing it right.

This wasn't really news to him, not after Gamergate happened a few years ago, when harassed women in all aspects of the gaming world came forward to speak out about the issue.

She continued, "The past few years the hottest games target a very specific male subset of the population. Anyway, this is one of my hot buttons. Sorry. Stepping off my high horse now." She pointed at the screen as the homepage popped up. "My game isn't virtual reality, but I think it's fun. I'll walk you through the first level. You ready?"

Sometime later he glanced at his watch. "Two hours? I didn't even feel it go by."

"Let's quit." She shut off the game.

Wait...no. I didn't mean stop. The last time he'd gotten hooked on a new game written by someone other than him had been years. Shocker number two was him being into a fantasy game. Usually, witches and magical bullshit with ever-changing rules drove him berserk, but the rules of her world made sense.

"What'd you think?" She was back to chewing on her lower lip.

"I didn't want to stop playing. I liked it, but I think I'm biased because I like you. You okay if I show it to Jake and get his opinion?"

She sighed and shook her head. "Noah, we're dating. Even if it's not real to us, to everyone else it is. If you suddenly develop my game, then it's an obvious leap to assume I slept my way into getting your attention. That'd be feeding the misogyny of the entire thing. I can't do that. I think it'd be smarter for me to walk with it. To do it on my own elsewhere. Maybe take it to Mongo Kats. I thought about them because they're an all-women organization, but this isn't really their kind of game."

He closed his hand around hers. "It's good work."

"Forget about the game." Her eyelids drooped to half-mast. She moistened her lips.

Looked like she wanted him to kiss her. Did he go in for

it? Or wait. What if it's not about being kissed?

"You like me?" she asked.

"God, yes." That came out a little too desperate. Very uncool.

She leaned in to press her lips to his. She pulled back to whisper. "I want to feel alive. Kiss me."

Yes, ma'am. Clear direction. That he could handle.

Chapter Fifteen

Tori's only anchor was to cling to Noah's shoulders, intoxicated by his taste. She slid her fingers up his neck into his hair.

"We shouldn't do this. You'll end up blaming me when this goes south," she mumbled as she ran her hand down his back.

"We don't know that." He kissed along her collarbone and gently nipped.

She jerked back with a groan.

He whispered, "Whatever we have isn't something I've ever felt before. Call it chemistry or whatever, but what's going on now didn't start today. Those jeans you wore today… Admit you chose them so I'd stare at your ass. Every time you moved I imagined the dragon on the inside of your thigh and got hard."

Air whooshed out of her lungs. To know she'd turned him on that much made her feel ridiculously sexy. It made her bolder and crazy for more.

He stopped kissing her. "If your no is real, tell me now. I'll stop."

"Don't. Please, don't stop."

"I want to see all your tattoos, dragonfly. I want to make you come for every tattoo you've got."

She gripped the fabric of his shirt in her fist and tugged him down, over her on the sofa. He opened at the first touch of her lips against his. She slid her tongue into his mouth and kissed him deep. Everything else faded away. Worry about the FBI, Symphis, escaping the Stadium faded. All that mattered was this.

All she needed was him.

He changed the angle of the kiss, licked into her mouth with long, deep strokes and moved his hands down her sides.

"Undress," she ordered, pulling away.

His eyes widened as she shimmied out of the borrowed shirt. He remained frozen, staring at her skin, or maybe it was her underwear. Good for her on wearing a matched set, not that she'd counted on getting naked with him today.

She smiled and fiddled with the fastening on his jeans. "Yeah, you earned a chance at the full visual. But…" She reached for his pants. "These off first. Fair warning, I suck at the button openings on pants. Wouldn't want to, uh, damage anything."

He brushed her hands away and undid the jeans himself, sliding them over his hips and off.

She lifted his shirt to put her hands on his abs. "Oh my…that's sexy."

He glanced down her body to her thighs. "I want to see it."

She slowly smiled. "You promise to make me scream in pleasure, huh?"

He scooped her off her feet and put her beneath him, bracketing her with his arms to lean over her. "You will be."

"God, I hope so. I want to scream hard."

Then his lips were back on hers. He slipped his hands down to her breasts. Her body went electric as he touched, teasing her through the fabric of the bra. He dragged his mouth from hers and gazed down, rubbing his thumbs over the tattoo above her breasts until she trembled.

"You are so beautiful. Smart, brave, and talented." He nuzzled her bra-clad breasts, but moved south to the mini dragon tattoo encircling her bellybutton. His tongue swirled around it, and he nipped her gently over the area. Shockwaves of sensation scattered through her nerve endings.

She arched up with a groan. "Noah…"

His hands smoothed along her skin while he continued to stroke his tongue over the tattoo. All remnants of anxiety over the rights or wrongs of doing this disappeared. Her fingers tangled in his soft hair. He continued to suck and nip at her inked area while his hand slipped between her legs. A groan slipped out of her when he teased her slick folds. She spread her thighs, needing more of that agonizingly slow and gentle touch.

"Are you ready to scream for me yet, dragonfly?"

"I won't…not that easy," she admitted.

He chuckled as he kissed down her abdomen and arrived at the tattoo on her thigh. "Licking or blowing fire?"

"What does it look like to you?"

He kissed up the tattoo on the inside of her thigh and licked toward her core. "Not sure yet. I need a closer look."

He pulled away to slide off her panties.

She bucked off the sofa when his mouth licked along the tattoo again and latched onto her. He released to breathe out, "Blowing fire."

His finger slipped inside her, massing until he found an internal spot that made her buck with a scream of pleasure. He synced his internal touch to his mouth on her.

"That's it. Let go for me, Tori."

"Holy fuck, Noah…"

"I'll catch you, dragonfly. I promise. You can let go." He increased his rhythm. Her world exploded. She choked on a sob against a moan when he sucked her too-sensitive bud.

He stopped to kiss back up her stomach.

"How the hell did you learn to do that? It was great, don't get me wrong." It sounded coherent, even though her mind remained fuzzy. For all his odd awkward moments, *that* hadn't been the act of a novice or someone consumed with insecurity.

"I'm a studier. This and programming were the only things that interested me in college. Turns out if you're willing to learn, there're girls willing to teach. They might not have wanted to be seen with me in the daylight, but learn a few skills and even I'm acceptable in the dark." The sadness of the words melted her heart.

"Their loss."

"You only say that because I look like this now. This look took a couple of trainers, a lot of daily work, and the stress of running a business to shed the pounds."

She cupped his cheek. "I don't care if you have the body of a Greek god. We're back to clichés and unreasonable social standards. If you prefer to eat Twinkies and pizza for the rest of your life, then I'm good." But she added, "I might also need some decent gaming competition from time to time, too."

He grinned and laughed. "I'm not big on cakey processed food. My weakness is ice cream. To have a high quality Rocky Road..." He rolled his eyes heavenward.

"I'll remember that."

"I like exercising. It helps to free my mind when I'm trying to figure something out. Biking isn't my thing, though. Had a crash and broke my collarbone a few years back. Swimming. That I'm pretty good at. Shit, I'm ruining the moment, aren't I?"

She shook her head and suppressed a giggle. With a tug, she pulled his lips to hers. "What else did you learn?"

He groaned but stilled her roaming hands to step away. She moaned complaint.

"I'll be right there, dragonfly. Hang on." He fumbled to find his wallet and slid on a condom. Then he was back.

"My turn." She leaned forward but he pulled back.

"I'm so close to the edge that I can't right now. I need to be inside you the first time." He leaned over her and caught her mouth in a kiss. "Tell me you're sure. That this isn't just the product of fear."

"God, yes. Stop asking. I need you deep. I need you to shuck the nice guy right now. Be bad with me, Noah."

"I promise we'll get there, dragonfly. You haven't done this in a while, I assume. Let's take it slow at first." He eased himself inside her with an agonizing slowness, stretching and filling. Her mind wanted it hard, but he was right. Her body needed time to adjust.

"Relax for me," he whispered. "I'm going to get you there as hard as you want, but in a minute."

A sound escaped her, half acceptance and half distress as he worked himself inside. It was so, so good. He surged the rest of his length into her.

"Oh my God. So fucking good." His head dropped forward. She ran her hands beneath his shirt desperate to feel the planes of his back. Hot skin slid beneath her fingers.

"Maybe it's been a while since either of us did this." She leaned upward and kissed the side of his exposed neck, gently scraping her teeth. "I need hard and fast, baby. And deep."

Something in him snapped. With a groan his fingers speared into her hair and tilted her head for his kiss. "Hold on tight."

She grabbed his arms as he scooped a hand beneath her ass to angle her upward and pistoned hard and deep. Over and over.

Pleasure rose within her, spiraling and twisting.

"Deeper?" He waited for her nod to flip her over and pull her ass in the air. This time when he slid in, it was so deep her body shuddered. He kissed along her neck, his body arching over hers with the warm skin of his chest in contact with her back. "You feel me?"

"Yes. So good."

He braced an arm around her waist to keep her upright as he began to move. Slow. Then he increased his rhythm until he pounded into her. Over and over until her body shattered for the second time. Several more hard thrusts and he came.

His head dropped onto her back as he held them there,

motionless, pulsating and swollen for endless seconds. He gently withdrew and helped her turn so she could rest her head against his chest. His rapid heartbeat pounded in her ear. When she finally glanced up, his blissed-out gaze brought on a surge of tenderness.

"Now come the regrets," she whispered.

The warmth in his gaze cooled. Something almost dangerous entered his eyes. "No regrets. We sure as hell should've done that. Don't tell me anything about that was wrong."

"No, it was all good. Everything so right. But..."

"No buts. No psychoanalysis."

"Okay, no psychoanalysis. So, now what?" she asked.

He scooped her up and carried her to his bedroom. The bed wasn't made, not that she cared. He tripped and dropped her onto it. She landed harder than expected with her head wedged between two pillows.

He ended up sprawled across her legs. "That went a lot smoother in my mind. Sorry."

She laughed. "I like that you're real and not perfect."

He nipped her thigh as he got off her.

"Oww." She batted at him.

He traced the mini dragon over her breast. "I like your tattoos. Why dragons?"

"What?"

"Dragons?" he prompted.

"They're a symbol of power, courage, and strength. They represent to me being fearless of my own life changes. I want to see yours. Where are they?"

"My back."

"Roll over." She pulled off his button down and undershirt, and pushed at him until he rolled over. She straddled him just north of his ass. Spiraling tribal-type designs snaked down his spine. "This is beautiful. Does it have any significance?" She leaned forward and kissed the design following it down to its end at the base of his spine.

"That feels good," he muttered.

She kissed the base of his spine. "Why'd you get this? Looks recent."

He raised up on his elbows and gazed at her over his shoulder. God, had there ever been anything sexier than his eyes dilated until there was almost no blue left?

"Got it a few years ago. It was a breaking free of the past thing. It was phase one. I just never got to the next phase," he admitted.

"An attempt to leave Chicken Boy thing in the past?"

"Yeah, something like that. I haven't gotten up the nerve to get in front of a camera to do PR or an interview. That's phase two."

"The ink is sexy. I love it." She resumed kissing her way along the tattoo. "You'll find your way to phase two when you're ready."

She wanted to see him as mindlessly crazy for her as he'd made her minutes ago. With deliberate slowness she kissed her way down his hard abdomen. She dropped to her knees and licked the tip of his cock.

Noah groaned.

Hoarsely, "You don't have to—"

She wanted to. Needed to. She traced a finger around the flared tip. God, he was big and long. Uncertainty shattered her concentration. She cast him a startled upward gaze.

"Only do what you want, dragonfly."

She licked his tip and sucked him as deep as she could. His words strangled into a moan of bliss. For the first time ever she wanted to rock her partner's world to the point he'd lose control. Something about Noah tempted her, pushed her. Maybe it was her competitive nature. He'd already demonstrated ownership of her body. Now she needed to prove she could command his. Years ago at the prompting of a particularly nasty ex she'd studied how to do this, but never used the info. Now directions surged to the fore of her mind. Relax and breathe. After a few seconds it worked. His cock bumped against the back of her throat.

"Oh God," he groaned.

She chuckled, feeling him tense at the vibrations. With each deep movement he became more rigid. She teased, pumped and sucked.

"I'm so close," he groaned. And then he was pumping his release into her mouth. In this moment she owned a small piece of this man. She wiped her lips as his eyelids drifted closed. "Let's rest for a bit."

She tucked in close to him with her head on his shoulder. She liked this. Hell, she liked him a lot. Liking led to love.

No, she was not in love. Not this fast.

He touched her face. "You sure you're okay."

"I'm good with all this, but I'm remembering why I'm in your life. This isn't supposed to be real. It's about your brother and saving the future of gaming."

He kissed her gently. "No regrets. Remember? Did I mention how beautiful you are?"

"I think you already said that."

"Good." He pulled her close.

Damn it, she liked him too much.

***

Tori stared at the night shadows teasing across the ceiling, wondering where Noah was. The digital clock on the nightstand read ten p.m. She should probably go home. A sleepover seemed more permanent than she'd signed up for, although it'd look great to Symphis.

He'd folded her clothes and put them on the side table.

Thoughtful. They were still warm from the dryer. So, they hadn't been there long. With a smile, she slowly dressed.

She padded barefoot to the TV room where she retrieved her shoes. No Noah.

His voice came from the kitchen. She marched in that direction but slowed, realizing he was on the phone.

Noah said, "She's got tentacle arms, Jake. You know how that goes. Hard to avoid." Pause. "Yeah, I know. Why couldn't it have been someone else? Someone not a girl? Then I wouldn't have to deal with this." Another pause and a long sigh. "Yeah, I got it. I'll handle it. Swear I won't screw it up. It's only temporary, right?"

He thought…that about her?

Why couldn't it have been someone else? Someone not a girl?

All he'd said before about her not being alone in this had been total bullshit. She couldn't breathe over the pain as her heart fractured into a zillion pieces and her dignity deflated. She was an inconvenience; a problem he couldn't wait to be done with.

She had no regrets, right?

Almost none. She'd given him everything and like an idiot thought he'd been there with her, feeling the same…giving the same.

Oh, hell. She'd fallen for him. Totally. But he hadn't fallen for her, too.

Chapter Sixteen

Going home? Nope. Not when she was hurting and bitchy. She'd lash out at one of her roommates. Then they'd tease out of her what happened. She'd never hear the end of it for being so gullible about Noah.

After sneaking out of Noah's place to avoid goodbyes, Tori did the only thing that didn't make her feel powerless. Computer research. She stretched her neck as she leaned away from the computer. The computer lab at NYU reeked of Indian takeout, but it offered easy twenty-four-hour Internet access that was free and virtually untraceable to her. Alex, her roommate, attended a night class here once a week. He'd given her his password months ago when her laptop had gone on the fritz and it'd taken her weeks to earn enough money to get it repaired. Neither of her roommates were good at fixing hardware.

Two hours of digging and she wanted to say she was a lot closer to IDing Symphis, but she wasn't. If he lived in Jersey City his place would use a higher than normal amount of electricity from computer usage than other residentials. That data wasn't public. She'd have to beg for hacking help to get into the electric company's database. Alex or Quan might do it, but the help would come at a price. Last time she'd asked for hacking help Alex demanded her framed *Firefly* poster, the one signed by everyone in the original cast. Parting with it hurt. A lot.

No giving up. Not yet. Her only hope was to get to Symphis first, but her eyelids drooped.

***

Noah switched off the gaming system and turned up the overhead lights. A second time around and it still rocked.

Jake rose from his gaming chair and tossed his gamepad on the sofa. "Needs tweaking. The AI is okay but needs work. It'll need a soundtrack and better voices...packaging. I like the ability to customize whatever avatar the player wants and that everyone gets the same starting weapons." He tapped a finger against his lip, lost in thought. "I can sell this."

Noah grabbed his and Jake's gaming pad and returned them to the storage shelves. "Can we do it in five months? Use it to launch the virtual reality goggles?"

Jake sucked air through his teeth. "Tight. We'd have to pull teams off other projects. Get marketing on it now. Do a full press junket within the next two weeks to get buzz started. That means mock covers, casting and interviews." He glanced up to make eye contact. "My end's doable. How about yours...the tweaking?"

He cringed. "It's a lot of work, but pretty sure we can do it."

"It's going to make her career."

"You agree, then, that it's exactly what we need to branch into fantasy. Tori's game is eons better than the *Orc Zone* we reviewed last week. It's next level with avatars that aren't predictable or formulaic. "

"The game is right, but this isn't simple. The game we already own. That's easy, although I'd renegotiate her contract. Her, though. Noah, man..." Jake scratched his scalp. "I'm worried about you. You're not the kind of person to do a fake relationship."

"Tori is...something else. She's talented and funny and badass."

Jake said, "Dating Tori isn't fake, is it? You and she—"

"I never said Tori and I slept together."

"I didn't. You did." Jake punched him in the shoulder. "Happy for you."

"We kissed. We're going to leave it at that."

Jake emitted a sarcastic snort. "If you say so."

Noah wondered if Jake planned to make a play for Tori. "It's real."

"You cut me deep. You know me better than that, Noah. Don't look at me like I'm going to sneak in and make her my next weekend fling. She's only got eyes for you."

"You made eyes at her?"

"Look at you getting territorial. Never seen you like this. Are you actually going to hit me?" Jake threw up his hands. "Chill."

"Hell." Noah cast himself onto the leather sofa and threw his head against the back to stare at the ceiling. He rubbed the stubble on his chin. "We probably would never have met if it hadn't been for the FBI case...Kaleb's death."

"You might've eventually met her with Emma as your assistant and Jason working for us. Maybe a year from now. 'Course, we might not've been looking for the game next year. We might've jumped behind *Orc World.* All that aside, I don't know if you making it a real thing is the best idea, if we plan to produce her game for real."

"Why can't it be simple? She's smart...a Trekkie. I like her, we date, and then whatever. Why can't we have normal relationship problems? But, no. She has to be the ticket to all this FBI shit. And she designed the answer to our professional problems." He covered his face with his hands and sat on the sofa. He slammed his fists into the sofa. "Damn it."

"I'm sorry, man."

"Symphis phoned her yesterday. Threatened her and messed with Emma's bank accounts. When I told Tom he said no one else he'd had infiltrated had ever been personally called.

That means she's special to the psycho. I don't like it because I don't know what it means."

"She's okay?" Jake asked.

"She came over. Things got intense. I must've done something or said the wrong thing because she left without a goodbye or anything. Now she won't answer my calls or texts. Hell if I know what I said." He wrung his hands. "I'm shit with reading people and always say the wrong thing."

"You put Tom and Sam on figuring out who called her?"

"Done hours ago." Noah jumped up and stalked to the mini-refrigerator for a water. "They're tracing the call, but not much to go on. Sam did the evil laugh, which I normally find disturbing but right now I think it's good." Noah collapsed onto the sofa.

"Chill out before you have a heart attack. Or give me one," Jake muttered. Louder, he said, "I want to hire her to work on her game and whatever else comes out of her brain."

He twisted the top off the water bottle and chugged half of it before answering. "We can't hire her. It'd mess up Tom's master plan. She also won't go for it because it looks like she used her body to get us interested in her game. And it's true. No, it's not. I mean, I got to see her game because of it but not because she wanted me to. Had to twist her arm into it once Emma told me Conjur had acquired it." He slammed down the bottled water so hard water exploded out the top and went everywhere on the sofa. "Damn it."

He wiped at the water droplets, pushing them to the edge of the sofa, which didn't help. Now the wetness locked itself to the cloth.

"To hell with what's right or FBI plans. Hiring her to work on her game makes business sense. I don't care how complicated it makes the FBI crap. The company needs this. Her career needs this. Maybe this is what she needs to get free." Jake parked himself at the opposite end of the sofa. They both stared at the blank screen for a while in silence.

Jake said quietly, "Maybe we can spin it that I saw the game before I knew she was dating you."

"That's weak. I don't think she'll go for it. She's been the brunt of a lot of shit as a hot gaming girl for years. Her being perceived as sleeping her way into it or even using a date as a way to suck up to us might kill her."

"We need to make this work. The company's in a bind " Jake squeezed his shoulder. "I don't want to be an ass, but I had a feeling this fake dating plan would implode. A week and you fell in love."

"You're an ass. I'm not in love with her."

Can't be.

Shit, maybe I am.

"Look at it this way. If we make her famous, it'll be tougher for that freak to kill her."

"Or it'll make her death all the more sensational." Noah dialed Tori for the sixth time today. It went straight to voicemail. "Damn it. Why won't she answer?"

Chapter Seventeen

"Did I give you a wet handshake?" Tori's date asked.

"What?" She pulled her gaze away from the airy palatial architecture of the restaurant to focus on her date. The guy's abstract level of communication since being seated over fifteen minutes ago put her off. Maybe his distraction had been the product of him working all day in a cubicle or the restaurant clamor surrounding them.

"I'm sitting here and all I can think is that I gave you a wet handshake when we first met." He smoothed a hand over the impeccably styled dark hair. A hurricane probably wouldn't ruffle the dark, shellacked shell on his head. The blast would disintegrate his body, but leave the hair-dome intact. She bit her lip against a giggle.

"Don't worry about it." She took a huge swallow of her chardonnay. If she hadn't been clued in this straight-laced lawyer wasn't her type, then the OCD nature of this conversation was a huge red flag. Talk about blind dates from hell. *Job interview. Steady paycheck at an entry level coding position at a gaming company. A foot in the door. No cursing and be polite.*

"I just wanted it out there in the open rather than worrying about it all night." His delicate wine sip put her gulps to shame.

"I guess that's good." Another swig of wine down the gullet. Its cheap acidity burned her throat. "So, you're a lawyer?"

"Yeah."

"You work for a cell phone company?" She shifted, restless.

"Sure do."

Oh. My. God. This date was going to kill her before the main course arrived. All she could think about—had thought about for the past day—was Noah. She was crap at choosing the right guys to develop feelings toward. She shouldn't be out with anyone, not with a flayed heart. It made her vulnerable and likely to make poor life choices, whether it was drinking too much of this crap wine or doing a second date with this guy.

She asked, "So, what's your favorite play right now?"

A broad smile broke across his face. "I've been stuck on level fifteen in *Drone Wars* for two weeks. Any hints?"

"It's really best if you figure that level out yourself. Gives you a huge sense of accomplishment." She nudged the candle in the middle of the table toward him to make it more centered.

"Come on. I heard you mastered it. You've got to know."

"*Drone Wars*...what level did you say? Fifteen? What's going on at that level?" She tried to inject enthusiasm into her voice.

"It's a jungle mission in the Congo. The trees are hell on getting a visual on the targets," he prompted.

"The jungle." She didn't love *Drone Wars*. It lacked the complexity and sophistication of games that let you do some building. "Try flying below the canopy."

"That's hell on avoiding crashing."

"It's a level about flying skill." Crap, that came out catty.

"That's all you've got for me? Improve my flying skills and go below the trees?" He frowned. "There's some guy bee-lining for us."

She craned her neck to look toward the entrance behind her. Her pulse pounded in her ears. The rapidly approaching, totally gorgeous Noah couldn't be aiming for her. She turned to gaze past her date, trying to find Noah's target. Only one table was set behind them, with an older couple. She twisted around to stare at Noah again.

He halted next to the table, inches away from her. She lifted her gaze. The intensity in his eyes stole her breath. Images of him naked, of tracing his spectacular tattoo haunted her.

He pulled a chair from a nearby empty table to sit.

"Can I help you with something?" She jumped when his knee bumped into hers under the made-for-two table. She rotated her legs away from him.

"We need to talk," Noah said.

"Right now? Kind of on a date here." Her eyes darted across the table, but her date hadn't yet passed beyond silent outrage.

"I noticed." Noah's voice dropped an octave. His eyes narrowed in the direction of her date.

Was he jealous?

His leg hit hers again. A second time meant the bump was on purpose. Her body electrified. This zing of nervous anticipation is what she'd missed with every other guy she'd dated before Noah, and apparently after.

No. There will be no anticipating anything with this asshole. "I'm no longer your *problem.*"

"*We* were supposed to have a date tonight," Noah said. Oh, yeah, he was completely off-the-range jealous.

Why? It didn't make sense.

"I don't remember having anything about you and me on my calendar. Can whatever has a burr up your ass wait until another time? I'm busy." She cast her date an apologetic smile.

"Now works best for me. It's important." He held his hand out to her date. "I'm Noah Harrison."

Her date didn't know who he was. "You want me to ask him to leave, Tori?"

Noah's focus rolled from her date back to her. "First date?"

"Yes."

"Going better than ours went?"

"Everything was rip roaring awesome until you crashed." She'd gone a little too heavy on the sarcasm.

"We need to get things straight between us." Noah leaned close to her.

She gripped her hands tight in her lap. "What *things* are you talking about? We had two dates. That's hardly what I'd label as an *us*. We're done. I am no longer something you need to *handle*." The reality of him here hit her. "How'd you know where to find me here?" She unleashed a string of mental curses. "Emma."

Or he could've had the FBI track her on the button device. She'd forgotten it was inside her jacket. *Oh, crap...the FBI.* That's probably why he was here. She wasn't done with her side of the deal.

"Whatever is going on here isn't going." Noah's gaze darted to her date. "Now, you and I, we're going."

What a great line. If only it was true.

Her date's scowl didn't bode well.

"How would you know my date with...?" Her mind blanked on her date's name.

"Paul," her date supplied.

"I knew that. How would you know whether or not Paul and I were sharing a connection?" She asked. "My life doesn't revolve around you."

Paul pushed his chair back as if he was about to get up. "Noah, you should leave."

"Hold on, hotshot. This is between Tori and I." Noah held a hand to Paul and faced her. "We need to talk. Maybe in private. I only need a few minutes."

Her breath stilled while her heart continued to race. A mixture of unparalleled attraction and fury electrified her. And scared her. This man already annihilated her heart. Yet, he stood here acting like he was still into her. Maybe this was a show for the FBI Fake Date Operation. He had to be the greatest actor of all time.

Her date interrupted, "Are you dating this guy, Tori?"

She met Paul's gaze briefly and wanted to bark, *catch the fuck up* but figured it'd be rude. "We had two dates. I'm not sure we could call that serious dating, but, yes, we've been out."

"Oh, we've been more than *out*." The angles of Noah's jaw sharpened. A flare of vulnerability, possibly hurt, skittered through his eyes, which squeezed her heart. Then his striking face molded into indifference. He slapped a business card onto the table next to her. "Jake wants to see you in the office tomorrow. Ten a.m. We're going to discuss our plans for *Dragon Spy*. It needs work to get it fully 3-D and maybe even virtual reality ready, but we like the concept and the twists. We also want to discuss you running the project to get it ready for launch."

What?

He was *not* here about them as an us. It was about him. Oh. My. God. They liked her game!

She sat up straighter. "Jake liked it? No, scratch that. I made myself clear yesterday, didn't I?"

Noah leaned in to whisper in her ear. "I'm not into sharing. I'm leaving before I show you just how not good at sharing I can be." Louder he said, "Enjoy your *date*."

Noah stormed out without a backwards glance.

Her entire body felt frozen. *That* sure sounded like it was about them as a couple.

Several silent moments passed while she and Paul stared at Noah's card.

They liked her game. Jake had liked it. This was her big chance to do what she loved. Be a game designer in the big leagues.

Maybe it was a pity offer. They messed up her life. So, here was her olive branch.

That sucked, if so. This wasn't a path she wanted to take.

She'd be forever immortalized as the programming gamer who fucked her way into a deal.

Paul rotated the card to read it. He broke the silence. "You made a game and NJ Legacy wants it? This is a legit NJ Legacy business card, isn't it? *The* NJ Legacy that put out *Zoneworld,* right?"

"I guess so." She picked up the card and flipped it over. Noah had written: *Call me, dragonfly.* Now she had a choice: deal with NJ Legacy and the stress of working with Noah or shop her game elsewhere. The latter sounded good, but she'd shopped it for the past few months with Conjur being her first nibble.

"I think you need to work out whatever's going on with Noah before you and I start thinking about anything here."

"Was there something going on here? Really?" She reached for the wine but couldn't bring herself to take another sip of the acidic liquid.

"We both know this date wasn't going anywhere." He didn't hold back on chugging his wine.

"Paul, I'm sorry." Her phone dinged.

Incoming text from Symphis: *Tonight. Bring it with you.*

Great. An unplanned night in gaming hell.

Paul waved at the waiter. "I was only here to find out what you knew about the game since I heard you were a decent gamer, even though you're a girl. I'm going to get the check and cancel the meal."

Chapter Eighteen

Tori reviewed her preparations in her mind as she descended into the basement of the commercial high rise in Queens that served as the Stadium tonight. After what happened to Emma, she wasn't taking chances. She'd backed up her bank records, credit from four different credit rating agencies, printed out her credit card transactions for three years, and printed out her criminal record, which was all misdemeanors or dropped charges. She'd saved them on a flash drive and given it to Quan before she left. He'd been pissed, but understood without being told.

She'd forgotten to copy school records and medical records. Damn it. She was tempted to return home, do it, and then be late.

A hulking man in dark camos and a long-sleeved dark shirt stopped her and the guy who'd been a few yards ahead of her. "No coats or jackets today. New security protocol. Check them and then get frisked. No weapons inside."

She resented the leer that crossed the security guard's face when his eyes dropped down her body. As soon as she'd checked her coat the guy was reaching in to frisk her.

Her eyes narrowed. "This isn't a green light for you to feel me up. One finger in the wrong spot on purpose and I'll make you a eunuch."

Her frisk did get a bit too personal when he stuck his hand into her front jeans pocket to remove the zip drive.

She said, "Call Rand. Tell him it's Selene and I've

brought what he wants. It's on that drive."

The guy texted on his cell. Moments later he handed back the zip drive without a word and chin nodded her inside.

The atmosphere of the Stadium was different tonight. It was *Battlefield West* night, which was always exciting. In legitimate competitions it drew some of the most talented gamers. Here, she couldn't predict who'd show up. The gambling was fierce in the minutes leading up to start time. This was how she'd gotten into trouble a few months ago.

She fingered the zip drive in her pocket and realized the FBI button had been in her coat. Guess she really was flying solo tonight.

"Where's Rand?" she asked a guy she recognized vaguely from years of non-illegal gaming.

The guy pulled the ear buds of his headphones out. "What?"

"Seen Rand?"

"He's around." Headphones went back on as he continued his pre-game prep.

She rounded the first row of computer tables and almost smacked into the fifteen-year-old from the other night. "You seen Rand?"

"Heard you were dating Noah Harrison." He whistled.

"My personal life has nothing to do with here. Seen Rand?" She ignored his obnoxious boob scan.

"Check the pizza table. I hear we're on a team tonight again. Guess they liked my style of play. Made it to thirty-four the other day." He flashed a nasty grin.

"Guess you're the man," she said sarcastically. "Gotta chat with the boss man for a few. Later." She scooted away.

Bingo on Rand at the food table. Rand shoved an entire slice of pepperoni into his mouth while jabbering to some guy about his new sound system. Without any hint of a conversation detour he passed a packet of two small pills to the listener.

"It'll give you a boost tonight. Take it now. Works for about two hours."

She waited for the other guy to move away before stepping into Rand's space. "Got a minute?"

"Want a piece?" Rand extended a slice of pepperoni her way. Zits in various stages dotted his forehead, made prominent by his tight ponytail.

"I already ate. Thanks."

"You on your game today?" Warning reflected in his gaze. She handed him the flash drive.

He slowly put down his pizza and rolled the drive between his fingers. "All of it?"

"I got code for the first three levels. Cost me a lot for this. Way more than a blowjob."

His demeanor shifted as if someone ran over his favorite dog. He snarled, "The first three levels? That's not what he asked for. We want the complete code. What the hell good is a few levels?"

"It's what I was able to get. That shit's more locked down than the Pentagon. I hacked this off his personal computer at his place."

"I could hack the Pentagon with my eyes closed."

A snort laugh escaped her. "Really? Then why are you playing the heavy for some Jersey kid?"

"He pays well." Rand leaned in. "You don't know jack shit about what I can do."

Score on confirming location of Symphis. "Are we done with this stealing code shit? I prefer to get back to gaming." Her heart pounded so hard she was certain he could hear it rattling her ribcage.

He waved the flash drive. "This isn't what we asked for." He pressed his ear communicator. "We expect the full code."

"It's not possible. Hell, I don't even know where to look for it."

"We don't care how you get it. But..." He pushed his earpiece again. "Heard through the grapevine NJ Legacy wants your game."

"How would you know that?" Chills skirted down her spine as she wondered if they had a mole at NJ Legacy.

He shrugged with an eerie smile. "Take whatever NJ Legacy's offering for your game. Once there to do negotiations I'm sure you can break into their system and get us the code." He smiled an eerie lift of his lips. "We want it in two days when we convene again."

"That's not enough time." Said in a much calmer voice than the *oh shit* detonating inside her brain. "I'm not sure getting the full code is possible. I need to be in the building unmonitored. I'm not a level one hacker. Even if I got through paperwork this week regarding developing my game, this kind of hacking wouldn't be doable until next week. It may never be possible. They've got some security guru who's locked down the whole place."

"Two days. You better have the code." He didn't need to say *or else*. It hovered in the air, thick and menacing. "We're very disappointed about this."

She bit back the *fuck you* on the tip of her tongue. "I'm not up to snuff tonight. Haven't slept well in the past few nights. I shouldn't play."

"I don't care. You're on Green Team. Do you need something to keep you awake or give you a boost?"

"Nope." She spun away to search for the Green table. Tonight's performance from her wouldn't be great. Passable, perhaps, but overall crappy.

The Green Team turned out to be the reject table. Again. She'd played with two of the guys other than the narcissistic fifteen-year-old and knew the other two rounding out their six-some as low rankers locked into Symphis's ring. Her sitting at the table brought up the average age by almost a decade.

No *hey-how're-you's* came her way, only hate glares. How had she ever thought this was a great place to spend nights?

Two days. Noah would never give her the full code. And, damn it, no choice but to negotiate for NJ Legacy to produce her game. Nothing like a little fuck you on caring about her image to the non-illegal gaming world.

***

Hours later, Tori stared at the red digital numbers on her bedside clock. *I need to sleep.*

Every shadow in her bedroom looked suspicious. None moved. None were new. The bathroom light, intentionally left on, reduced the number of wall shadows. If she hadn't been alone in the apartment, she'd be gaming with Quan or Alex. But Quan had a date that looked to have ended in an overnight. Good for him, since it was the first date he'd had in about six months. Alex's father had knee surgery yesterday. He'd gone out to stay with his parents for a few days on Long Island.

Being alone usually didn't bother her.

A creak sounded outside. She jacked upright, ears straining. Was it inside her apartment or outside? She'd dead bolted the door, hadn't she? Crap, she couldn't remember. Pretty sure.

Double-checking the door meant leaving her room. No way in hell she was leaving her room or the bed, as if it the area had a magic protective ring around it. The person who went to check out noises at night in movies was always the one who died first.

A new minute on her digital bedside clock, now 3:46 a.m.

Her phone dinged with an incoming message. She dove for it, anticipating something from Noah. Her smile fell. As she read her stomach churned.

Symphis: *Thursday night. Disappointment will be*

expensive.

She had no hope of getting the code and no clue how to steal it. A hacker she wasn't. Gaming, yes. Breaking into heavily fortified secured networks? No. Maybe Noah would do this for her. Doubtful, since he was only around to *handle* her. No way she'd use sex to get this. That was a line she'd never cross. Oh God, she'd actually considered it.

She clamped a hand over her mouth and ran for the toilet, bringing up everything in her stomach.

A mouthwash swish burned away the foul taste in her mouth, but not her dread. If Noah and Jake had wanted her to have the full code, wouldn't they have given her it to begin with? She didn't want to have this conversation with Noah.

First, you have to say yes to NJ Legacy buying your game.

A yes didn't mean she'd call Noah tonight, though. Noah's business card lay on her bedside table. She returned to the bed, sat, and stared at the card, inches out of reach. *Don't touch it.*

She yanked her hand away from the card when she realized she'd started reaching. Too late to call him tonight.

She sat and cradled her head. She had to negotiate with NJ Legacy to do her game. This was no longer about getting free, which probably wasn't possible. Her sister might get hurt if she didn't do this. She slammed her fist into her pillow.

If she allowed NJ Legacy to produce her game, she'd make sure she was with her creation every step of the way. No peon programmer was allowed to muck up her ideas.

She fingered her phone. Calling Noah wouldn't only be about the game. He'd make her feel less alone in this mess. Even if he didn't want to deal with her on a girlfriend level, her gut still trusted him.

She unlocked her phone. Her finger hovered over the green call button beneath Noah's number. One short call. She'd make sure it stayed on the phone. No visiting.

He answered on the second ring. "Hello? Tori?"

"Hi." Her stomach flip-flopped as the deep baritone of his voice washed over her. God, it was good to hear another human. She wanted to tell him about the text from Symphis and the Stadium tonight, but remembered how much he didn't want her as his problem.

"Are you okay?" he asked.

"I'm not dead, if that's what you mean. Beyond that, I'm handling things." *Not well, though.* She cleared the raspiness from her throat. "I didn't sleep with you to get you to like the game. I didn't want anything to do with you guys producing the game because everyone's going to assume the online trolls are right that I'm a slutty whore. Whatever the future holds, you and I...it's not happening again just because you buy my game."

"We should talk face to face. Come to my place. Or, no, don't come alone at this time of night. I'll send my driver to pick you up."

"Hell, no. I don't want to see you again in a one-on-one setting. You stay there. I stay here. I'll see whomever I'm supposed to meet about the game tomorrow morning. Keep your distance from me. We'll make us become as professional as possible. Officially, we broke up...are broken up, right?"

"That sounds smart. We have a dramatic breakup before we officially sign paperwork to renegotiate your contract to produce your game. That makes it believable and you did nothing to, uh, sway me."

"God, you really are a misogynistic asshole, aren't you?"

"No, I didn't mean it that way. I'm trying to help. What is this about? I thought we really liked each other. Why'd you leave the other night without saying anything?" He sounded so earnest and heartbroken. Her chest clenched.

No heart hurting. No feelings could get involved with all this. "We don't have anything else to talk about. Let this be my confirmation I'll be there tomorrow."

"Tori, I want to see you. I need to make sure you're okay after…tonight. Your date and other things. Seeing you with that guy tonight… I didn't like it. Please, let me come over."

"No." She ended the call.

Chapter Nineteen

As if sleep had been possible after the phone call with Noah. Ha.

Tori cradled her third cup of coffee and stared at her laptop screen that flashed news stories, not that she registered anything. When she couldn't sleep after the call she got hooked on a telenovela three-season story, which left her strung out and beat this morning.

Her phone dinged with an incoming text.

Symphis: *Thought you needed inspiration this morning.*

The loud knock at her door made her jump, almost dumping the coffee. A peephole check found her sister stood outside. Emma?

"Why're you here?" Tori asked as she opened the door. She glanced around the hallway seeing no one else.

"I had the freakiest thing happen. I got all messed up in the head about it. I haven't seen you. I got worried." Emma pushed into Tori's apartment, threw her hand against the wall and panted.

"Why're you out of breath?" Tori's heart pounded hard.

"Took the stairs. Twenty goddamned flights in stilettos." Emma pulled her into a brief hug. "No way in hell I was getting in your elevator."

"You weren't in the elevator? What happened?"

"I was in the elevator of my apartment building this morning and it stopped. Then it fell three floors pretty fast before it stopped. I pushed the red button. I've never pushed that button before. When I pressed it nothing happened. What good is an emergency button that doesn't work?"

Oh God. Not again. Symphis messed with Emma? Tori's throat closed to the point she doubled over and grasped the edge of the futon. "This is my fault."

"I'm fine. Chill. My neighbor said it's been acting up all week." Emma put a hand on her back.

"It was him. Shit, can't breathe." Tori hit her chest.

Emma stomped into the kitchen and reappeared with a plastic bag. "I don't know if this works like a paper bag, but breathe into it."

Tori breathed into the bag. "This seems stupid."

"But you're breathing."

Tori collapsed into a sit on her futon and dropped the bag. "I can't take this anymore. This has to stop."

"We don't know what happened to me was related."

Tori held up her phone to show Emma her most recent text.

Emma sat hard text to her. "Maybe it was. Crap. Now I'm freaked." She smoothed her hair. "I'm fine. The elevator did stop. The doors opened on a different level. I got out and that was it."

Tori felt her chest closing up again. "Maybe it was random." *It's not. Fuck, it's not.* "Elevators in some buildings are technically hackable. Yours is a newer building. You sure you weren't hurt?"

Emma shook her head. "Shaken. You're okay?"

"Fine. Had to go in and play at the Stadium last night. They didn't like what I took. At all."

Emma popped up and paced. "I want all of this over. All of it."

"Me too, but I don't know how. I don't want to do this thing with my game and them. The world will perceive me as a manipulative bitch who dated Noah to get noticed."

Emma wiped moisture from her eyes. "Sorry about

barging in, but I needed to clear my head, not that me here is helping. Good news about your game, huh?"

"I knew you told Noah where I was last tonight. He crashed my date."

"Oh? He was a tad persuasive to get the information when I mentioned it. I think he's got it bad for you, but I agree you two should give up the dating crap, especially if you decide to work for the company."

"I called him. Broke up officially."

"That went okay?"

Tori shrugged. "The other night when I went over there to give him the phone I overheard him on a phone call say he didn't want to be dealing with me anymore. Called me some other things. So, breaking up isn't a biggie."

"You overheard that? You sure it was about you. I didn't get anything like that from him. He seemed irrational to get info on where you'd be last night when I mentioned you were going on a date. I totally read he liked you off that."

"He doesn't."

"I can't believe he'd give up on the two of you dating this easily. I don't get it." Emma nibbled on a nail. "They're nuts about the game. I'm a total jerk not to tell you the second I walked in how awesome it is that we're going to offer to keep your game and make it a headliner."

"Noah and I weren't all fake, but based on what I heard him saying on the phone, he preferred it over."

"Relationships and work mixed together is trouble. Maybe this is a blessing to give you a way to walk away from the emotional craziness that comes from dating your boss. This is your dream to see your game published with a big-time company. Kiss him once, you can call it a one-off thing. More than once can be a problem."

How about a bit of sex? Total disaster.

***

Noah stood at the front of the midsize conference room, hands on his hips, scrutinizing everything through critical eyes. Thirty minutes before Tori's arrival. He wanted to impress her with what they could offer. He'd already summoned the department heads to ensure their presentations were loaded and ready to go.

This was about her. And he was going to make sure it went well.

"Ready?" Jake strode into the conference room. After a busy morning of announcements, meetings, and a lot of employee surprise about the rapid launch of Tori's game Jake still managed to come off cool and organized. Every strand of Jake's brown hair rested in perfect place. His togetherness enhanced Noah's irritation.

"Can't wait to get this started." Jake rubbed his hands together. The gleam in his eyes reflected a wolfish anticipation. "What's wrong? Did you speak with her yesterday?" Jake crossed his arms. "I told you phone only."

"We did some talking in person."

"Did it stay professional?"

Noah averted his gaze.

"Aw, shit. What'd you do?"

Noah folded his arms across his chest.

Jake rolled his eyes. "I need you to think with your head right now, not with your dick."

"You can be such an asshole sometimes. Remind me why we're friends." He brushed past Jake to exit, bumping his shoulder intentionally hard.

Jake grabbed his arm. "Sit."

He yanked out of Jake's grip. "Go screw yourself."

"Don't make me prove who's the better fighter." Jake pushed him into a chair and swung a chair to face him. "I may be an ass, but I'm the ass who made us rich."

Noah crossed his arms. "I'm the one who had the original concept for *Zoneworld*. Without me you'd be living in your aunt's basement developing a concentration style game that involved shooting things, which is the dumbest idea ever."

"I still think it's a viable concept."

Noah cracked a smile at his best friend. "You've got to be kidding."

"You're right. It's for toddlers. It'd suck. I could sell the shit out of it, though. Tell me what happened."

Noah ran a hand through his hair and crossed him arms in silent communication: *not talking.*

Jake said, "I worried acquiring her game with your balls in a wad over her might be problematic, but the game is important to us. I know you get that and can keep it professional. Aside from her career and our need for her game, my top concern is the FBI stuff will go south before the game is ready. Tom really didn't like us producing her game. He painted all kinds of gloom and doom. I don't want it to go bad for her, but with that agent turning up dead, we have to figure out how to get her free of all this."

He scrubbed a hand over his scalp, which no doubt screwed up his hair, but he didn't care. "If this Symphis guy is smart, he'll never let her out. She's a talented gamer likely making bucketloads for him. If she can hook him up with the code for our games, too, that's gold. What happens when she's not useful?"

Jake leaned forward and tented his hands in front of his mouth. "We can send her to our satellite office in the Bahamas or open a new one in another country."

Noah blew out an agitated breath, which did nothing to settle the emotional tornado in his brain. "She'd be online, though. We can't make security tight enough for him not to find her the moment she logs on. Could we beef up security here in

New York and buy her out of the illegal stuff? How about we give her the money to pay him off and be out of debt?"

"We can give her the money up front today. She can pay Symphis off. See how he reacts. Maybe he'll let her leave."

"This is how I lost Kaleb."

"We're doing everything we can to keep her safe. We can use the press to make her known. We can make it clear she's not on drugs so they can't use a heroin OD. We can hire security. Whatever it takes. We won't leave her out there, dangling." Jake paused. "Tell me what the hell you did."

"I crashed her date."

"Tori had a date? I thought you and her weren't fake? That she was really into you."

"Me too, but when she called me to confirm she'd show up today she was pissed. Made it clear we were broken up." He covered his face. "I must've done something or said something stupid. For the life of me I can't figure out what."

Jake put a hand on his back. "You know I have your back no matter what happens. Always, man."

Sam walked in, bouncing like a beagle who'd just been given his favorite treat. "I traced the cell phone call. It's kind of fun to be able to have FBI access to dig through phone company records."

"Who was it?" Noah asked.

"An entry level hacker in Tribeca. The FBI pulled him in for questioning a few hours ago based on my information. I waited to report to you to find out if my trace had been right. It was. The guy claims Symphis forced him to patch him through on the phone. That he threatened to alert the government his Green Card expired. Like Tori, he doesn't know who Symphis is or where he lives. But he did have a more direct email account for him that he communicated."

"You're on it?" Noah trusted Sam's ability more than anyone in the FBI.

"Of course. I'll let you know more toward the end of the day. But I think I've narrowed his location down to Jersey City."

Chapter Twenty

Emma stalked into the lobby of the NJ Legacy building. She waved for Tori to follow to the keycard access elevators.

"You look perfect. Stay cool."

"Don't be the personal assistant to me. I can't take that fake sucking-up crap," Tori snapped.

"I wasn't. You look nice."

"Sorry. I'm nervous about all of this." Mostly about seeing Noah again in person. After long deliberation and emptying her entire closet onto her bed, Tori settled on skinny jeans, boots, and a relaxed black top for the meeting. Emma hadn't thought the outfit worked at first, but when she explained this reflected the height of dressed up for her, Emma went with it. A programmer didn't need a suit. She brought herself and her talent, potty mouth, piercings, and all. Her hair she left down, although debated on putting it into a familiar ponytail. Something about Noah saying he liked it down made her leave it. Now she regretted and considered pulling it up with the band she had around her wrist.

She clenched her shaking hands around the strap of her computer briefcase.

Selling her game, the need to hack NJ Legacy's system for the code, and seeing Noah again was too much. She'd either have a stroke from high blood pressure or a core meltdown.

In the elevator, Emma scrolled through several screens on her iPad. "Relax. Noah will take one look at you and let you have whatever you want. This is a great deal for you."

"Oh, that makes me feel so much better. That I'm not the slut everyone will soon call me." She glanced around. "You seem okay in the elevator. You sure you're okay?"

"Sam says he has everything in this building super protected. I believe him. Remember him? The IT security guy?" Emma stress smiled.

"Your smile's freaking me out. You sure you don't prefer the stairs?"

Emma grabbed her finger before she could push the button for the next floor. "I'm not walking twenty more flights of stairs right now, not with the blister on my foot."

She crossed her arms and fixated on the increasing numbers. "Them buying my game is about my skill, right?"

She saw Emma lower the iPad in the metal wall's reflection. "Of course, it's about your skill. These guys don't mess around if they find something they like. The world might misconstrue the events leading up to the game's acquisition, but the company would never want your game for something this big. Look, they've been shopping for a game to launch in six months for about a year. They'd settled on something last week out of desperation and were about to sign that developer with a contract until they saw your work."

That did somewhat soothe her ego.

"Are you planning to decline their offer?" Emma's brows drew in. "This isn't about dating Noah or you and the FBI. This isn't some new angle to work the gaming case." Emma snapped her fingers in front of her fixated gaze to get her attention.

"Everyone will still think I slept my way into this. The shits who troll me online will be doing cartwheels over this."

"Screw the trolls."

Easier said than done. Words hurt.

The elevator dinged and the doors opened.

Emma stepped out ahead to lead. "Ask Sam his opinion. He's brutally honest about almost everything. He'll tell you that's wrong with your game and what works. Follow me."

The conference room wasn't a typical oblong configuration with beige carpet and some sort of screen. It had a semicircular table, festive carpeting, several tree-sized plants, and huge windows that were open. She'd expected Jake, Noah, and maybe Emma at this meeting, not a crowd of about fifteen unknowns.

A twenty-something guy jumped in front of her with a grin and held out his hand. "I'm Jonathan, Jake's assistant. Your sister's equivalent. Is there anything I can get you? Water, coffee, tea, maybe a sandwich or doughnut?" He pumped her hand with enthusiasm. "Stoked to have you come on board."

"I'm good." Was everybody some freaking nice here? She'd prepared herself to pull out the hard-ass gamer bitch.

"I'll grab you a water. Everyone needs water." Jonathan was like an animated character, filled with a bubbly, ingenuous eagerness.

Noah closed in on her. God, he looked great in jeans and a white button-down shirt.

"Be fierce," he whispered as she passed by him.

What the hell? She halted and whispered, "You can drop the act."

"What act?"

"The part where you pretend to like me. The fake dating crap is over."

He frowned. "But I do like you. I meant everything I said. This isn't fake."

"I heard you on the phone. So, you can—"

"Let's all sit," Jake boomed from the head of the table.

Noah's frown deepened. She could've sworn she heard him say, "What phone call?" before she was directed to a chair.

Jake introduced the people in the room in an onslaught of names she had no hope of remembering. They turned out to be graphic designers, programmers, marketing specialists and a token lawyer.

A half-hour of presentations later, Tori understood their vision for her game. To be the game used to launch the virtual reality goggles was humbling. Even so, she needed to be here to help them understand *her* vision for the game.

When everyone quieted and stared at her as if expecting some sort of enthusiastic wahoo she asked Sam, who'd been silent throughout the presentations, "What do you think of the game?"

Sam tapped his pen against his lips. He scratched his head. His gaze met that of Jake before looking back to her. "I like the idea and the fundamentals, but the AI isn't up to par. Witches have never been my hometown."

She'd judged him a hardcore gamer. "Would you play it?"

He stared at his fingers on the desk and nodded. "A few big tweaks, the right voices, a decent soundtrack and, yeah, I could see myself playing it so long as I got to annihilate a few witches."

"Everyone, give us a few minutes alone. You too, Emma," Jake requested. All but Noah and Jake shuffled out of the room. Jake pushed a folder in front of her, which contained their proposal and a contract for payment.

She scanned the documents.

Jake said, "We're offering a team of specialists to enhance your game, and a once in a lifetime chance to launch next level technology. We want to use your game to launch our virtual reality goggles."

Be chill. Don't scream yes. This was beyond her wildest dreams for her game. Instinct urged her to jump before they rescinded the offer.

No. Negotiate.

She scanned the paperwork, although didn't comprehend a thing. "This is all great, but I want ten percent of sales in addition to artistic control."

"How about five percent?" Jake didn't even flinch.

"Seven."

"I can do six," Jake said.

"Okay. And artistic control?"

Jake wobbled his head and scratched his hair. "I need some give and take on that. There might be things that you won't understand or like, but once done will improve the game. I can't have you saying no out of the gate to everything."

"That's fair. Then I need to see the improvements and sign off on them. I want it in writing."

"Okay."

Boom. Game production on its way.

Noah chimed in for the first time. "Did you have anyone help on the games? Do we need to write someone else in on the contract or worry about rights issues?"

"There was another guy who did some help back in undergrad. I talked to him weeks ago when Conjur contracted it. He's good with just having a credit when the game is published. He doesn't want money."

"Everyone wants money. Why wouldn't he?" Jake asked.

"Ed inherited well from his father. Said it'd just be one more thing on taxes that he didn't need."

Jake said, "We'll need him to sign a waiver, then. We'd also like to offer you a position as a developer with us. There's information in there about compensation for this—"

"Is working for you a requirement?"

Jake grimaced as if he didn't like being interrupted. "No. But if you want to be involved in modifications, then you'll need to be employed by us."

"I prefer not to be locked into a long-term agreement."

"We can do at a short-term contract position with an option to continue."

"Hire me as a contract employee for the upgrades. If it works well, then before I work on the next in the series, which I have already partially developed, we can renegotiate. I also want to have my lawyer review an updated contract copy with these amendments before I sign."

That sounded professional. But a lawyer? *Where the hell am I supposed to find someone who won't charge me to review this?* Legal Aid? Maybe her failed date from last night.

Jake flashed a wide expanse of pearly white teeth. "Sounds like a deal."

"They traced the call. It led to some guy that was controlled by Symphis. Another likely dead end." Noah pushed a manila envelope across the table. "Pay him off when you go again. See if he'll let you go."

"Not unless that comes with a zip drive of the full code to *Zoneworld Two.*" She stared at the envelope full of more cash than she'd ever touched.

"The money is yours free and clear in addition to what's in the contract. A signing bonus," Noah said.

She stared at the money in silence.

Jake said softly, "We can't give you the code. I'm sorry. We were clear to the FBI about this. There's too much risk. Since they stole the code to *Zoneworld One* we've fought pirating and weird online modification complaints to the point it costs as much to do this as the game now brings in. I've got a whole departments whose sole job is to deal with it." Sorrow filled Jake's gaze when he met Noah's glare and then glanced back to Tori. "I'm worried about you as a person, Tori, but I have to be hardass about this. It's my job to look out for the company first."

"I get it." All hope of getting the code free and clear vanished.

"You're under a lot of pressure from a psycho. That makes you a big risk from my perspective. Let me be very clear about this." Jake stared at her in silence until she met his gaze. "If you do anything in an attempt to steal the code, we will be forced to prosecute you for the theft. We will no matter what. You will go to jail and never work in this field again."

She glanced to Noah who wouldn't meet her gaze, but he fiddled with his pen as if agitated.

Jake said, "On a lighter note, we're doing a press junket tomorrow to launch the virtual reality goggles. I figured we can combine it with an announcement about your game. It's kind of a rush but I had the team do some mockups that look pretty good. We can review them in the morning while our PR guru goes over sound bites with you."

"A press junket? You mean answering questions about the game?" Tori asked.

Jake nodded.

"I'm not doing it unless Noah participates. No reason I can't claim fear of the media, too."

Jake rolled his eyes. "Fine. Noah will be there."

"What?" Noah sat up straighter.

Jake shut off his laptop and closed it. "I've been doing them for years alone. Time for you to get out there. Maybe Tori there will distract the press piranhas from how thoroughly unprepared we'll be for launching this game."

"How're you planning to angle the fact we dated before all this came about?" She stared at Noah, her heart in her throat.

Jake sighed and glared at Noah. "We could call it a disaster date where we fortuitously discovered you're a programmer."

"You implying I need to apologize to you for something, Jake?" Noah asked. "The only one who needs apologizing to is Tori for us fucking up her competition."

"You're supposed to be the sensible one, Noah." Jake's shoulders slumped. "You've always made sound choices. I'm usually the one with personal messes."

Now even Jake admitted she wasn't a "sound choice" for Noah? This hurt so much.

Noah stood and picked up Tori's laptop bag for her. "Come with me. We need to talk."

"No, thank you. Email me the updated contract so I can get a lawyer to look at it tomorrow." She stood and took her bag from Noah.

Noah followed her out to the elevator. "What phone call are you talking about?"

"Stop." She held out a hand to warn him to keep his distance. "As usual, my life's a confusing mess. You and me? We're not dating. It's done. It's for the best. You guys are nice to offer me a way to see if I can get out of the Stadium. It's more than I had last week, even if I'm not feeling optimistic it'll work. If something should happen to me before the launch, you guys should do whatever you need in order to make it ready. I'm sure there's a death clause in the contract."

"I don't know what happened or what you think you heard, but you have to tell me."

"I heard what you said." She dropped her gaze, unable to meet his. "There's no need for you to stress about us. We're over. No more confusion over what's real. Us working together is real."

The elevator opened and she stepped on, jabbing at the door-close icon.

The door slid shut before he said anything more. One floor down, she hopped out and took the stairs from the twentieth floor, not out of fear of the elevator but to fight the tears threatening to spill.

Chapter Twenty-one

Tori padded to the refrigerator, unable to sleep. Quan sat on the futon. He wasn't watching TV. "Late night?"

"Why're you up?" Quan glanced up from his phone.

She shrugged.

"I didn't ask questions about the flash drive you handed me, but I did check it out. As if I wouldn't. No reason for you to back up your life unless you were worried that gaming freak was about to fuck you over. I warned you."

Tori turned on the kitchen light, which didn't flood the apartment with light like she'd hoped, but made it less dim. "What do you want to hear? You were right? I'm fucked. You'll probably hear I was found dead next week."

"You need help." He hadn't moved, remaining stiff with his arms crossed.

"Got so much *help* I don't know how to deal with it." Her stomach churned at the lie.

His eyes narrowed. "Come with me. I've got something to show you."

"I'm exhausted. Can this wait until tomorrow?"

"No." He marched to his bedroom door and held it open for her.

Quan had transformed the room into an electronics lab with a futon. Clothes littered every vertical surface. He flicked on his sound system, which emitted a high-pitched screech.

"Ow." She cuffed her ears.

"Put these on." He handed her a pair of noise-canceling head phones with a microphone.

"Better." No more ear piercing pain.

"This is a conversation I don't want monitored by anyone. Tell me what's really going on."

Quan knew something, which meant he knew a lot, probably everything. "Why don't you tell me what you know and what you figured out?"

"You're smart, but my IQ is about fifteen points more than yours."

She rolled her eyes. "You better not be basing that off the online Mensa quiz we did last year. I wasn't even trying."

He scowled. "Trying to pull shit over on me is stupid. Let's start with you and Noah Harrison. Him messing you up at the competition that his gaming company supported made no sense. I mean, hell, him making a public appearance made no sense. Then him dating you? Bizarre."

"You don't think I'm good enough him?" She crossed her arms and bit back a list of defensive arguments.

"Oh, you're plenty attractive and smart. There's not a gamer man alive who wouldn't think you hot as hell. But you're too prickly for a man like Noah Harrison to handle. I don't mean that in a bad way so don't get your feathers ruffled. Him noticing you at his competition in what was a dark room 99 percent of the time? Nope. Him having the cojones to hit on you with your bitch warrior armor on? Oh hell no. This man won't even talk to reporters, not even online interviewers."

"I admit it was a set up for the FBI to find out about Symphis. Them liking my game, though, had nothing to do with all this. It was a positive side effect. Conjur acquired it. NJ Legacy just bought Conjur. It's a future."

"Which you're not going to live to see the way your life's going." He rocked his head back and forth. "Congrats on the game. You deserve that, but what really happened?"

"I met Noah in jail last week when I got hauled in during a police raid on the Stadium right before the D.C. competition."

"Yeah, I matched up arrest records. Seemed too coincidental with you there and him there. So, I called a friend of mine in the NSA to find out what he knew about any operations going on out here with any government agencies. With Noah Harrison's brother dying in weird circumstances and then him caught in the gaming raid… I can put two and two together. Someone's using you. Now I know for sure it's the FBI."

"I don't think Noah intended for us to meet in jail. That I think was coincidence."

Quan's face scrunched up in a sarcastic *really?* "Someone could've manipulated him to be there. Or maybe he wanted to be there to meet you. You thought about that, right?"

Maybe if someone gave him the offhand information on the next location of the Stadium he'd have been tempted to go. Someone could've tipped off police and then made sure they got discharged together. Could be done electronically. Maybe Noah was involved in "handling" her more than she thought. Tori pulled her nail away from her mouth when she realized she'd been chewing. "What'd your NSA friend say?"

"There's one FBI sanctioned operation against a video gaming ring in New York run by an agent who's gotten into trouble for running civilians instead of agents in the past. People…civilians died twice during his ops to bring down gambling rings. Then one of the two authorized agents who was on his team showed up dead in the Bronx the other day." Quan tilted his head as if waited for her reaction.

"Ravi?"

Quan nodded. "I did some research on other gamers I heard got sucked into the Stadium. Called a few friends. Most don't last more than a few months before something bad happens either technologically like bank accounts tanked or framed for a crime. Or, they end up dead, usually from a fake drug OD. What's Tom Smith making you do?"

"I'm supposed to provide info to help them bring down

the organization and to get Symphis for Noah's brother's murder, maybe other murders. In exchange they help me get out alive. They made me fake date Noah to provide a link to communicate. It got real between Noah and I. Then it wasn't real. I don't even know what's going on with the FBI anymore."

"Shit timing to find something real in the dating world. I think Noah's on the legit side of this, which is good because if not I'd firestorm him. That self-absorbed narcissist who calls himself Symphis doesn't hold the monopoly on destroying people with technology." His eyes drifted closed as if he sought calm. "What does this Symphis want from you other than you to play on his teams?"

"I've been playing like shit. So, not helping him there, unless he's having people bet against me to win some money." She squirmed on the seat. "He wants the code to break through the security on *Zoneworld Warrior Two*. The FBI via one of Noah's IT security experts allowed me to give him levels one through three security free."

"Had a back door or something I'm sure. Stupid of them to give you a few levels. They put you in danger for no reason. Makes no sense. Why didn't they give you the full code to begin with and when Symphis opened it they'd have him?" Quan asked.

"They can't give me the real thing. They've already had too much backlash from the code for the first one getting out. What if he wasn't the one to open it? Then NJ Legacy would be on the losing end of it."

"Did anyone open the drive you gave them?"

"Not that I've been told, but I'm not in the loop. They were super pissed it wasn't the whole thing. Rand, the guy who's Symphis's heavy onsite, got really scary about me bringing him all of it in two days. Tomorrow."

Quan sighed loudly and reclined in his gaming seat. He started messing with a Rubik's cube. "This stinks of foul shit. If all the FBI needed was intel on the Stadium or Symphis, then you could've told them where the next meet was."

"They're trying to stop the serial killing of programmers and people sucked in. They claim this is about saving the future of all gaming. I don't—"

Quan held up a hand for silence. Distractedly he mumbled, "The one thing Symphis wants more than anything is the game code? Doesn't make sense. Other than illegal bootlegs what's he done with the code for *Zoneworld One?*"

"I think he's had his programmers modify it to make certain levels unwinnable. It doesn't play like the true version."

"I don't think this is about gambling money or the stupid code. They could find some way to hack NJ Legacy for it or hack the game itself. It's a test of you. Or it's just some sort of deranged game he's playing with you. Perhaps, revenge for something. Or, he likes you, which is even more twisted. No one can guess the goal of a sociopath."

Nausea twisted through her gut. "Don't you mean psychopath?"

"No. The guy's too cautious to do this out of pure psychosis. This is deliberate. It's a big game for him. I get a back feeling you're no more than a small time distraction." He met her gaze. "We've got to figure out who Symphis is."

"He lives in Jersey. I need to break into the electric company grid to pinpoint where it might be usage hikes and see names."

"That's easy." Quan fired up his computer. He patted the chair next to him for her to sit. Within minutes Quan was in the electric company's records. He found high utilizing residentials and scrolled this list.

"Stop." *No way. Maybe.* She pointed at the name on the screen. Martin Rodríguez. "That's got to be him."

"Martin? That teenager dipshit? Can't be." Quan paused and smiled at her. "I heard what you did to him in D.C. Bet no one else had the balls to point out his grundies."

She rolled her eyes. "Tell me it wasn't online."

"It was everywhere. You're a hero to gamer women and gave hope to a lot of guys who were already half in love with you. Guys who want you aware they know how to properly wear the pants in a relationship."

"Glad I missed reading those messages." She massaged her head. "I remember hearing rumors about Martin when he appeared on the scene last year. He'd come up from Honduras with his mom. He was related to someone involved with drugs."

Quan did a search. A hundred articles on Matías Rodríguez popped up. "No mention of a Martin, but did say his mom moved to the U.S. a few years ago. They've tried leveraging her to find out about her son, but Matías cut ties." He met her gaze. "That's bullshit. What good Hispanic son cuts ties with his mother?"

"This may be way more complicated than we thought. There's only one way for me to get out. I need to confront Martin. I can take him the code, personally. Or pretend I got the code. I can take it to his house instead of the Stadium."

"Very dangerous. But ballsy. We're going to need help. We'll need a recording device to record what he says, but the device can't be something activated remotely. He's going to have blockers on that sort of tech. Who wrote the back door into the code you gave them before?"

"Sam at NJ Legacy. I don't know his last name. You know him?"

Quan searched NJ Legacy's employee list on his screen until he found Sam Miller. He tapped a finger against his lip as he stared at Sam's headshot. "I remember this guy. We met a few years ago at a Tolkien Con in Vegas. Let me find out if the back door was opened."

"How in the world are you going to contact him?"

Quan logged on to his mainframe on the desk and then

into what looked like a forum for fantasy junkies. He posted a question. "Now we wait."

A minute later there was a reply. Quan typed what read as a bunch of gibberish. She knew a lot about computers and technical jargon, but this wasn't English. "What language is that?"

"Elvin language. No universal translator for it. The serious Tolkeinites memorized it to talk on this forum."

"You learned a fictional language to talk on a fantasy forum?" She stared at him. "You aren't really doing contract work for a financial firm are you?"

"Love you, Tori. I do. This is why I'm going the distance to save your ass. But there're some things I can't talk about. This would be one of them." Quan didn't lose focus on his typing.

"If you have some sort of security job or whatever the hell you really do, why are you slumming like a penniless post-college kid and rooming with us? Why claim to be taking sucky contracting jobs to pay rent?"

"I like living here. I like gaming with you guys. I'm pissed they sucked you into this illegal racket, though. This also points out how much I need to ramp up security in this apartment. I'll be doing that in the next two days." For the first time he stopped typing and glanced at her. "The back door wasn't opened. Sam agreed there's something not right, and with the possible Rodríguez cartel connection…not good. You'll need the full code to try to get out of this, but Noah can't know about you getting the code. Sam thinks there's a mole at NJ Legacy."

"You suggesting steal it?" She'd never done something that illegal. Noah would also never trust her again.

Quan laughed. "I don't think you could hack it off their secure server. Sam will help, but you can't mention him when this is over. They have to assume you are good enough to hack it."

"I think Noah should know about it."

"No. Too many possible spies. He might tell Tom and there might be someone on the FBI team that's working for Symphis."

"You're on the good guy team, right?"

"Does it matter?" Quan smiled in an eerie way.

Probably not.

Chapter Twenty-two

"This is Tori Duarte, designer of *Dragon Spy,* which we have scheduled to release in six months." Jake waved her way from where he sat to her right on an elevated platform. Cameras flashed. Video cameras documented their every twitch. At least thirty reporters yelled at once and waved hands for attention. This was the big league of techie world media.

Her first press conference and she should be freaked out. Yet, she wasn't nervous about the questions flying their way or about the attention. Her mind remained stuck on the image Symphis sent her fifteen minutes ago.

Alex had been slumped against a building, his face covered in cuts and bruising from a recent fight. Only, Alex didn't even know how to throw a good punch. Someone had beat the crap out of him.

Symphis had texted: *Tonight. The code. Next time he might not be so lucky.*

She'd called Quan moments before walking onto this elevated platform. He'd said, "Two guys jumped Alex last night while he was pumping gas. He went to an urgent care and might need some nose work, but he's making it."

Had someone asked her a question? Crap, she needed to focus.

Mere inches of air separated her from Noah on her left. Her foot accidentally bumped against Noah's, or had he done the bump intentionally? Her shoulders ached from holding them stiffly in an effort not to glance his way. *Don't look.* One glance and everyone in this room, and the international world of gaming, would guess she was in love with him.

Was she?

Yeah, she probably still was. But like Quan said, it was shit timing.

Maybe it wouldn't be a crisis to be caught Noah-gazing. Every woman who'd crossed his path while they'd been ushered into this conference shot him googly eyes. Half the questions coming their way were from reporters hungry to grill the one person they'd been denied speaking with for years.

From the front row of reporters a brunette with cleavage pushed to the spillover point in a low-cut blouse threw Noah an I'll-do anything-with-you smile followed by a less than subtle lip moisten.

Tori wanted to watch Noah, to see if he responded to the woman in the front row. The need to study him and her determination to resist led to a throbbing headache.

If he responded to the woman in the front row, then what? She had no claim on him. She was about to screw him and his company by stealing the code.

A focus on slow breathing didn't help to soothe her escalating headache. She mentally talked herself off the edge of a mental breakdown. A calm glance at the press corps helped her conclude most here probably assumed she had a minor crush on Noah and Jake. Few would deduce her feelings surpassed the crush level.

Noah leaned into the microphone in answer to a question "Fast paced, upgradable skill tree, online and offline modes..." She zoned out as he launched into her game's technicals. All she registered was the sexy low vibrations of his voice. Even though they weren't touching, the heat from his body warmed her in the chilled air-conditioned hotel convention room. His tone sent chills across her shoulders and down her spine. Memories of his voice, hoarse after he... *You will not go there.*

She planned to reaffirm they were on a professional-only basis with him after the press conference. Speaking calmly would hopefully reset the two of them to sail into friends territory. In her mind she'd practiced her what-happened-is-over speech dozens of times. Although, why put out the effort when she was about to fuck him and his company over by fake stealing the code?

What if he gave her the cold shoulder? She'd be miserable because she was hooked on him. Totally, irrevocably. Okay, that was not a professional-only attitude.

You need him to give you the cold shoulder. She needed him to verbalize a clear it's-over and reaffirm he didn't want to deal with her anymore to push her into the move-on process. Getting over Noah might require a lot more ice cream and *Firefly* reruns than any previous guy, though.

Stop thinking about it. Focus on being here. On getting code today. And calling Quan when this is done. You'll get clobbered by some dumb question if you don't pay attention.

The next reporter asked, "Noah, what did you first notice about Tori that grabbed your interest."

Her mind snapped to attention.

Jail.

Tori held her breath. Her gaze met Noah's for the first time during the press conference, remembering their moment in jail.

"I liked her...outfit?" His lips broke into a silly grin over pointing out the mistake in the question. The press erupted into laughter. Noah said, "Her work is visually exciting."

Visually exciting? Did he really mean her work or was there a subtext? *Get your mind out of the gutter.*

The same woman reporter yelled, "Tori, what's it like to work with two of the world's sexiest CEOs?"

Speak into the microphone, but not too close. She leaned in. "The team at NJ Legacy is amazing. I couldn't be happier."

Success. She'd delivered line three on the worksheet of news bites she'd memorized this morning under orders from NJ Legacy's press guru. Her gaze darted to Noah. He smiled at her, supportive. Sexy. Her stomach squeezed.

Look away. Now.

She glanced back into the throng of reporters.

A male reporter said, "So, Noah, Tori's sister is your assistant and we have reports that you and Tori went on a date? Are you two dating? She does look a little like the avatar Giselle from *Zoneworld One.*"

Noah shook his head. "No. No, no, no. Nothing to do with Giselle."

Tori read between the lines. "Would you ask what that question implies if I owned the company and Noah was my newest game designer?"

The reporter shrugged. "It is awfully coincidental. And with your gamer background..."

Tori saw red. "I'm a woman. I'm attractive. Is that a problem for you? Do you assume because of that I must've slept my way into this? For your information, I'm an internationally top-rated gamer. I attended MIT. I can develop games better than most men in this building. It's this kind of pervasive gender bias that's got to stop in the gaming industry."

She chanced a glance at Noah, who looked impressed, but the horror on Jake's face didn't bode well.

Jake leaned into his microphone. "We discovered her game in the backlist of Conjur's acquisitions. Conjur hadn't gotten around to producing it yet. We recognized its brilliance and had to develop it."

Noah's gaze narrowed on the reporter that asked the question. "Why would it matter who I dated? What does that have to do with her ability to have designed an incredible game that I predict will go viral? Any one of us would be a lucky son of a bitch if she decided to go on a date with us."

Noah totally saved her. Was that her heart squeezing? No, it was her heart reminding her she was punch drunk in love with this man.

He thought her talented to the world. Wow. She smiled gratitude his way, perhaps mixed with a tad bit of a lot more.

***

Noah leaned against the wall and gazed at the hotel's high paneled ceiling in the dark, quiet hallway. *Get your head tight.*

The press conference had been nonstop torture. Sitting so close to Tori, teased by small touches here and there, but forbidden to acknowledge what scorched between them...pure hell. Thank God for the tablecloth or the press corps would've discovered exactly how much he wanted the beautiful brunette game designer—so much that he'd had trouble walking out of the conference at its conclusion.

He'd promised Jake he'd keep his shit together when all he wanted to do was ask her about the fucking phone call during which she claimed he'd said something derogatory about her. Not so sure he made high points on the goal of keeping it together, given how he'd gone off on the reporter about dating Tori.

Now he had to survive a launch luncheon with an intimate group of reporters. *You cannot stare at her tight T-shirt.* Since the moment he first saw her today he had a hard time keeping his eyes off her spectacular breasts encased in a pushup bra miracle.

He'd wasted enough time hiding from the press junket. Time to get the next ninety minutes of hell over with. As he rounded the corner into the hallway he smacked into a small woman moving at high speed. When she stepped back...damn. The object of his inability to think straight gazed up in wet shock.

A full plastic cup of what he assumed had been water had

exploded down the front of Tori's white T-shirt. Based on the new wetness on his abdomen, the water was all over his front, too. What had been a sexy T-shirt on her, hinting at the secrets hidden beneath, turned into a no-imagination-required peep show. He made out the intricate lace connecting the smooth cups of her bra and her now pebbled nipples. And, the dragon tattoos above her bellybutton and her left breast.

"Crap," she said, wiping at the shirt, which did little more than plaster the drenched fabric tight to her wet skin. He almost groaned at the effect.

"I'm sorry," he managed lamely. Two of the notoriously snarkier online tech reporters headed their way up the hallway. Before the guys noticed them he grabbed her hand and pulled her around the corner into the restroom.

"This is the men's room." Her outraged tone faded as she walked toward the mirror. "Oh my God!" She set the empty cup on the counter and fanned the front of her soaked shirt. "I look like I stopped off for a wet T-shirt contest. Why did I choose to wear white today?"

"You'd have my vote to win."

She rolled her eyes. The edges of her lips crept upward into a weak smile. "Serves me right for being in a hurry with water. I shouldn't have eaten those pretzels this morning. They make me too thirsty all day."

"You wouldn't happen to have a change of clothes in your purse?" He glanced at her small handbag.

"Not unless I'm carrying around a bikini top for a just-in-case swim. Nothing fits in this thing." She waved the green hand-sized designer bag. "Emma said I needed something more hip than my usual and lent it to me, but I can't even get my wallet in here. It's a useless piece of fashion." She fanned her shirt in front of the mirror again. "I can't go to the luncheon looking like this."

"You have to be there. I'd give you my shirt, but—"

"Let's do that," she said sarcastically. "Then you can distract them with your naked chest. Everyone already thinks you're eccentric. This'll confirm you're slightly insane. The ladies would sigh and drool. I could spend the entire time trying to explain how I ended up in your shirt, yet we're still definitely *not* dating, while Jake has a stroke. Yeah, great plan."

"Too bad Emma isn't here today. You could change clothes with her. No paper towels in here." He clicked on the hand dryer and waved her over.

"You've got to be kidding." She crossed her arms.

He shrugged.

"Fine." She knelt below the pointed-downward air dryer and held out her shirt while it blew. "This is so freaking cold. Don't you dare look."

He bit his lower lip, but a laugh escaped. The show from his perspective was pretty damned good.

She glared at him, but then her gaze turned naughty. Her eyes dropped to his wet groin, now level with her head. She moistened her lips. "Got wet in the wrong area, did you?"

"Don't do that."

Her eyebrows quirked upward.

"Don't mess with me right now," he warned.

"Call it payback for staring down my shirt."

The blower ended its cycle. Noise from the bathroom's anteroom prompted him to grab her hand, yank her to a stand, and pulled her into a stall. "Someone's coming in."

"Are we supposed to pretend we're having wall sex in a public restroom now? Couldn't we get arrested for that?"

"Even I have standards, although there's a first time for everything. I don't want you caught by reporters while drying your shirt in a men's room. Go in that stall. I'll stay out here."

"Doing what? Pretending you have difficulty peeing? I mean you did pee your pants." She doubled over, laughing hysterically as he continued to push her into the stall.

"Lock it. Damn it, stop laughing." He heard a few residual snickers from her as two guys came in, did their business, did a cursory hand wash and left.

She walked out and resumed drying her shirt with the blower. "How'd it go out here? Able to perform and all that jazz?" Laughter burst out of her when he resumed drying his pants in front of the dryer next to her.

Laughter burst out of him. The whole thing was absurd.

"You wet there...me wet here...this really doesn't look good." She fanned her shirt and pointed at his pants.

After a few minutes of blow-drying, or maybe it'd been ten minutes he asked, "What phone call?"

She glared at him. "My shirt's dry enough. Don't want to get caught in the men's room. See you in there."

Damn it.

***

Tori plucked at her stiff T-shirt, thankful it had dried enough to no longer be see-through, although it'd lost its fresh look. She'd left Noah in the bathroom still trying to dry off.

He hadn't returned. Showing up independently to avoid speculation had probably been smart. The press did love scandal. What better than to feed them a story of the two of them messing around during the press event?

On her way into the conference room she heard, "Tori, great job."

A head swivel found Sam over by a table full of coffee carafes looking a lot less cheery than his tone. "Just wanted to shake your hand. Welcome you on board."

When her hand connected with his she felt the small drive in her palm.

"It's a one-time read," he said quietly as he turned to fill a cup with coffee. One time meant it'd corrode after the first time it was opened. Symphis could confirm the code was there, but then he couldn't do anything with it after opening.

Sam poured creamer in the coffee and whispered, "This has to be on you. You need to go to Noah's office on the twelfth floor before he gets back from the hotel. He and Jake are scheduled to remain after the luncheon to speak privately with a marketing group for about twenty minutes. I gave you access to the building. Just show your driver's license. His password is NH762. There's no other way. I'm sorry. Think we have a spy for Symphis working for us. You caught on camera getting into his system will help the illusion."

"Thanks."

Louder he said, "See you around."

She stuffed the flash drive into her jeans, saying goodbye to everything she had with Noah. This had to be dark and dirty. And fast. Would he forgive her?

Jake squeezed her shoulder supportively as he took his seat on her right. He leaned in a whispered, "You're doing great. And Noah? Damn, I'm proud of him. He's only here because of you. I can't thank you enough for that."

Before she could reply Jake initiated conversation with the guy next to him. Charming, witty. He was really good at this.

She sensed a familiar blue gaze burning into her and she glanced up. The power of Noah's gaze strengthened as he closed in, making it hard for her to concentrate on anything else, although she had to. Her body cranked up to preheat.

"Ready for lunch?" Noah asked her, his tone edgy.

She shrugged, trying to appear unaffected when he rubbed against her hip as he slid into his seat.

"I'm starved." He politely greeted the blonde next to him. Tori barely held back the urge to shift her body just a little to the left, to push herself into him and keep his attention on her, not the blonde.

Lunch service began. She chatted with the senior editor of

an online tech magazine seated next to Jake until the guy and Jake launched into an economics debate. Her interest in the conversation dropped. She picked at her food in silence but noticed the perfectly manicured blonde magazine editor next to Noah kept angling herself to allow him a view down her low shirt. Maybe it wasn't on purpose. An editor important enough to end up at their table had to have worked her ass off to get to this position and rest her reputation on her professionalism.

Tori grabbed her water and tried not to pay attention when the editor erupted in laughter and leaned intimately toward Noah. Noah's body stiffened as he leaned away from the editor and into Tori. His face flushed red and he jerked away from Tori, which bumped him into the editor's legs.

His granted the lady an apologetic smile. Every bit of care to keep the attraction between she and Noah secret vanished. Bad time for jealousy to rear its head.

Jake asked Tori, "How're you holding up?"

"What?" Her cheeks heated in a you-caught-me blush. "Great," she forced out followed by a fake smile. Feminine giggles erupted next to Noah. Tori clenched her teeth. This had to be her imagination.

"We're in the home stretch." Jake's gaze bounced from her to Noah for a moment. His voice dropped to a whisper, "You will keep it together." He turned away to chat with the male editor again.

The blonde editor reached across the table to get the pitcher of water from the center of the table and brushed Noah's chest with her arm. Whether intentional or not, Noah's hand jerked, knocking over Tori's water. It soaked both Tori and Noah.

Noah jumped up with a gasp. "Shit, I'm sorry."

Noah stared her shirt. Oh, crap. Take two on wet T-shirts. This time, the shirt was soaked lower than her chest.

Waiters appeared to take care of the mess.

"Why don't we go dry off," Noah suggested. He grabbed her arm and escorted her out of the room.

She yanked her arm free once outside the luncheon hall.

Noah took her hand and pulled her into a vacant conference room. Once inside he closed the door.

"Admit you were flirting with the blonde editor," she said.

"She's the senior editor of *Wired*. I wasn't flirting. I was trying to avoid her touching me."

"Oh?"

Noah massaged his forehead and mumbled, "This is insane."

"What's insane? That fact you were flirting with someone to make me jealous on purpose?" She let her gaze drop to his groin. Bad decision. The hard length of him pressed against his zipper. Her cheeks flushed hot.

"There's nothing going on with…with…whatever the fuck her name was. I'm no good at flirting."

"Sure as hell looked like you were rocking it."

"I'm trying to help launch a game. Apparently, whatever the hell was going on with flirting or talking charming is a part of it."

"Flirting, then, is a part of the marketing plan?" Her eyes narrowed. She put her hands on her hips. "You're saying me having a slightly transparent shirt might be a good thing? I think the editor next to Jake might have the hots for me, or be into staring at this wet mess." She waved at her chest. "You think I should push 'em up a bit more before we go back and be sure to lean his way to ensure he gets a good show? It's for the game, right?"

Anger and something far more potent flared in his eyes. "No."

"It's okay for you, but not me?" She poked him in the chest.

He leaned in toward her, pressing her flush to his chest

191

and caging her against the wall with his hands. Her body went haywire. Lust. Hope. Want. All the emotions tangled in her chest, strangling the breath from her lungs.

He hit her with blistering eye contact. All she could focus on was the feel of his hard body pressed against her chest. Heat rolled off him, or maybe it was coming from the fire storming through her. She dragged in a deep breath.

"This isn't the right time for us to hash anything out. But we are going to talk about what you think you overheard to make you freak the fuck out." He scowled at her even as he stared at her lips.

Her eyes fluttered shut and she grew still, unable to take more than shallow breaths while his breath tickled her face. She whispered, "We need to hash, Noah. Whatever's going on here isn't a small problem. But not now."

His mouth crushed down onto hers. With sigh of "thank God" her world became him. The kiss was angry, raw, and soul searing as his tongue swept into her mouth over and over. It held a possessive edge as if he was staking his claim.

One of his hands came off the wall to gently touch her cheek, so at odds with the ferocity of his lips.

She melted into him.

"Tori," he whispered in a raw tone. He kissed down her neck. Her need for him turned to desperation. He kissed her hard, tongue claiming her. His hands seemed to caress everywhere as if memorizing each contour of her body.

"Was a mistake. Gotta keep my shit together," he mumbled.

Warning bells went off in her brain, but she was so mesmerized by his kisses that she lost interest in analysis of whatever he said.

Noah jerked back. Her eyes opened as she struggled for breath and equilibrium at his unexpected retreat.

He stumbled backward, putting several feet between them.

"That didn't happen. Can't happen. We're in the middle of a press luncheon. They're going to realize you slept with me."

As the fog cleared from her mind she stared up at him. "I didn't sleep my way into selling my game. I am *not* that kind of person. You're right. We are a mistake."

His expression turned guarded. "That's not what I said. Not what I meant."

"Sure sounded like what you said. Forget it. Forget me and all this interpersonal bullshit." She pivoted and stomped out of the room.

Chapter Twenty-three

Tonight.

She stared at the one word text from Symphis, and had been for forty-five minutes. She'd somehow made it to NJ Legacy and Noah's office before his meeting at the hotel ended. She'd managed to pretend to hack into his computer and not have a heart attack. If anyone who actually knew how to hack evaluated what she'd done, they'd realize she didn't have a clue. She'd slipped the flash drive she'd picked up at the store around the corner into the side of his computer and read a few boring memos but copied nothing onto the drive.

Tori sipped coffee at the Jersey City Waffle House where she'd been for the past hour, thinking. And waiting. Not that it got her anywhere other than paranoid and hopped up on sugar. Too much apple butter and raisin toast.

Where was Quan? She texted him for the fifth time. He hadn't replied to emails, either, and he usually responded within minutes. Maybe something happened to him.

She texted Noah: *Game on. Tonight.*

Noah didn't respond. She wondered if he'd found out she'd hacked his computer. She couldn't stand the thought of his disappointment. This was for him and his company. To find out answers and bring down Symphis. Hopefully, Noah would forgive her later.

Never had she felt this alone. She had to believe the plan would work.

When she handed the flash drive over, if the troops didn't

pour in, then Symphis's next step remained a mystery. But this might end in her dead.

Her stomach rolled and lurched. She barely made it to the stinky bathroom before it emptied.

Information on the location of the Stadium popped up on her cell phone. The thirty-minute countdown to arrival time had begun.

She phoned Emma. "I'm going to the Stadium."

Emma cleared her throat. "Don't go. Come here."

"I can't. Don't make decisions I wouldn't," Tori joked.

"Not funny."

"Love you. Bye." She hung up. Done. If her cell was being monitored, misdirection accomplished.

She flagged down a cab. Who cared about wasting the thirty bucks? There was a high chance she wouldn't be around tomorrow to regret it.

Her phone dinged with a text from Quan: *You got this.*

She needed that.

Martin's mother's house was in a gang-ridden part of town. The cabbie asked her three times if she was sure this was where she wanted to get out. A cockeyed sign on the yard's metal fence warned of a dog, but she didn't see any evidence of one before she walked through the open gate and up the steps. At eleven thirty p.m., they wouldn't be getting many house calls. The lights were on in the two-story.

She texted Quan: *Going in.*

Time to be gamer-bitch tough. She rang the doorbell and waited. No obvious cameras were mounted. That didn't mean they weren't there, but she didn't equate Martin with the concept of subtle. The concrete porch smelled of new paint, but the old house needed some serious work. The stairs had a few large breaks in the concrete. A crack snaked along most of the porch.

With the money Martin raked in why wasn't he using it on upgrades to the residence? Maybe he wasn't the guy. She'd gambled everything to be here. If Martin wasn't the guy, then showing up here would be so super bad. She couldn't make it to the Stadium before it ended.

A short Latin lady in a ratty robe with graying black hair pulled into a tight bun answered but remained behind the screen door. "¿Quién eres?" *Who are you?*

"Soy un amigo de Martin. Tengo algo para él." *I'm a friend of Martin. I've got something for him.*

The lady waved her hand for her to enter. "Sí. Sí. Entra."

From downstairs she heard Martin yell, "¿Mamá, quién es?" *Mamma, who is it?*

The woman shook her head and muttered, "Regresaré a la cama. Él está abajo." *I'm going back to bed. He's downstairs.*

The smell of stale air mixed with some sort of garlic food assaulted her as she descended into the shadowy basement. The tech setup that came into view was jaw-dropping. She'd give her left leg to have one of the five computers that were running. The capacity of those machines was a zillion times more than her laptop. Six seventy-inch screens showed views of the Stadium.

Bingo.

She pressed the recording device that looked like a pen, which she'd used to spin her hair into a messy bun.

"Hi, Martin. Thought I'd bring what you'd asked for directly to you. Rand irritates the shit out of me."

Martin whirled in his chair. No wannabe surfer dude tonight. He wore glasses, a trendy, refined V-neck sweater and jeans, a look she associated with a prep school kid. He'd be attractive if his glare didn't scare the hell out of her.

"Tori Duarte." He didn't move from his chair, his fingers poised over a cordless keyboard. He spoke low into a headset, probably calling in his security.

"How's play going tonight, *Symphis*?" She glanced up at the jumbo screens.

"You're a smart girl. I'll give you that." His gaze darted to the one screen that was darkened. She could swear he turned it off.

"Never underestimate a gamer bitch." She sauntered closer and leaned against a support column. She waved at his attire. "This is a better look for you."

"You shouldn't be here, Tori. I wondered where you were." He pushed a button to show Noah in his apartment, drinking a beer. The man looked miserable. "Weren't with your boyfriend." The screen flashed and showed Emma. "Not at your sister's." One more screen change showed Alex in the apartment on the futon, bruises covering his face. "Not at home." Martin faced her. "Going rogue? I respect that. But you here doesn't change things."

"I have what you requested. My life's changing. I'm done with gaming. All of it. The competitions, the Stadium, and online."

"You're done when we say you're done."

"That's scarier via text message than from a preppy teenager." She glanced around. "You've done wonders with your mom's basement, but really? You've raked in tons from the Stadium. Why do you live here?"

"It is what it is." His eyes darted nervously toward the dark computer screen. Was he, too, being monitored? By whom?

"Because you're like every other gamer teenager. You can't grow up. You like your mom cooking and cleaning for you." She shook her head and rolled her eyes. "You should pay to have her house fixed up a bit. It's disgraceful."

"You invade my home and lecture me?"

"I'm just giving you pointers to get some personal respect. Maybe even a decent girlfriend. Also to warn you Rand doesn't like you or respect you. It's all over his face at the Stadium. That fucker will stab you in the back the first chance he gets."

He turned away to speak into his microphone, probably calling in the kill squad.

"I think you like being a creepy, secretive asshole. I wouldn't be here if you hadn't ordered Kaleb killed and got the FBI on your ass. Do you have any idea what it's like to be purposefully messed up in a big time competition? And then used by the government? *That* is your fault. I'm done with that as much as you."

Martin rolled his eyes. "Kaleb...the pansy motherfucker. I should've had him dumped in the ocean or somewhere he'd never be found."

Gotcha, asshole. Let's see if you want to monologue.

"This is a pretty sweet setup, but what's the point of all this? Why not be open about who you are?"

"Government...FBI? Hello? I thought you were smart."

"If I can figure out where and who you are with a few clicks of my fingers, then you can bet your ass they're not going to be far behind."

"The Stadium is a first step."

"Planning to take over the world one dead programmer at a time?" Her heart pounded. *Come on, talk.*

"No one cares about geeky programmers other than their mothers." He shrugged. "So no one gives two shits when they OD."

"Have you ever actually killed someone, or is it like another game to you? Push a few buttons, give some orders, and a few people die. Hands not dirty."

"Everything's one big game, Tori." He laughed stiffly. "Symphis's game."

Okay, Quan, now'd be a super time to bring in the cavalry.

"I think you and I need to part ways," she said. "Not as friends. But with an understanding not to mess with each other anymore. I'm not interested in whatever you have going on here or in the Stadium. You're going to back off my people. You don't want me or the FBI up your ass anymore. Here's what you wanted." She threw the envelope of cash into his lap and held out the flash drive. "That's all I owe you guys. The code I stole for you is on the drive. If I don't go to jail for it, I'll lose my job. Definitely lost my *boyfriend* over it. Take it. Do whatever you need with it."

When he didn't take it she tossed it to him.

He stuck it in a drive and booted it up.

Please please work.

The program booted up to show lines of code. He chuckled. "Very good, Tori."

She spun on her heel for a quick evac.

"We're not done," he said. "Nowhere near done."

"You got into my head when I didn't know what you looked like. Now all I can see is a teenager pretending to be a doped-out surfer who isn't that great at gaming. If you need some pointers, call me."

Run! Her heart pounded like she was at a sprint as she walked up the stairs.

An arrow landed in the dry wall near her head. Arrows?

"You and I are not done," he growled.

She spun to face him. *I really, really, really don't want to die by bow-and-arrow.* "You going to murder me in your mother's house? Implicate her in all this shit?"

He chucked the bow and targeted her with a gun. "You and I are going for a drive."

"Are you old enough for a license?" She bit back a smile at his aggravated groan. Probably shouldn't aggravate him when he had a weapon pointed at her, but she was banking on him not messing up his mother's house.

He stormed up the stairs, gripped one of her arms behind her back, and propelled her in front of him out of the house.

Everything lit up around them the moment they stepped into the front yard. She squinted against spotlights. A lot of guys in tactical gear aimed big guns their way. She made out NSA on the sleeve of one guy and SWAT on another.

Over a megaphone boomed, "Martin, drop the gun."

"What the hell?" He pulled her tighter against him and pressed the muzzle of a gun to her head. "I'll shoot her."

"Drop the gun or we'll shoot," the megaphone voice replied.

Her body trembled to the point she thought her legs might give out. Even though terrified, a calm descended on her, the same calm that came when in the middle of the biggest gaming battles.

A gun fired. The armed men turned and began shooting at someone behind them. Her ears rang from all the gunfire.

Martin flinched and cursed. Maybe shot? But he didn't let go of her. He dragged her to the side of the house. Years of martial arts training surfaced. Dictated by instinct and adrenaline, she head butted him and hit his wrist. The gun flew out of his hand. An elbow to his abdomen got her freedom from his grip. She swung around to launch a knee strike to his groin. Direct hit.

As he rolled on the ground she poised to strike again.

"We got it, Tori," Quan said behind her. "Back away."

She jumped, noticing the gunfire had stopped. "Where'd you come from?"

"Never took my eyes off you." He rolled Martin to his stomach and cuffed him. "You get what we needed?"

"Yes." She took the pencil-like recording device out of her hair and handed it to him. "You're NSA?"

He yanked Martin to his feet. "I didn't know this kid was Symphis, Tori. You figured it out."

"You could've showed up a bit earlier, before he tried to kill me with a bow and arrow."

"I missed on purpose," Martin said.

"You have the right to remain silent." Quan pushed him toward the waiting van where other men took Martin away.

"This way," Quan directed. Once seated inside a plain sedan, just them, he said, "You okay? Did you get hurt?"

She covered her face with her shaking hands and rested her elbows on her knees in silence.

"Tori?"

"Is it over?" She wanted to forget the sight of Emma, Noah, and Alex on Martin's screen. Watched...hunted. Had he put anything in motion against them? "Have you checked in with Alex?"

"He's fine."

"Martin had cameras on everyone. Cameras in locations that say he'd sent someone into all of our places. We need better security in the apartment."

"I'm on it."

"I want to go home and find every camera, even if it takes all night." She fisted her hands and then wrung them together.

"We'll find them," Quan said too calmly.

"Don't be the patronizing fucker with me right now. You're not the one who had a gun to her head or an arrow land in the wall inches from your face. You used me just as much as the FBI. Please, just take me home. I don't want to talk."

"Sorry."

"Where's my money? Can you make sure I get that back?"

Quan nodded.

She texted Emma, who messaged back she was fine. Her fingers started a message to Noah, but she didn't know what to say. Finally she settled on: *I finished it.*

Chapter Twenty-four

Was she ever going to answer her door?

At this point, Noah wasn't sure. He'd knocked over a minute ago. Tentatively, he knocked again. He knew she was here. The one thing he'd wrangled out of Tom after he got the full story on what happened last night was where she'd gone afterward. He needed to talk to her this morning. After she confronted Symphis alone...after she stole the code...

He knocked harder. Actually, he was pounding on her door. Nothing.

Then it opened. Water dripped off the ends of Tori's dark hair onto a light blue zipped hoodie. She fiddled with the strings on it. Her long lashes lifted above her eyes. A complexity of emotion he couldn't interpret met his gaze.

"What are you doing here?"

His heart slammed into his sternum. He wanted to hug her, touch her, to confirm she was fine. *Talk. You have to talk.* "We need to discuss things. Should we go inside or talk out here about last night?"

She opened her door wide and waved him inside. "What happened was I ended it."

He pushed shut the door and crossed his arms. "You hacked my computer to steal the code."

"I'm sorry about that."

He shook his head and covered his face with a hand. "Officially, I'm here to tell you you're on probation until we have a meeting with our lawyer and company security to decide the right course of action to deal with it. It's scheduled for tomorrow. I don't want to, but prosecution's on the table as well as firing you."

She nodded. "I understand. There wasn't another way."

On a long sigh he said, "I know."

"The code I gave away was protected. A one-time read-only file. After he opened it, which he did, it'd be dead."

"I should go, but I still want to know what the hell you think you heard on the phone."

"What? After everything, *that's* what has a burr up your ass?"

"I need to know, Tori."

"I heard you saying to Jake that things were almost over, that you could see it through and handle it, but you obviously didn't want to."

He stared at her, his mind rewinding his call with Jake. They'd talked about a lot of topics for about twenty minutes. "We never talked about you. I think what you heard had to do with our accountant. She's always trying to pull off my clothes. It's sexual harassment and it scares the hell out of me. It's a big firm so we've asked for a new person to manage our account, but they're shorthanded right now and the new person can't be here until a week from now. Quarterly taxes are due so we're shit out of luck in dealing with someone else. Jake's going out of town on the day she's scheduled and wanted to be sure I could handle getting through the taxes."

"Oh."

"Tori…" He fisted his hands. "I can't believe you did that last night, not the code stealing, but faced off with that guy alone."

"It was the only way to get a confession out of him. He admitted to killing Kaleb. Well, maybe not directly, but he did put in the order to have him murdered." She fiddled with the strings on the hoodie.

"I was scared when I heard what you did." He snagged her around the waist to pull her close into his embrace.

She hugged him back. "I needed to get control back in my life." Her gaze met his. "I'm sorry I jumped to conclusions when you were on the phone. I'm sorry I left you in the dark and stole the code."

"You're fucking amazing. You beat down the reporter at the press junket and then faced your worst fear. I've never known anyone like you." His world closed around the feel of her lips against his. Her fingers curled into his shoulders through his jacket. A moan erupted from her when he deepened the kiss. He pulled her tighter and reached down to her waist, under her hoodie and soft T-shirt, and up the smooth skin of her back. Her hands slipped under his shirt to press against his lower stomach.

"This is insane. What is it about you? You're...you've got great abs." She slammed a hand over her mouth. "I didn't mean to say that out loud."

He held her. "My abs are probably all I've got to offer you. I don't deserve someone brave like you. Someone who can handle anything that comes her way alone. I always shit out my mouth at the wrong time. I'm an awful date."

She put her fingers over his mouth, stopping him. "You deserve someone a lot better than me. You're real, genuine. And good. Yes, it's good in a nice way, but not in a nice friends-only sort of way, if that makes sense. I'm not right for you and the timing of all this is total crap, but I need this...you."

With her melting into him he lost focus on the fact he should be leaving now that he'd delivered the probation message. Her hands explored the contours of his stomach and slipped lower.

He bowed his head and struggled to shake off the haze clouding his mind. Memories of her coming apart swamped him. Water dripped off the ends of her dark hair onto a light blue zipped hoodie. Her long lashes lifted above her eyes. God she was beautiful with her wet hair dampening her hoodie and big gray-blue eyes.

"Dragonfly," he muttered hoarsely. "I should go. I'm trying to do the right thing here."

She traced the edges of his collar. "What is the right thing?"

"Hell if I know anymore. We're going to make your game a best seller. I guarantee it. It's that good. But I don't know how it's going to go with the committee to decide if you stay on probation, come off it, or we fire you and take you to court. I don't want you thinking that if you and I do anything that it'll make me try to sway the committee."

She gave him a small smile, but soon lost it. "We can't have an us. I get it."

"You're right. No us." Yet, despite everything he wanted to fight for them.

She dropped her head, her chin resting on her chest. "Okay."

"It's not what I want, but it's the cards we've been dealt. I should go. Me here isn't helping." He backed away from her.

She caught his arm. Her feather light touch froze him.

Softly, she said, "Don't go. I'm impulsive. It's a handicap, but, after all that happened last night when I almost died, I want to feel alive. You make me feel that way. That's not what you want to hear, is it? Not when you came here to tell me you're going to fire me and probably a lot worse."

"Tori, we shouldn't, not if we're not together. And, there's everything else."

"Probably true, but we weren't ever technically together." She kissed along his jaw and down his neck. "Let's give ourselves right now. Tomorrow isn't here yet."

He scooped her up.

"No," she said.

"What? Should I go home?"

"Put me down."

He set her down, alarmed by the rejection turboing his way.

"Let's stay out here first. Kitchen table?"

"All right." He kissed her, more out of relief than desire to ignite them into the next phase.

She shoved the dark jacket from his shoulders. His shirt went next. She dropped it on the floor. "There's just now."

As he pulled away he gazed to the kitchen area, staring at the small semicircular table, then back to her. He'd make it work, but maybe he should suggest they have a kitchen experience at his house and choose a different piece of furniture here. At his place he was certain the table wouldn't collapse. The intensity in her gaze smothered that notion. No woman had ever looked at him as if she fantasized having him naked on every piece of furniture.

He was on board with that.

His lips met hers in a kiss again. This time it wasn't about slow seduction. She kissed him back just as fiercely. He felt her tremble against him and was amazed to realize it was he who shook with need for her. He groaned against her lips. "You have no idea what you do to me."

He unzipped her hoodie and pulled it off. Then he lifted the soft cotton shirt over her head, giving him a perfect view of her braless breasts. He lifted and carried her to the edge of the table where he set her on her feet. His hands sought to find the waistband of her stretchy pants. Fingers tucked under the elastic band, he pulled, catching her panties on the way. Her hand jumped to his shoulder for balance as he bared her lower half.

Her freshly bathed flowery scent hit him. Lust clawed down his spine and so did her hands, tracing his tattoo in butterfly strokes that activated every nerve. He lifted her onto the table and started a slow, kissing seduction down her neck. She gasped when his middle finger parted her swollen folds. Wetness coated his finger, easing his penetration. He ached to be inside her when her inner muscles clamped down on the intrusion.

"So wet for me," he murmured, keeping up his finger's movements gentle and coaxing.

He nipped her shoulder, smiling at her gasp.

"Noah," she breathed out on a moan. Her hips undulated against his hand.

"Don't move," he ordered as he stepped away to peel out of his pants and underwear and unfurl latex in a quick stroke.

He eased two fingers inside her again. Her inner muscles clamped down with a strength that surprised him. His breath came out ragged.

He lifted her knees to fit himself between her thighs. As he rubbed himself across her center, continuing the teasing movement, he enjoyed her responsiveness. She squirmed and angled her pelvis upward. "Stop teasing."

He chuckled low. Exactly what he'd been waiting to hear. Her fingernails dug into his forearms as he slowly parted her. She tossed her head back, taking all of him until he was deep within her.

"Tori," he breathed against her neck. He kissed her deep and desperate…real. "Have you thought about this as much as I have?"

As slowly as he entered he began to withdraw. The sensitive flesh he'd fought to get in now fought him to get out. Her only reply was a series of tiny whimpers.

"Have you?" He pressed inside her again.

She moaned. "God, yes."

"Me too." He cupped her ass with his hands and encouraged her to wrap her legs around him. "Hang on to me, dragonfly." He filled her hard and fast again and again.

He tamped down his beckoning release, coaxed her closer to detonation with each clench of her inner muscles. Noah focused on her. Head thrown back, eyes closed, giving herself over to pleasure. Her throaty cries pushed him close to the edge. Then her body quivered and clamped down as he ushered her into an orgasm. His muscles stiffened with force of his need to come. He groaned as she contracted around him but focused on not giving in to that release. With gentle movements he pulled away from her to let her recover.

***

Her mushy mind registered him carrying her to…had she waved toward her bedroom? God, it'd be embarrassing to end up in one of her roommates' beds. He grinned down at her.

"Did that take the edge off?"

"Mm-hmm."

He laced his hands through hers and pinned her to the mattress, easing down to lick a path to her breasts. She expected him to tease, but thank God he didn't. He took a nipple into his mouth and rolled and sucked. He released her hands and caressed his way to the area between her folds, but she slammed her thighs together against the too sensitive nature of the touch.

"Open for me," he coaxed. He slowly guided himself back into her and leaned down for a deep kiss. "You okay?"

"Don't stop."

He let go, unleashing his strength. She was more than ready, locking her ankles behind his back and hanging on again, letting him exorcise all his frustrations. Then he rolled over so she was on top and stopped.

She traced a finger through the moisture on his chest. His body was a beautiful study of sculpted planes. She squeezed her internal muscles and grinned at his blissed-out groan.

"Damn, Tori."

"You want me to go easy on you?" She rolled her hips and his voice trailed off in a growl.

"No." His hands traced her hips and then up her back.

She threw back her head and laughed, starting a fast, deep pace. His angle hit all the right places. She gasped his name as her climax crested. Usually her first was the most intense but this one worked up her spine and clamped all her muscles until her world exploded and her body closed around him.

He pushed upward and deep for several long strokes until he shuddered. She scored his sides as he came. Based on the way he shivered, he liked it. Then she collapsed onto his chest. "I don't think I can move. That was so good," she said. "Tell me if I'm too heavy."

"You're good right there. Don't move." He stroked mesmerizing circles on her back.

Her cell phone rang—her sister's ringtone. Perfect way to shatter a moment. She stared at the cell on the end table across the bed, unwilling to move. Its ringing finally ended.

"Did you need to get that?" He stared at the phone as the electronic song began again.

"Probably. It's Emma." She stared at it until it went silent. Then her phoned dinged with an incoming text. She rolled, eliciting a subtle complaint from him. "Guess I better see what's up."

The text from Emma read: *On my way up to your place.*

"Oh, crap." She jumped off the bed.

"What?" He sat up.

"Emma's on her way up. Now." She scrambled to find her clothes. In the process, she threw his clothes at him as she found the pieces. When his only movement was to prop himself upright on an elbow she yelled, "Get dressed. You have to go."

"Does your sister normally barge in at all hours?"

"We're close. I almost got killed in an FBI sting operation. If it'd been her out there tonight, then I'd be barging into her place." She yanked on her panties and a pair of yoga pants. Where was her sweatshirt?

He got up and went into bathroom for what she could only

assume was condom care. But he wasn't moving at the pace necessary to evacuate the apartment in time, especially if Emma was already in the elevator. She could only hope Emma hadn't yet entered the building.

With slow, deliberate movements he pulled his briefs over his muscular legs. He leaned against the wall near the bathroom door. She admired the planes of his abdomen right up until she registered the smirk on his face. Quickly, she pulled on a T-shirt and zipped her hoodie.

He folded his arms across his naked chest. "Emma already knows about us. What's the point of hiding from her?" He tried to catch her, but she avoided his reach. "Why're you freaking out?"

"You're her boss…in his underwear who's here to tell me I'm on probation, likely fired," she pointed out. He was a mouth-watering sight she could laze around and gape at all night. With a headshake she stopped ogling to mutter, "Put some clothes on. Please."

"Is that what you want?" He grinned.

"Your assistant is on her way up. I'm not doing an *oh-hey-here's-your-boss-in-his-underwear* confrontation with her."

She threw his shirt at him. "You without clothes is the last thing she wants to see." She paused, staring. "Okay, it'd be a gift for her to see you like this. I said that out loud again. Shouldn't have. Stop grinning. Be serious." She found his shoes and socks where they'd been discarded and deposited them in his arms. A push to propel him toward the door didn't work. "Take the stairs. She's likely in the elevator now."

"Why don't I take a seat? Maybe I'll put my shirt on, and turn on the TV. We could be having a perfectly normal visit." Instead of moving toward the door, he sat on the futon.

"We don't have regular TV. I stream movies and sometimes the news. Mostly, we use it for gaming."

"Playing a game, then." He grabbed the remote.

"In your briefs at seven-something in the morning? Sure, I'll strip down to my bra and panties and we'll be two normal gamers drinking coffee playing a friendly competition of strip video game. Lose a level, lose some clothes."

"Never played that, but I'd be into it. With you." He grinned and let his gaze roam down her body.

She shivered. "That wouldn't make sense in any universe, given the shitstorm going on around us. There's nothing normal going on here."

"I agree. There's nothing *normal* about us when we're together." He rose and took a few steps toward her.

"Stay over there. No, wait. Don't stay there." Was the elevator almost on this floor? "I need you to go."

"Calm down. There's no need to panic. You're an adult. Your roommates aren't here. Now, why is that? Where are they?"

"Snap out of it. Get moving." She glanced between the door and him, considering options to get him in motion. There wasn't enough time to get him safely between the door and the stairwell. "This was..."

"Don't you dare say it was a mistake," His eyes narrowed.

"Wasn't going to say that. It was great, but it was goodbye sex. It was me being weak because I was messed up from last night and you're...you."

He stalked to her, lifted her chin with two fingers and leaned in for a kiss. "It's going to be okay."

She ducked away. "Be serious." She yanked open her front door and poked her head out to see the elevator floor numbers. The elevator was three floors away. "Oh, hell."

She motioned hurry-up to him. "Get in Quan's room. Move."

He grumped as he hugged his shoes and shirt to his chest while she pushed him toward Quan's bedroom.

The elevator dinged outside the apartment. It was an

annoyingly loud sound, a noise she lamented on nights when she'd conked out on the futon.

Adrenaline surged through Tori's body.

She pushed him into Quan's room and slammed the door closed. "Don't say a single word. Nothing. Don't breathe heavy. Don't radiate sexy vibes through the door. Stay put. I'll get rid of her as soon as I can."

"Sexy vibes?" he asked through the closed door.

"Shh. Forget I said that."

"You feeling the vibes coming your way?" He laughed loudly. She imagined him doubled over and wiping at tears.

She hissed, "Quiet."

Knock. Knock.

Now she'd spend this entire visit worried Noah would appear.

"Are you okay after everything?" Emma pushed into Tori's apartment.

"You over your elevator issues?" Tori peeked behind her into the empty hallway.

Emma pulled her into a brief hug. "He's behind bars. No one to push buttons now. I can't believe you did that last night. That you left me in the dark to go play hero."

Tori glanced at the Quan's door. No sign of movement. Distractedly, she said, "I'm fine."

Emma paced. "I'm glad the gaming stuff is over. It is over, isn't it?"

"I think so." Her gaze caught on Noah's discarded jeans at the threshold of her bedroom. Crap, crap and super crap. Maybe Emma would think them one of her roommate's.

Emma wiped moisture from her eyes. "I'm here to give you the heads-up they know you were on Noah's computer. I'd say I can't believe you did that, but I know you did what you thought you had to in order to finish this."

"There wasn't any other options. I worked with the NSA

instead of the FBI."

Emma rocked back on her designer pumps. "Has Noah or Jake called you?"

Tori nodded. "Noah let me know I'm on probation."

"They can't fire you. You brought in that asshat last night for *them*. You put your life on the line for them. I'm calling him. Telling him he has to stick up for you and make this go away."

"No—"

Noah's phone rang from his jeans, lying in her bedroom doorway.

Emma's eyes went wide. "What the hell?" She pointed at Tori's face. "I thought you'd just come from the gym to be that red, but...holy crap, Tori. I can't believe you."

Noah emerged from Quan's room and picked up his jeans.

"Hi, Mr. Harrison." Emma glared a *how could you* at Tori with a little bit of shame thrown in.

Noah pulled on his jeans. In silence they watched him stalk to his jacket and pluck it off the back of the futon where he'd draped it.

Emma folded her arms across her chest. "Neither of you have anything to say for yourselves? Noah, you put her on probation. And, then the two of you... I have no words."

She couldn't meet Emma's gaze. "We're not together."

A snort laugh escaped Emma. "Then what the hell was this, then?"

"This isn't funny." She huffed, crossing her arms.

Noah nodded and stalked out without another word. Her heart urged her to run after him and soothe his battered ego, but it was best this way. They had to work together. She would not become the slut trolls claimed her to be nor give them ammo to toss in her face.

"Oh, you two are definitely a big problem about to turn into a train wreck," Emma said.

Chapter Twenty-five

Tori followed Leo, her gangly, twenty-something orientation director into what he called the "Early Weekly," a first-thing Thursday morning meeting. Who the hell did Thursday meetings?

I'm an NJ Legacy designer. Unreal.

Okay, a designer on probation for doing something highly illegal before even starting. However, seemed like the whole probation thing remained top tier information only. Everyone they'd met on her orientation tour welcomed her.

"Most of the time we slowly integrate designers with our system, but since your game has to go from zero to launch at hyper speed, there's no time to take it easy." Leo led her out of the "game room," a no-expense-spared playroom, which made her inner techie geek swoon. Although, moments later it swan dived into panic as the reality of the other side of her life took over.

Leo led her into a spacious, naturally lit room set up like a lecture hall with huge screens at the front but without the sloping floor. Many people chatted, some were already seated and some milled near the food. Nerves squeezed her stomach. She prayed they wouldn't make her stand up front like the new show-and-tell toy. She was probably the news of the week, maybe even of the year. This meeting would be all about her.

She scanned the room for Noah, coming up with a big zilch. She didn't need Noah's validation. She wasn't addicted to him, either. If both of those statements were true, then why did she feel jittery? She hadn't been this nuts over a guy since high school.

Stop obsessing about him. He was the boss, the big cheese, the guy everyone here deferred to and probably didn't even call by first name.

"Grab yourself a coffee or if you're hungry..." Leo waved at the table of pastries and morning drinks at the back of the room. He pushed his wire frames up his nose and cleared his throat. "Heard the big press meeting went well."

"Thanks but I'm not hungry."

His eyes darted around and his voice lowered, "So, you know Quan Lee?"

She smiled at his conspiratorial whisper. She whispered back, "He's my roommate. We do some gaming together. Well, did. I don't think I'll be allowed to continue since I work here."

Out loud he said, "Crapsters! You're really her, aren't you? You're the third of the *Dynasty?*"

"It's not a secret." She shrugged.

He shot her a goofy grin. "I'm a huge fan. You guys are so totally cool. You were one of the first to form an alliance online and fight the *Zoneworlds* as a group. I didn't believe Quan when he said you designed games in addition to playing. He and I have been friends since Comic-Con San Diego six years ago. We bonded over an episode of getting piss-assed drunk and running the hotel hallways in capes and underwear."

"I think I need to know more about that."

He drew an imaginary X over his heart. "The code of Comic-Con brothers is no details, especially when it involves states of partial naked."

"I'm texting Quan right now." She pulled out her phone and shot Quan a text. Her phone dinged back almost immediately with a picture of a group of four in superhero underwear and towel capes. She compressed her lips against laughing and rotated her phone to show Leo.

Leo's face turned dark scarlet. "There's a picture?"

"It'll be our secret." A snort laugh escaped her.

"Everyone sit," Jake ordered over the PA system.

"Later," Leo murmured to her.

She moved down an aisle toward an empty set of chairs.

Noah slid into the room. He leaned against the wall near the door as if he needed a quick exit, or didn't want to garner much attention. Her heart hammered against her ribs. God, he looked amazing in jeans and a T-shirt. His familiar gaze burned over her. She felt its continued scorch as she turned away from him. She imagined him scanning her shoulders down to her butt, outlined perfectly in her skinny jeans. She tripped over a chair leg, landing hip first onto her target chair's seat. She caught herself on her neighbor's arm and uttered an apology.

Smooth. Real smooth.

Her gaze shot to Noah as she pushed away from the cute guy whose chest she'd almost face-planted into. Maybe Noah hadn't noticed her fall. Noah glowered at the guy she'd tripped into as if it'd been the guy's fault she fell. Then his gaze locked with hers. So much for not him not seeing her klutzy moment. Anticipation quivered in her belly. She felt stripped bare in a way unsuitable for this public venue. The noises around her faded.

Pull out of the stare. She should care if others thought she was sleeping with the boss.

Leo plopped into the vacant chair on the far side of her, cutting off her staredown. He nodded toward Noah. "What you think of him?"

"He's, uh...not what I expected."

"The rumor is you two dated a bit? Maybe still dating?" Leo seemed to be holding his breath in anticipation of a juicy piece of gossip.

"We might've gone out once or twice."

"That's unbelievable. All he does is work. The guy doesn't seem to date. And you're—" Someone signaled to Leo. "Sorry. Gotta go for a minute. This is going to be a blast of a meeting." He popped up with a mysterious smile and trotted away.

Jake paced back-and-forth across the elevated platform down front. He tapped the microphone for attention. The noise died down. "I see everyone's buzzing this morning. Glad you're all adequately caffeinated. We're not going to talk about the new email protocols again today."

A few "*Thank Gods*" echoed around the room.

Jake said, "So, we've got a new game and we were lucky enough to snag its designer to come on board. She's going to help us get it through final production, which as you know needs to be accelerated. May I introduce Tori Duarte." He waved her way. "She's—"

The lights dimmed. Jake glanced around, startled. The screens behind Jake flickered. Jake said something into the microphone, but nothing transmitted. He tapped it and threw his arms in the air. He said something to Emma, who shrugged at him.

The theme from *Zoneworld* boomed while the avatar of Evelle sauntered into view on the screens. Oh, crap. This was about to get embarrassing.

A low voice reminiscent of a baritone movie voice-over boomed through the room, "Selene has entered the game."

Her face couldn't get any hotter.

The lights popped back on.

"What was that?" Jake said into his now working microphone.

"Sorry to ruin your intro, Mr. Allen, but mine was light-years better," Leo said over the PA system from the back of the room. "Ladies, gents, geeks, and gamers...royalty is in our midst. Selene of the *Dynasty* is here." He paused for dramatic effect as everyone craned around, searching neighbors for this unknown person.

"She's none other than Tori Duarte, designer of our newest project, *Dragon Spy*." Gasps echoed through the audience. Then clapping and whistles deafened the room.

"I told you guys I'd eventually get one of the *Dynasty* down here. Stand up, Tori," Leo ordered as he approached her.

She stood.

"All hail, Selene." Leo pumped his arms up and down in praise-bows toward her. He covered the mic and whispered to her. "The *Dynasty* trio are gods here. I've been begging Quan to come here for over a year just so we can pick his brain on how you guys do what you do."

She leaned toward him and grabbed the microphone. Into it she said, "Thanks, guys. Super excited to be here."

She waved. Her gaze slid past Noah. Her pulse jumped in response to the sexy double eyebrow raise he threw her. She resumed her seat.

"Right. Thanks, Leo. That sure was something," Jake said from the front. He didn't look pleased. "Like I said, we've got a new project. If anyone wants to volunteer to be on her team…"

A lot of hands shot up in the audience. Many screamed variations of *"pick me."*

Jake said. "Maybe you want to hear a bit more about the game before you jump to volunteer. Most of you already have projects… Noah, any words about *Dragon Spy*?"

Tori glanced to Noah. Leo shoved the microphone into Noah's hands. Noah locked gazes with her for a second. "It's going to be next level. We wanted to break into the fantasy market and this is it."

"Any more?" Jake asked.

"It's addictive." He smiled.

She suspected he wasn't referring to the game.

"Well, there you have it, folks. That's it in a nutshell.

Addictive."

***

Four days. Three restless nights.

Not one iota of communication from Noah. At first she'd been relieved, but now she missed him.

If not for double shot mochas and Skittles, she'd be a zombie.

A rumor circulated that the top-secret meetings about a security breach over the past few days had come to a conclusion early this morning. No one here seemed to stop work on the weekends. According to Leo, everyone believed by the end of the day someone would be fired. They didn't know about the code stealing or that it'd be her carrying her small box of belongings under an arm out the front door.

She'd been instructed to report to Jake with issues or anything to do with development of her game, which, according to the others on her team, wasn't normal. Jake rarely managed the day-to-day of any project. For most big projects Noah ran point.

She'd seen Noah from a distance on Friday, but he hadn't noticed her. He hadn't even attempted to make eye contact with her.

The past few days demonstrated whatever they shared wasn't as easily left in the past as it should be, if they were a doomed mistake. His communication silence she interpreted to be his way of ending things without further confrontation. It would make it easier when he and Jake fired her. Or maybe they'd send the HR manager to do it.

Time for her to buck up and move on. So much easier said in her head than reality. Aside from missing Noah, she liked it here between the top-level talent, the personalities, and the resources.

Her heartbeat pounded through her ears as she strode up to Noah's new assistant since her sister had been reassigned to work with Jake after Jake's assistant had to leave on a lurch when his father got hospitalized. That was the cover story, but she believed they moved Emma on purpose because of her.

Noah's new assistant had positioned his desk to blockade Noah's office.

"Is he available yet, Josh?" Tori asked. Ditching the gamer bitch for a courteous professional sucked when it came to hard-asses like Josh.

Cynical, tough eyes met hers. Josh reminded her of the high school kid who'd had a toilet head swish one too many times. Now he enjoyed riding his power high. He tapped his pencil on his desk. Who even used pencils beyond grade school?

"He's busy, like I told you three hours ago."

"I've got a few weeks to produce a fully functional product. We need Sam to write in security code before the virtual reality folks do their bit. He doesn't share his secrets. Arguably, it's ridiculous to have only one person who does this, but it's the way it is."

"Sam is working for Mr. Harrison on a different project. He's not available." Josh twirled his pencil between his fingers and glared at her over the upper rim of his glasses as if she was an annoying insect. "Did you try emailing Mr. Harrison?"

"There's something wrong with his interoffice account, or so I've been told. *Mr. Harrison* can take a break and help me with this. I need to discuss it today. With him. Not you."

"Why don't you tell me exactly what you need Sam to do and I might be able to help you." He gave her a condescending smile and tapped his pencil against his desk again.

"How are you going to do the necessary coding to make *Dragon Spy* safe from hackers?" Probably should've toned that down.

Josh's gaze narrowed as he typed on his computer with an

air of importance, which was total bullshit posturing. She considered shoving the pencil up his nose.

She gritted out, "According to people on my team, Sam is the only one in this building who can do the next step. Since Sam's work isn't assigned by me, I need to speak with Noah about this."

"You mean Mr. Harrison, don't you?"

What a jerk.

"Where is *Mr. Harrison*?" She tried smiling but suspected it came across a bit scary. She fantasized hand jabbing Josh in the throat just to see him gasp for a few seconds until his muscles unclenched enough to move air.

Josh scanned through a few screens on his iPhone. A total dismissal.

He finally said, "Like I told you twice already today, as soon as he's free I'll ask. Right now he's busy. We'll get back to you tomorrow."

She slammed her back molars together and forced out, "Tomorrow doesn't work for me."

Josh slowly rose from his desk to tower over her. His face splotched with color. "Mr. Harrison doesn't care what works for you. He isn't interested in seeing you right now."

She stepped backward.

This had to be the little tight-ass trying to flex his muscles. It didn't make sense to be a direct personal denial from Noah.

Through glass windows of Noah's office a slender blonde came into view. The elegant woman slithered around Noah in a designer skin-tight hip-hugging dress. Noah's face came into view, but turned before she could read his emotions. The woman touched him in a way that suggested easy familiarity and intimacy.

What. The. Hell.

Noah was here. And not busy with work.

He'd moved on to someone new?

Her heart snapped into two. She'd never be a polished and poised fake blonde who could pull off designer wear in five-inch heels. She was Tori, the tattooed gaming dork who was only sexy when hiding behind a game avatar—not the kind of girl who belonged with a man like Noah.

Wait a second.

No.

She didn't need Noah or any man to define her. She'd rocked as a top scorer for two years on *Zoneworld* online. She faced off with Symphis. She totally rocked Noah's world to the point he lost his mind in the middle of a press conference.

Not pitiful. She was strong and self-reliant.

Her brain wasn't buying her pep talk. She was about to get fired from her dream job for unfair reasons.

If Noah didn't want her, then it was his loss. Not hers.

But I miss him so much. Hold it together and leave. She refused to vent in front of this prick.

Josh mimed his hands in a run-away signal.

Oh no he did not.

She leaned toward Josh. The gamer bitch emerged. "Look, you little prick, I need to hear from *Mr. Harrison* about Sam. Not you. So, get off your lazy ass and do your fucking job."

She pivoted and walked stiffly to the elevator, regretting her behavior. Maybe she wasn't cut out for a corporate life.

The door opened to reveal Jake.

Great.

Maybe she could swivel a one-eighty and take the stairs.

Jake said, "You're just the person I was looking for. We need to talk."

Fucktastic. Here comes the pink slip.

With a nod she stepped inside the elevator, ensuring several feet of air rested between the two of them. She didn't dare meet his eyes, not while in this dangerous mood.

Her mind whirled with images of Noah and the blonde

woman. How had he so easily moved on when she couldn't contemplate another man touching her? She was tempted to march back into Noah's office, push him against the wall and remind him exactly what it meant to have good chemistry.

The elevator opened one floor down.

"Come to my office." Jake marched out of the elevator, expecting her to follow. When she didn't immediately move, he glanced over his shoulder.

She nodded, not trusting herself to speak politely.

If he hadn't been her boss, she'd come up with an excuse and flee. She needed alone time to lick her wounds and glue together the pieces of her heart.

Jake waved her into a seat on the opposite side of his desk. She found him difficult to read, but based on his rigid stance when he took his seat, he didn't plan to shoot the breeze about marketing strategies.

He gazed at her in silence for several uncomfortable seconds. "We've been trying to figure out what to do with the hacking incident."

She kept silent.

"I watched the tape. Whatever you did on Noah's computer was for show. That was our problem. Someone else gave you the code, didn't they?"

She continued to stare at him, silent.

"Jesus, Tori. Let me help you. Tell me who gave you the code and secured it."

"Why would you think I couldn't hack it and then reprogram it to be a one-time read-only file?"

"Perhaps you could." He leaned back and tented his hands. "This is a problem."

"What's more of a problem is you and Noah roadblocking me from doing my job."

Jake combed a hand threw his hair and stared at his ceiling for a moment. "I owe you for getting Noah beyond his media paranoia. Not sure what you did, but he did a magazine interview yesterday that included photos. Two months ago, before you, that never would've happened. The company needs him to be more out front like this. I'll also grant you that the work you and the team have been doing has been great. But Josh says you've been making waves. I don't want you losing momentum because you feel the need to have some sort of come to Jesus confrontation with Noah. What you two had wasn't real. You fake dated. I'll give you twenty-four hours to tell me who gave you the code. If you don't, I'm afraid we'll have to let you take the fall."

She tried to rationalize the emotional avalanche clenching her mind and rolling her stomach. Caring about her job should be her top priority. She should be agonizing over tattling, but her mind wouldn't quit hashing out the details of Noah and the blonde. Maybe he'd not only turned over a new leaf with regard to the media, but also with getting out there and dating.

Then it hit her like a ton of bricks. She was miserable without him, drowning herself in work and avoiding communication with anyone that mattered. She'd been dodging her sister all week, which wasn't easy since Emma emailed, texted, and called almost hourly. She'd also missed the past two Sunday nights at her brother's, where all the siblings converged for dinner.

Love sucked.

Noah didn't want her. He'd moved on.

That's what she needed to do. Love was for losers. But she wanted to wallow. For the first time ever she believed a man wasn't in her life just to fuck her or use her skills, but because he'd liked her for who she was.

She shoved all the self-realizations way. "My team needs Sam to do his security coding before it can become virtual reality compatible. The only one who can redirect Sam's efforts to accomplish this is Noah, or so I've been told. I might've been rough on Josh, but he's been…" She pasted on a smile. If she finished the statement she'd call Josh something far more than a prick, which she considered generous.

"I'll look into it. Let me make myself perfectly clear." He paused to glower straight into her eyes. "Stay away from Noah. Twenty-four hours."

"When can I expect Sam to help us?"

Unease skittered through Jake's gaze. Maybe he didn't have the ability to move Sam off whatever he was doing. "I'll let you know. Maybe later in the week."

"As I told Josh, waiting doesn't work for me. I need to know now. We need to get the game through some trials before moving it to the next phase. You were the one who said we had to get this done fast. Not doing this may put us way behind. Sounds like Noah really is the person who controls Sam's schedule."

Jake shot to a stand. His mouth opened and shut. His placed his closed fists on the desk. "I will handle it."

After shooting him a squinty eye she had no doubt conveyed the skepticism and annoyance burning her from the inside out, she left. Staying with NJ Legacy now was about her game, not the long term. She didn't want anyone else messing with what she'd slaved over for years.

She marched down the hall, feeling like a building whose basement had just been dynamited. Taking a sharp right she pushed into her sister's office. She closed the door behind her, leaned back against the door for support.

"Tori?" Emma jumped up from behind her desk. "What's wrong?"

"I can't do this anymore, Em. I can't work here under this kind of stress. All I want is to do my job and get this game ready." She swiped the back of her hand across her eyes.

"Stop it. Now your makeup is smeary. I didn't even think you wore mascara." Emma held out a box of tissues. "Here."

"I am not a crier. Damn all of this." She took the whole box of tissues and sat on her sister's "emergency" futon. Even though Emma claimed the college-esque futon ruined the ambiance of her office, Emma sometimes crashed here after a long day or had a nap after an intense workout.

Emma said, "Start from the beginning. What happened?"

"You already know what happened with Noah. I wish to hell I could make these tears stop leaking. So freaking embarrassing."

"What happened today?"

"I need to ask Noah if he'd be willing to reassign Sam to my project for a short while. That little jerk, Josh, seems to take great joy in blocking me. Josh told me, well implied, Noah doesn't want to see me. Later in the week is too long to wait."

"I know you get impatient when you need something done. Maybe it could wait a bit?"

"Stop being the personal assistant and be on my side."

"I am on your side. Just trying tone the drama down a level." Emma held out a bottled water.

Tori shook her head to decline. "This can't wait. Leo thinks Sam could do this in a few hours. We need it virtual reality ready to test run the game and problem shoot, but it can't go to the gurus for virtual reality until Sam does his thing. We have to remain on pause until this happens. That's wasted time." She used a tissue to dab moisture from the corners of her eyes.

"Did you try sending someone else on your team to see if it was just you Josh was blocking?"

"No. I hadn't thought of that. I thought it was my problem to deal with. I'm in charge."

"Ask Leo to do it. He can be pretty tough. If he comes back with the same blowoff, then you'll know it's not you."

"That makes sense."

"Then what happened afterward with Jake?" Emma asked.

"He pretty much chewed me out for harassing Noah. Said

I was itching to have a come to Jesus moment with him. I haven't even tried to talk to Noah since he showed up at my place that morning you were there. Look at me. I'm a catastrophe. This is not me."

"It's been a lot of stress for the past few weeks. Someone just told me Josh was being a bit of an ass to you for some reason. Your team is really protective of you, you know. It's fascinating. I think their loyalty is not only driving Jake crazy, but also he's jealous of you."

"Really? Jake is jealous?"

"Yep. The team is supposed to give him details when he asks, but they all hedge and tell him to ask you. Then you give him nothing, which means he has no idea what's going on with one of the biggest projects set to launch this year. He asked me to try to get info from the team, which means you. I didn't want to get in the middle of his problem. So, perhaps his attitude toward you has more to do with frustration. And..." She scrunched up her face. "He's pissed at you for taking the code. They came to a conclusion this morning on what to do, but I wasn't allowed in on that meeting. No one seemed happy."

"The code. Yes, that is a problem." How she wanted to blurt the whole story, but she'd promised Sam. He needed time to figure out if there was someone who'd been working for Symphis in the company.

"I tried to help. To explain to them why you did it. That you got him. I think they understood that. From their perspective, though, it puts their whole company at risk if you did it once." Emma sat next to her and nibbled on one of her French manicured nails. "I saw Mr. Harrison, er Noah, yesterday. He looks like baked-over roadkill. I've never seen him look so bad."

"Did he say anything about me?"

Emma laughed. "Want me to slip him a note in homeroom for you?"

"That came out wrong. I don't really want to know. No, that's bullshit. I do want to know." She pressed the heels of her hands into her eyeballs.

"You're ruining your makeup more. You've got it bad for him, don't you?"

"Is it that obvious?"

"You've practically got stars in your eyes when you say his name."

She blew her nose again, indelicate and loud. "Should I quit? I'm crying on your sofa during work hours over a man I'm not sure I even had a real relationship with. A man who's our boss. Putting aside the FBI and being used to take down illegal gaming, which almost got me killed, everything with Noah felt real."

"You're not going to quit your job, and you're not going to quit Noah, either."

"I don't want to be like this."

Emma waved her hand dismissively. "You're Tori. Tough-ass, hardcore bitch who doesn't bawl about guys on her sister's sofa. Get it together over there. First, send in Leo. Find out if it's just you Josh is keeping away from Noah. Maybe Josh is also worried Noah isn't running on all cylinders right now. If he's blocking everyone, then barge your way into Noah's office. He can't deny you face-to-face. I have a feeling he wouldn't deny you very much if you asked him nicely. Wearing skimpy clothes might help."

She frowned. "I resent the skimpy clothes statement."

Emma laughed. "That's the Tori we need."

"I saw him with another woman."

"Who? What other woman?" Emma made a no-way face.

"The woman was all over him."

"Noah has women all over him all the time. Sometimes he has trouble getting them off him because he's so worried about hurting their feelings. The poor man has no clue how to deal with them. The first time he reciprocated feelings back, that I'm aware of since I started as his assistant, was with you. Based on the pitiful few details you provided I think he's very into you. Jake might be behaving oddly in order to damage control this situation and get the old Noah back, the one who only liked to work and not chase after a girl. Jake doesn't handle drastic change well. You and Noah would equal catastrophic change in his mind."

That made sense. "I owe you."

"I know you do. Now, let's fix your makeup and find out if Noah is as into you and I think he is."

As she left Emma's office her phone dinged with a voice mail message. She cursed the building's unpredictable reception. The message was from Quan.

Quan sounded rushed. "Tori. I'm not sure when I can call you again. I'm in Baltimore right now. Probably not back until tomorrow. Martin's dead. He was killed somehow. Looks like poison. No one's even sure how it's possible since he was in a high security FBI detention center. He said something last night during questioning that... Shit, I don't think it's over. When someone asked about why he'd phoned you when Symphis never did personal calls before he'd been surprised. Martin said: 'He likes her. A girl's good for the Stadium.' Crap, Tori. I don't think Martin was Symphis."

Chapter Twenty-six

Tori hadn't stolen the code.

Sam's admission to both he and Jake of the deception ricocheted around inside Noah's brain. Sam had needed time to find the culprit loyal to Symphis. An entry-level programmer who'd started six months ago had been identified as the spy. It still hurt that neither of them had trusted him, but deep down he understood everything could've been monitored on video.

Noah needed to see Tori. To apologize. To praise her courage. No, all that was great, but he needed to be honest with her and himself. He was shitfaced drunk in love with her.

Jake's words about crippling Tori's reputation and hindering her professional development held him in limbo. He didn't want to be the reason Tori lost her dreams.

Altruism aside, he couldn't survive much longer without righting everything with her. He didn't know if seeing her would improve anything interpersonally between them. It was a first step. It might put an end to the absurd stress dreams. They hadn't surfaced in over a year, only torturing him when under duress. The dreams always featured a college class he'd signed up for but couldn't find where the class took place. The dream had nothing to do with reality. He even recognized the dream as ludicrous while having it, but he couldn't escape the angst of needing to find the class.

He ran his hand along his rough jaw, staring at himself in his office bathroom mirror. His eyes were reddened from insomnia. The last time he looked this bad had been the morning after an all night Vegas bachelor party a few years ago. He'd consumed too much vodka and awoken naked and hugging a stuffed tiger with no memory. Jake offered to tell him the story many times. Noah didn't want to know. What happened in Vegas…and all that shit.

This probably wasn't the best time to hunt down Tori.

Certainty of his feelings toward Tori pushed him to action. Amazing how he'd gone thirty years and never truly fallen in love—until now. Now that he had, he was in a rush to let her know. To fight for her and for them. He might even step down as CEO, maybe go back to designing instead of running things, if that's what it took to make this work. It didn't matter. He wasn't willing to let her go without a fight to figure out how he fit into her life.

Maybe they could figure out how to pause their relationship until she had a solid grip on her career. Based on experience that might take a year, maybe even two. He didn't think he could wait that long to be with her again.

The only way to resolve this was to find her.

He glanced at his watch, wondering if she'd still be in the building at eight thirty p.m. It was Friday. She might have plans. He was willing to kiss Emma's ass to get info on Tori's plans, if needed. It just might come to that.

He rounded the corner out of the bathroom into his office and slid to a halt. His jaw dropped.

There she stood. Next to his desk, so damned sexy in jeans and a dark T-shirt that molded her chest in all the right places. And those boots…

Her dark hair was pulled up into a messy bun. He swallowed past the dryness in his throat. "Tori?"

"I'm sorry to bother you like this. I know you're super busy. That you prefer not to have a one-on-one conversation with me, but we need to talk." The soft pitch of her voice triggered a montage of memories in his brain. Her taste, her smell and how perfect she felt surrounding him.

"You look like you're leaving but..." The glassiness of her eyes suggested frustration close to tears. Tori crying?

He pulled her into his arms, feeling the rightness of her there. "What's wrong?"

Her arms wrapped around him. "I'm sorry. I just...he told me you didn't want anything to do with me. Then Leo couldn't get through him, either. So, I knew it wasn't only me. Then Quan called about Martin. Crap, I shouldn't be here when I'm this worked up."

"One thing at a time. Who said I didn't want to see you and blocked Leo?" His tone came out harsher than intended. He'd crush the asshole who'd kept her from him.

She buried her face against him for a few seconds before rolling outwards with her ear to his chest, but she didn't release him from her hug. "Josh...and then Jake pretty much banned me from being near you. I probably shouldn't be here. If you're trying to get on with your life, then I don't want to ruin that for you."

Assholes. Both of them.

She pushed out of his arms and wiped her eyes. "This is very unprofessional of me. I'm sorry. Jake is right that maybe I was itching to have some sort of confrontation with you. I'll go through Jake to speak with you in the future like you both want. I hate being the clingy psychotic girl who you probably consider an in-the-past one-nighter. Okay, maybe a time beyond one night, but you get the idea." She rolled her eyes upward. "This is so embarrassing, especially since you have a new girlfriend."

"I'm not dating anyone else. There's no one else."

"What?" He found her baffled uncertainty cute, especially on a girl who usually had all her confidence chips in a row.

"We're sure as hell not resolved or over. From a professional respect, Jake's trying to do the right thing to protect you. I don't want to mess up your chance to make it big by throwing a relationship into the mix. This is your moment, but if your reputation is damaged because of me or what people perceive about us, then you might get hurt by what people say. It might damage your career. You're too talented for that."

"Then why was I banned by your assistant?"

"I don't know what Josh said, but he's a temp. I never told him I didn't want to see you. Maybe Jake said something to him."

"Josh was a hard-ass all day about me not seeing you. Then Jake pretty much laid down the law against me seeking you out."

"Were you trying to talk business or was your visit personal?"

"Both." Her gaze darted around as if she was uncertain. "I'm at a roadblock on the game. We need you to authorize Sam help us get do some security coding before it can be made virtual reality compatible. Josh informed me Sam's not available."

"It'll be tough but we'll work out Sam's schedule. No biggie."

"Thanks for helping me with the Sam situation. That's a huge relief." A small smile teased her lips. "Then I saw the woman in your office...blonde."

"A woman? Please tell me you don't mean Cheryl."

"Tall, blonde, touchy feely."

"That's Cheryl, the accountant I didn't want to deal with when I was on the phone with Jake. Even though we've fired her twice and asked the firm replace her as our rep the word *no* doesn't seem to work on her. There's nothing going on there and never was. And Sam told me about the deception."

"I'm sorry for all that."

"He found a Symphis spy." He swept her back into his arms and kissed her, releasing weeks of denied passion and the love burning his chest. Tori's arms encircled his neck. He moaned as he held her tight against him. It felt so good to hold her, to feel the press of her breasts against his chest. He wasn't sure how he'd survived so long without her. They kissed until a breathing break became necessary.

Noah smoothed the hair away from her forehead. "I don't want to see anyone other than you." Couldn't she tell he was messed up over her?

"Okay."

"But I don't want you to be embarrassed by me or us. I can't be jumping behind furniture every time someone gets too close. You're worried about perception and I want you to make it on your own. You're really talented."

"I'm not embarrassed. I..." She hugged him tight. In a small voice she said, "I don't know what you did to me, but I'm a mess. I'm not a crying kind of girl. Ever. This is your fault. But—"

She pushed away and stood in front of him, wringing her hands.

"What's wrong?"

"Give me a sec. There're two things. Let me try to get out the hard one. This doesn't come easy for me." She wrung her hands harder. "Fuck, this is hard. You and me...it's never been like this with anyone else. It scares me. Not much scares me, but I don't want to walk away from it. I don't care what other people think in the gaming world. I like you. No, I'm likely in love with you. I want us to be real, if that's what you want, too."

He grinned. "So, you'll consider going on a date with me? A real date? Tonight? Right now?"

"No motorcycles. Maybe some gaming afterward?"

"Deal." He pulled her into a hug again.

She nodded against his chest. "Or maybe we could just go to your place."

"I'm not doing this half-ass. If we're real, then no secret dating. I want it all. Dates, you staying at my place, everyone at work in the know, and you attending events with me. I prefer my place. Roommates in the morning might be weird."

She said, "I'm worried about things getting complicated here, but I'd like to see my game through to the end. I can quit after that, if you think that'll help. I can design another game on my own. I don't need all this." She waved around her. "Although, what you've built is pretty great. Especially the employee playroom."

He interlaced their fingers without thinking about it and tightened his hand around hers. "Your game needs you. You and me, here and working together...it won't be simple. We'll figure it out."

She fell silent, pulled back and stared at him.

"Too fast? Not ready for moving-in talk? How about we start with a date?" He tamped down his anxiety. *Please don't say no.*

Finally she said, "Quan left me a message on my cell. Martin was poisoned last night at the FBI facility. He said something weird the night before that makes them think he wasn't Symphis. It's not over."

"Did you get any texts or anything else from Symphis?"

She shook her head. "The Stadium doesn't play until this weekend again."

"You're not going back. Never again."

Her hands fisted his shirt. "I hate hiding or being monitored by some asshat. He's got reach, though, Noah. I'm scared, more for everyone around me than myself."

He held her against him. "I've always said I'm with you in this and I meant it. No matter what. Unless the FBI objects, we think the best way to handle what happened with the security breach and to try to save the world of gaming is to come clean to the press about the Stadium. We can work to help close down other Stadiums across the country. That was our conclusion between us and the lawyers and even Sam over the past few days."

"It's lucrative. If Symphis isn't really gone, he's going to fight."

"If we can get the best of the best in the industry on our side before he sucks them into the illegal world, then that's a first step. To do that we need to go public on what's going on. You don't have to be a part of the fight, though."

"Fighting is what I do best." She smiled up at him. "If I go public and then die with evidence that points to Symphis then that makes him an epically big target."

"I don't want you dead over this." Wrinkles furrowed his forehead.

"Then we better make the best of all the time we have."

Jake strolled in.

Noah saw red. He released her. His fist hit Jake's face with a *whack*.

The impact wrenched Jake's neck to the side, but he didn't fight back. Jake backed up with his hands in the air. "Hold on. I realize you're in love with her." He massaged his chin and nailed Noah with a hard glare. "I needed you to be sure yourself."

Noah gritted out, "You blocked her from seeing me?"

Jake turned to Tori. "I'm sorry about today. I was afraid I'd pushed you so far you'd truly walk away from Noah." His voice tight with emotion, Jake said, "Noah, I want to see you happy, but you needed to step back. You needed to see the risks to her and her career. You also needed to figure out if whatever this was had lasting power." His gaze fell to Tori. "It does. She's as messed up over this as you."

"Are you in love with me?" she asked Noah.

"Maybe. I don't know. Probably." Noah released a long sigh. "Yes."

"Right answer. I think I might love you, too." She pulled his head to her and kissed him. Her tentative smile lit up his world.

Noah grinned. She loved him.

Jake cleared his throat. "In my opinion, the only way to avoid gossip is for you two to be open about this to everyone—the company, family, and the world. That leaves no room for anyone to judge or talk." He pivoted but then paused, "I'm outta here before this goes rated R. I do have one request of both of you."

Noah stared a get-on-with-it.

"Noah, will you please run point on her project. Her team is so annoying with their unwillingness to tell me anything. I feel like the Queen of England whom everyone defers to but can't actually do or know anything. Please?"

Noah glanced down at Tori. "I'll only do it if you don't think it'll be uncomfortable with us dating." His gaze returned to Jake's. "We will be dating. I don't want any uncertainty on that."

Tori said, "I'm okay with it, but if there's something I want done and I think I can get my way when you're being tough, I might have to resort to *drastic measures*." He tone dropped to suggestive on the last words.

"Christ," Jake muttered. "This is why we shouldn't condone interoffice romance. Please wait to break up until after the game launches."

"I'm totally running your project and being a bastard all the time." Noah laughed when she shot him an irritated glare. "I'm kidding."

"I'm leaving." Jake waved dismissively at them.

"Wait," Noah said. "Tori just told me she has information that they didn't catch Symphis the other night. Martin wasn't the one."

Jake compressed his lips. "Sam mentioned this as a possible scenario. Bite off the head of the snake and another will rise up. Or, in this case, we didn't get it. Going public seems like the only way to save gaming the way we know it."

"You'll be at risk. He might try to retaliate against you

guys," Tori said.

Jake sighed and started a Noah. "We went into a coalition with the FBI and three other gaming firms knowing the risks. The only way we can beat this is for the gamers to be on our side. They have to see there's an escape aside from drugs or death." He squeezed Noah's shoulder as he headed toward the door. "Live. Love hard. Game harder. Now is all we may have."

"Sorry about the shiner you'll have tomorrow," Noah called.

"No you're not," Jake called out as he left. "I'll get you back one day."

Noah announced, "Let's do this date."

"Right now?" She plucked at her T-shirt and glanced despairingly at her jeans.

"Yes, right now. Come to Antonio's with me."

"I look awful."

"You're beautiful." He leaned in and kissed her briefly.

"A second first date?" She traced her fingertip over his brow, down his temple and across his cheek like she was committing it to memory. "Think we'll make it to dinner this time?"

"If we don't, it won't be the last date." He pulled her in for a longer kiss.

Grinning, she wrapped her arms around his neck. "Does this mean you'll let me beat you on level forty-three?"

Noah burst out laughing, the sound came out carefree. "I don't think so."

"Good, because I can't wait to see your face when I smoke your ass.

Acknowledgements

First I have to thank YOU for welcoming my characters into your life and imagination. I take this crazy journey to amuse, distract, and entertain you.

Every story takes a team to get it across the finish line. Tera Cuskaden's editing guidance was invaluable, especially in pushing Noah to be real. Gotta love that character, but he wasn't easy. Sasha Knight, you provided early insight to get this story moving in the direction it needed to go.

Nichole Severn...girl, you read so many versions of this story from when it started as a novella and then expanded into a fully fleshed out novel. Each new version you cheered me on and critiqued the bejesus out of it to make it better.

Quincy Marin created a beautiful cover yet again. Always amazed you can make my crazy vision a reality.

None of this would be possible without my family who tolerated me writing well into the wee hours after all went to bed. Yeah, there were some ultra rough mornings when even coffee wasn't enough. During the writing and rewriting of this novel one of our dogs in a moment overeager craziness ripped her underside on a trailer hitch, necessitating many surgeries and months of daily bandaging. Thank goodness her mom's a veterinarian and that manuka honey is truly magical for wound healing.

About the Author

Zoe Forward might admit to you she's almost prepared for the zombie apocalypse before the fact she writes contemporary and paranormal romances. She's best known for her sexy, laugh-out-loud Keepers of the Veil series, which has won numerous awards. She's a veterinarian by day. Sure, you can ask her about your pet's problem, but be warned she's into integrative medicine so her answer might involve treatments you've never heard of. You can find her residing in North Carolina with the love of her life, a menagerie of four-legged beasts and two wild kids.

Visit her online: www.zoeforward.com.

Other Books by Zoe Forward

Keepers of the Veil Series
Protecting His Witch
His Witch to Keep
Playing the Witch's Game
Hooked on a Witch
One Night With a Witch

Scimitar Magi Series
Dawn of a Dark Knight
Forgotten In Darkness
Darkness Unbound

Stand Alone Books
The Way You Bite

Next in the Game Lords series: Don't Game Me

Made in United States
North Haven, CT
05 January 2023

30683161R00134